DUSK MUSIC

DUSK MUSIC

Rob Chapman

First published in Great Britain in 2008 by Flambard Press
Stable Cottage, East Fourstones, Hexham NE47 5DX
www.flambardpress.co.uk

Typeset by BookType
Cover Design by Gainford Design Associates
Cover image © Shutterstock
Printed in Great Britain by Cromwell Press, Trowbridge, Wiltshire

A CIP catalogue record for this book
is available from the British Library.
ISBN: 978-1-873226-95-7

Flambard Press wishes to thank Arts Council England
for its financial support.

Flambard Press is a member of Inpress,
and of Independent Northern Publishers.

For Robert Wyatt, Bill Fay, Syd B, Simon Finn, Biff Rose, Allan Mostert, Julius Eastman, Davy Graham and all those who tread the other path.

RAINY DAY, DREAM AWAY

1966–69

'Hey, it's that other cat who plays left-handed.'

Keith Gear looked up from his guitar. He would have known that lispy drawl anywhere.

Hendrix narrowed his eyes and surveyed the other left-handed cat. 'Wanna sit in?'

'Wanna pick and grin?' said a voice behind him, a black black voice parodying those white white Nashville cats who spoke like that. It was Tennessee tinged and goofy and came from somewhere in the studio darkness. And from behind that, from further back in the studio darkness, came a sycophantic cackle. Like 'wanna pick and grin' was the funniest thing anyone had ever said.

Keith Gear was there in the first place because he wanted to sit in. He'd bumped into Hendrix on the corner of 3rd and Bleeker in the Village. Electric Lady, Hendrix's recording studio, was five blocks away on 8th Street. It was a cold morning in February 1968, the kind of cold New York morning that encases the brain in ice. Hendrix was swaddled in scarves and animal skins. He was accompanied by a tall, slim Afro-haired woman, who wrapped her arms tightly around him as he stood there on the corner of 3rd and Bleeker inviting the other left-handed cat down to the studio 'to jam and shit and see, y'know, what occurs'. He spoke through chattering teeth. Keith Gear assumed this was because of the cold.

From a nearby record shop, Arthur Conley's 'Funky Street' began to play. That swayed it somehow. Keith Gear coolly accepted the offer to jam and shit and see, y'know, what occurs.

What was occurring was a studio full of freeloaders and liggers. Earlier that evening Noel Redding had walked in, done a double take, and surveyed the scene with disdain. Seeing nowhere to sit he wandered the room for a while before adjourning to the nearest bar. Returning at midnight, a little less sober, a little more forthright, Noel perched himself on the edge of a sofa where a languid longhaired ligger was sprawled. With the minimum effort required the longhair shifted his body weight to see who had disturbed his stoned reverie. Spying this uneasy-looking dude in circular glasses squeezed up beside him, he lazily stretched his legs and draped his cowboy boots over the intruder's pin-thin thighs.

'Who are you?' he drawled.

'Who am I?' said Noel Redding in his thin reedy voice. 'I'm just the fucking bass player, man.' The fucking bass player, man, sat seething for some time, but not many more times after that.

Keith Gear couldn't remember if Chas Chandler was there that night. In his mind's eye, he could see Chas pacing up and down by the sixteen-track consul, occasionally hoovering up surplus hippies and depositing them unceremoniously into the corridor. But maybe he just imagined that. Wish fulfilment apparitioned into fact. He may not have liked Chas's conservative tendencies. Or the way he told Jimi that singles were where it was at when it was patently obvious that singles were no longer where it was at. Or the way he kept telling Jimi that the Animals had cut their first LP in an afternoon, oblivious to the fact that Jimi and the band mockingly mouthed the words behind his back whenever he went into that stale old riff. But for all his misgivings, Keith Gear did admire the no-nonsense way in which Chas dealt with the hangers on. Or thought he dealt with them. Because that's how he would have liked to deal with them, if he hadn't been seventeen and outnumbered and out of his depth. Like Chas in fact.

Chas cut a pretty demoralised figure by that time. This six-foot-four no-nonsense Geordie who had ridden the new gunslinger, Hendrix, into London town in 1966 and handed him the sheriff's badge when all the other contenders could only look on, open mouthed and amazed. Now he was reduced like Noel to spare part. Who am I? I'm just the fucking manager, that's all. I'm just the fucker who rescued Jimi from Chitlin' Circuit obscurity and passing the hat for dimes and nickels in nowheresville bars. Yeah, said another voice in Keith Gear's head, and maybe you're just the guy who got lucky. The guy who got in five minutes before everyone else noticed the genius in their midst. Or mist. Or myth.

Over time, memories condense and elongate, distort and dilate. From a distance, Keith Gear could no longer trace the sequence of events with any certainty.

Maybe it wasn't February 1968. Maybe it was later. And maybe it wasn't Electric Lady. Surely, that didn't open until 1970. Maybe Jimi had just talked about his plans to open his own recording studio. Jimi was always talking up plans about something. Maybe it was the Power Plant instead. And maybe it wasn't 'Funky Street' by Arthur Conley. Maybe it was some other record of the period, the significance of which had long since been forgotten. At various times, jolted into recall by the vagaries of cognition, he remembered the record as 'Green Tambourine' by The Lemon Pipers, 'Tighten Up' by Archie Bell and The Drells, 'Green Light' by The American Breed. All of these suggested possibilities, some tangible, some tenable, some so farcical they mocked the purity of the moment. For instance, whenever he remembered the record as being 'Tighten Up' by Archie Bell and The Drells, he recalled Hendrix executing this nimble little James Brown dance step. He knew this couldn't be true. Jimi never danced. Like Kay, his English girlfriend, said. Too cool. Too pigeon-toed too. But he could see it all the same. Jimi getting on his good foot. On the corner of 3rd and Bleeker.

It was 3rd and Bleeker. He was sure about that.

* * *

Another time it had been Wardour and Broadwick. The sixteen-year-old Gear stood opposite the MQ Club pondering how he was going to get past the bruiser on the door. He was tall for his age – but tall for his age wasn't necessarily going to get him past the bruiser on the door. It was a cold November night in 1966 and the Soho neon crackled with promise and expectation. Keith Gear had taken the train up from Purley Oaks to Charing Cross. He'd made the same journey the week before and the week before that. On each occasion, he had just walked confidently into the club, guitar in hand, looking the part. Tipped off by a friend of a friend whose hip older brother had a hip music teacher, he'd turned up for the Thursday-night sit-in session, fearless and confident and not altogether wet behind the ears. That first night he bided his time, waited for the opportune moment, joined London's musoratti on stage and impressed everyone.

Impressed was good. Double good. The best some people aimed for was not to blow it or be blown away. He'd seen that happen on the very first night and he'd seen it on numerous other nights since. Stage fright hit some people like a ten-ton truck. Masters of their own destiny in the privacy of their bedrooms, they froze in the company of their betters, fingers turning to putty as unsympathetic road-hardened pros looked on. Eyes blinded by the houselights, ears confused by the lack of foldback from the stage monitors, they could neither see nor hear what everyone else was playing. Indeed it had never occurred to them until that moment to either look or listen. It had certainly never occurred to them until that moment that a live band was a living, breathing, organic entity and not a gramophone record which plays exactly the same way every time you put it on, regardless of whether it's Andrés Segovia or Charlie Christian or Bert Weedon going about his unvaried business at thirty-three or forty-five revs per minute.

Keith Gear didn't blow it. He stood stock-still and supreme and sixteen, turning heads while his instincts did the talking.

He clocked the precise moment an old ringside jazzer shed his prejudice; one second the guy had his back half turned to the stage, tapping an untipped cigarette on a beer-stained table, the next moment he was swivelling round in one effortless impulsive motion as he heard the chord sequence that said, *Christ, this kid can play.*

Keith Gear didn't blow it. He locked eyes with a girl, made up and shimmy dancing and not much older than him, who had bluffed her way in too. Tall and leggy, and shock-haired just like Jimi, she stood out from the other dollied-up dancers who thronged to the left side of the stage jostling for prime position and eye line and attention from the musicians. She smiled a split-second smile, just long enough to say, *I'm cool, I'm yours.* Keith Gear was cool enough not to smile back.

And now his guitar was inside the MQ Club and he was outside on the pavement, kicking his heels on the corner of Wardour and Broadwick. Waiting, wishing and hoping that the jobsworth on the door would slip away so he could slip back inside.

Time was wasting. Anxious minutes passed. The jukebox in the adjacent caff played 'Reach Out (I'll Be There)' by the Four Tops. A working girl asked him if he was looking for company. He didn't appreciate the synchronicity.

He'd followed the same protocol as before. Walk right in as if you belong. Like you do this every night.

The resident road crew was setting up. The main guy, Gully, recognised him from previous weeks and gesturing towards a door at the side of the stage had said, 'Hey, kid, park your guitar in there. It'll be safe. I'm locking up.'

It turned out there was some electrical fault and there was going to be a bit of a delay in getting the club open that night.

'Might as well go and get yourself a bite to eat, kid,' Gully said.

So the kid went and got himself a bite to eat, and when he came back an hour later, still picking sweetcorn from his teeth, a sizeable crowd was slowly filing in. The kid marched confidently to the front of the queue and the bruiser on the door took one look at him, saw through his bluff and bluster and surmised his age in an instant.

'Come back when you're legal,' he said, barring the way with a thick arm.

'But my guitar is in there.'

'Don't come it with me.' The bruiser peered contemptuously into a vacant space just above Keith Gear's head, like doormen do.

'But it is,' he pleaded, suddenly subservient sixteen again, rather than cocksure sixteen.

'You're trying my patience, kid.'

'But, but, but,' he stuttered. He was locked out and found out and rapidly shedding his cool in front of the punters, none who knew this kid from Adam. Not one of them would vouch for him. Most just sneered curtly at his gauche free-loading tactics.

So now Keith Gear was skulking in the doorway of a chemist shop on the corner of Wardour and Broadwick. Lurking like all the other Soho lowlife. Back to the road, staring into the curved glass of the shop window, studying the reflected movements of the MQ crowd, and the non-movements of the MQ Club bruiser.

That's when he first saw Hendrix. That's how he first perceived the legend. Distorted in the curved glass, all elongated and out of shape. It seemed appropriate later on, the more he thought about it, which was often. A taxi pulled up right outside the club and deposited its passengers on the pavement.

Keith Gear watched them emerge from the taxi one by one. A tall heavily built bloke with an incongruously boyish mop of hair wearing a businessman's overcoat. That was Chas.

A slim dark-haired girl in a crocheted black beret and a blue velvet trouser suit, who stumbled on a loose paving stone and glanced at her snagged heel with a hint of annoyance. That was Kay.

And then this slow elegant apparition. He didn't so much emerge as uncoil from the cab. Easing his limbs from the passenger seat, he paused on the pavement and took stock of his habitat. He looked like he belonged to the night. Dark skinned, whip-hipped and slender, he ran his fingers through a tangle of barbed-wire hair and put his right arm round the waist of the slim dark-haired girl. He wore black hipster trousers and a bottle-green cord jacket, undone to reveal a lacy white shirt with a frill down the front. Pop star clothes. Even though he wasn't yet a pop star he already looked the part.

Keith Gear turned away from the image in the distorted glass of the chemist shop window and gazed the same awestruck gaze as the MQ crowd. Jimi looked like nothing else in that street at that moment, or possibly ever. The line of punters parted as Chas, arm raised like some Roman standard bearer, advanced towards the door, his charge and his lady friend huddled close behind him.

The kid walked across the road, drawn to the apparition, sensing that this was where the action was. At the door, Chas engaged the bruiser in friendly banter, as if he did this every night. Which he pretty much did. His thickset stature acted as a physical barrier, dwarfing the doorman's view of the queue, eclipsing the moment when a sixteen-year-old kid seized his microsecond of opportunity and slipped into the club in order to reacquaint himself with his Fender Telecaster.

Had he looked back he would have seen Jimi and Kay exchanging knowing glances, recognising a chancer when they saw one. Indeed that was Kay's opening line, later when she introduced herself to the fresh-faced kid who had just played on stage with her boyfriend.

'I used to sneak into clubs like that all the time when I first came to London,' she confided. 'The secret is never look nervous. Never look back.'

Keith Gear never looked back.

* * *

And now it was a year and a bit later. And here he was in a room full of strangers. The incense smelt like camel dung. So did the pot that was being smoked. So did the people who were smoking it. The whole studio reeked of Afghan fur and leather hide and sweat-drenched sofa and stale recycled air. In one corner, a red silk shawl that somebody had draped around a lampshade began to smoulder and singe, the burnt material forming a slow scorched corona while everyone lay slumped, oblivious.

All this and no Jimi.

Keith Gear slowly felt his way through the semi-darkened throng to a studio booth, partitioned off by soundproofed hardboard. He picked up a guitar, a white Fender Stratocaster, and eased it into regular tuning. In the dimly lit sanctuary of that studio corner, he sat quietly strumming, the studio booth absorbing the mosquito drone of fret buzz and the tinny unamplified rattle of slack strings.

Through the glass darkly he saw a match being struck. A line of smoke rising. Indistinct slow shifting shapes silhouetted by the bordello-red lampshade. That's how life often looked to him, then and later. Glimpsed through plate glass. The world going on on the other side.

That's what had brought him to New York the first time. The expectation that something might be going on. That American guy in the MQ Club. Or was it the other club? The one in Frith Street. The one that was no longer there. Sandy his name was. Said he'd followed Chas and Jimi over. From Café Wha? to Wardour Street. Friendly guy. Sandy said, *Come and stay at my place in the East Village. Whenever you're in town.*

So that's where Keith Gear had gone in the summer of 1967 to get away from plastic flower power and bogus 'wow-it's-a-hep-scene cats' and Kings Road louche lizards and jaded jazzers and predatory managers promising the earth but only ever offering cigar-butt halitosis.

He emerged from the 14th Street subway to a summer in the

cityscape, familiar from a thousand flicks, which he learned to call movies soon enough. There were the low-rise brownstone buildings with the fire escapes up the front. There were the bakeries and bagel stalls and the steam rising from ventilation ducts. There was Washington Square Park with a stray Fug busking. There was Ginsburg walking from West to East with a huge pile of Vedantist literature under his arm. There was Roland Kirk with a sax (just the one) under his. And there, in the weeks that followed, went doe-eyed boys and brown-eyed girls and Warhol and Moondog and Mothers and brothers and others.

That first night at Sandy's place on the corner of St Marks and 1st, elation gave way to jet-lag exhaustion around two in the morning. His metabolism told him it was breakfast time. His brain said *sleepy, so sleepy. Get some rest.* Sandy slipped away to his girlfriend's. Also called Sandy. 'I'll catch you in the morning.' Door slam.

Keith Gear went to the window, five floors up. There was New York in all its nocturnal glory. A living breathing pop art poster bathed in neon and framed in cinemascope. A Walk, Don't Walk sign blinked vacantly, its instruction superfluous to the flow of those who inhabited the city at this hour. EAT said the blood-red bulbs in the diner across the street. LIQUOR said the flickering blue strip along the block. Somewhere a police car siren wailed. All these sights and sounds to take in. Merging with his slumber all night long.

He woke to find Sandy back in his own bed, alone and snoring loudly. Tiptoeing around the kitchen and quietly opening cupboard doors, he found no food. Nothing but a carton of orange juice in the fridge and roaches the size of thumbnails climbing the walls. He let himself out of the apartment and tried to fix the door on the latch but it snapped shut behind him. His body clock told him it was nearly midday – which it was back in Purley Oaks, so many miles away.

Locked out, he didn't want to hammer on the door and wake Sandy to let him back in, so he walked down four flights of bare wooden stairs and out onto the street. 1st Avenue was desolate and deserted. The Jewish bakery two doors down was just opening its shutters so he peered in through the window at all the bread twists, bagels, blintzes and sweetmeats laid out in their multitudes. Abundance quite unknown to him. The clock on the wall said six fifteen in the morning.

Once he'd figured out what he was going to do with all this unwanted time he experienced a world he'd never seen before. He sat in a bar with the early-shift cab drivers, pear-shaped men who perched their gargantuan butts on bar stools and devoured a mountain of pancakes and maple syrup and talked of what they'd seen the night before in the back of their cabs – they'd seen everything – oblivious to the wide-eyed kid who ear-wigged away and struggled to finish one of his inch-thick pancakes and didn't feel the need to eat again all day.

He walked across town from East to West, amazed at how little time it took to get from funky East Side neighbourhoods to genteel tree-lined Greenwich squares. He wandered around the West Village for a while, got lost where the block system went awry and the grid lines got wonky and curved and doubled back on themselves, and then he walked all the way back again. Saw nothing but early morning garbage trucks and newspaper vendors arranging their displays and the first of the early-bird school kids emerging.

Later he wrote a song about it all: 'Greenwich Dream Time'. It was on the *Dominion* album. Everyone assumed it was about Greenwich in London, but it wasn't. It was about Keith Gear's own private New York. The one you have to get up early for. The one he only saw accidentally because his body was out of synch, traversing its own meridian.

In some ways he would always live like that.

* * *

He acquitted himself well that first time on stage with Hendrix. Just lay back and augmented. Mature enough to know whose thunder was rumbling that night. There was already a buzz about Jimi and the MQ crowd gasped as he tore up the rules before their eyes. Keith Gear watched his hands. Strong hands.

Afterwards Kay came over and spoke. Confirmed she'd seen him sneak in between Chas's bulk and the total eclipse of the doorman. Kay was friendly and unstuffy; he liked her from the start. Sure, she wore that veneer of cool that everyone wore that winter, but it was never more than that, a veneer. And sure she never seemed to have any money and was forever scrounging taxi fares, drinks and cigarettes but Kay knew the scene like the back of her jasmine-scented hand. She took the sixteen year old on board like an older sister would, telling him who was in and who was a must to avoid and what was what in the general disorder of things.

Keith Gear never got the chance to talk to Jimi that first night. Sycophants surrounded Jimi the moment he came off stage, and by the time he had freed himself Chas was ready to whisk him off to a new stamping ground.

'We're off to The Speak,' said Kay. 'You won't get in.'

Keith Gear appreciated the honesty but was crushed all the same.

The same scenario was enacted several times over the following weeks. The entourage would turn up at the MQ. Hendrix would jam with whoever was available and capable (which was not always the same thing), then the party would split to groovier climes – The Speakeasy, The Scotch of St James or The Cromwellian – leaving Keith Gear to make his way home alone.

That night he missed his last train and stood on the rainy Soho pavement, tuppence in his pocket, guitar case in hand, glowing with it all. He was prepared to walk all the way back to Purley Oaks. He suspected his feet probably wouldn't touch the ground. Some night.

A voice behind him said, 'Hi.' He turned round and it was the shock-haired girl he'd locked eyes with. 'Wanna get a hot dog?'

Keith Gear started to explain his predicament. How he was broke and had to be heading home.

'Where's that?' she said.

'Purley Oaks.'

'Where's that?' She threw back her shoulders and thrust out a stiff hand in a parody of manners. 'Sonya.'

'How do you do?' said Keith Gear, playing along and poshing up his voice, although he didn't have to posh it up as much as she did.

Sonya laughed a deep bass laugh that suggested friendliness, madness and on-somethingness all at the same time.

They sheltered under the canopy of the hot-dog stall and chatted through mustard-smeared lips.

'How old are you?' she said, a bit blasé but quizzical all the same.

'I'm sixteen and a quarter,' he deadpanned and she laughed her deep bass laugh again.

'I'm seventeen and a half. You can sleep at my house if you like.'

'Where do you live?'

'Battersea. It's not far.'

It is when you are carrying a guitar, it's starting to rain heavily and you have school in the morning.

Sonya gabbled all the way there. About how she was working at a laundromat. About how she was thinking of doing Foundation Art at college. Or maybe Fashion. Or maybe Theatre. She said her parents wouldn't be up. She said she sometimes hitched out to the all-nighters at The Cruiserweight Club in Romford and got lifts with the newspaper lorries or the bread vans. She gave the impression that she spent a lot of time climbing into newspaper lorries and bread vans.

'I know lots of the guys in the bands,' she said. 'I never have to pay. What did you think of the spade?'

'The who?'

'I noticed he was left-handed like you. Paul, out of The Allsorts, he's left-handed as well. He plays bass. Do you like The Allsorts? They used to be soul but they've gone freaky.'

Keith Gear hadn't heard of The Allsorts. Or The Nomads. Or Granny's Apples. Or Uncle Sideways (formerly The Missiles) or most of the other groups that Sonya jabbered on about as they crossed the dirty old river and followed the full moon all the way back to Battersea.

'You should come down the MQ on Saturdays,' she said. 'It's on all night. You get the yanks in after midnight. Airmen.'

'I'm mainly interested in the sit-in session,' he said sniffily. 'I'm not really a punter by nature.'

Sonya gave him a look. 'Get you.'

'How much further,' he said, switching his guitar case from aching left hand to aching right hand.

'Not far,' said Sonya, striding on ahead. By the time they got to Battersea it was gone one and raining heavily. 'This is my street.' They emerged from an unlit alleyway into a narrow terraced road overlooked by a railway cutting. 'Oh shit.'

He looked around and thought the same. *Oh shit*. The things a sixteen-year-old boy will do for a grope on a sofa. Sonya was standing outside a house looking at a chink of light escaping through not-quite-drawn curtains.

'Oh shit, shit, shit,' she said again. 'They're still up.'

Not only were 'they' still up, they were having a blazing row which was attracting the attention of the neighbours. Next door's bedroom curtains twitched. A hall light went on in an adjacent house.

'Aw, sorry,' said Sonya, meaning *you'll have to go*, meaning *some other time, eh?* She gave him a sympathetic look and put a cautious shoulder to an unlocked front door, as if checking to see if it was safe to enter.

On the other side of the road, a bedroom window creaked open. 'Put a bloody sock in it,' shrieked a woman in curlers, leaning out to have a look. Behind her stood a burly husband in a vest, arms folded, face like thunder. 'It's those bloody Drapers again,' the woman said. The burly husband leaned out to have a look. He scowled suspiciously at the rain-soaked boy on the pavement and brought the window down with a resounding slam.

In that dimly lit deserted street, the rain-soaked boy suddenly felt a long way from Purley Oaks. He heard the sound of crockery smashing in the Drapers' hallway. 'And what bloody time do you call this?' a woman screeched.

He found a phone box and dialled PURley 483.

'Where are you?' asked his tired mother.

He looked out through the phone box window. He couldn't see any street signs. Just a burned-out Vespa propped up against someone's front wall. 'I don't know,' said scatter-brained son to sleepy mother.

'Stop playing that guitar,' said a voice over the studio intercom. It was a drawling sarcastic voice. The same mocking voice that said, 'Wanna pick and grin?' when Jimi walked in. 'Aah said, stop playing that guitar, boy. That's Jimi's geetah.'

The sycophantic chorus swelled up again. More stoned laughs and cackles. Keith Gear heard a fumbling sound, then feedback, as the intercom mike was dropped onto the carpet. More hysterical giggles. He went on playing Jimi's geetah.

Jimi and entourage walked in at around three in the morning. 'Hey, it's that other cat who plays left-handed.'

Keith Gear looked up. Jimi had two members of Traffic with him, a stray Jefferson Airplane, and a super session master or two, all sworn to anonymity due to record company intransigence. Jimi was accompanied by the same tall black woman he'd been with earlier that day on the corner of Bleeker and 3rd Street. In daylight, Keith Gear took her to be an Upper East Side socialite, one of those radical chic types that Tom Wolfe would later write about, but in the bordello-red light of the studio she looked more dishevelled and wasted. She still had her arms wrapped tight around Jimi, except now it didn't look so much like affection, more like she was leaning on him to support herself, propping herself up.

'Wanna sit in?'

'Is every one of these guitars strung up leftie?' said a disgruntled voice in a broad Brooklyn accent.

Jimi addressed him as Al. 'Play keyboards, Al.'

'Uh, Stevie's on the Hammond,' said someone.

'There's two Hammonds,' someone else said. 'There's two of everything.'

Keith Gear had no idea how many people were in that studio. Prone and comatose liggers suddenly sprung into life and became percussion players. A Bronx taxi driver who had been sitting there with the meter running for an hour said he could play sax, so someone found him a tenor sax.

'Do you know "Got My Mojo Woiking"?' he rasped.

'Hey somebody send for King Curtis,' said Hendrix and the more knowing members of the gathering laughed.

Everybody jammed the blues endlessly. Keith Gear was there for three nights of this, although not a single note of his ended up on the record. None that he could detect at any rate. He remembered playing on a version of 'Rainy Day, Dream Away', but he couldn't ever recall Hendrix doing that talking wah-wah bit at the end, not on the night he played anyway. Or maybe it was 'Still Raining, Still Dreaming'. And maybe the talking wah-wah bit was at the beginning. Or maybe it was just one long jam that they spliced in half for the record and maybe he was there for all of it and played on half of it. But which half? Or maybe Hendrix dubbed on the wah-wah bit some other time.

He remembered sitting out 'Voodoo Chile'. He definitely remembered that. Having endured one blues vamp too many he went and sat with the liggers, sharing joints and sipping Coke as Jimi cooked up magic through the smoked glass. 'Voodoo Chile' sounded good when he eventually heard the *Electric Ladyland* record, better than he remembered it, even though some of that tired tainted atmosphere had somehow permeated its way into the grooves.

Best of all was '1983'. He thought '1983' was the best thing Hendrix had ever done. The way he heard it, seventeen going on infinity, that was the way forward, the pathway to the outer beyond. The rest of the time there was too much of that blues trad thing going on. He kept his reservations under wraps but Keith Gear could never see the obsession with the blues trad thing. Right from the first night at the MQ Club he'd noticed that whenever more than three musicians gather for a jam they'll resolve any known situation with a blues run. No matter how exploratory and exciting it gets there will always be someone guaranteed to drag it all back to the twelve-bar boogie. Even that night he sat in with Jimi and all those R & B legends at Le Beat in Leicester Square, the night some belligerent old beret head tried to bar his way onto the stage. That night he'd sensed Jimi getting a little baroque so he'd thrown in a delicate little J. S. Bach motif and this grizzled old soprano sax player threw him a look that said, *This ain't the time or place, kid.* That night he'd matched Jimi flourish for flourish. That night he'd watched Jimi inventing the space-age variations. But even then, there was some lowest common denominator primed and ready with his Elmore James lick. Jamming, he learned soon enough, was only ever as innovative as the weakest link would allow.

Keith Gear came to hate jamming.

That second night in the East Village Sandy took him out to dinner. Sidewalk pizza served in a paper towel, which they ate on the steps of a derelict brownstone with a couple of Sandy's buddies as they watched the street sights, the living theatre. Scuzzbags and hustlers and preachers and poets and painters. The ever-drifting, ever-shifting moving backdrop of the Lower East Side. Keith Gear discovered that night that, contrary to what he'd led him to believe, Sandy didn't really know Hendrix too well. His connection, tenuous as it was, came through his dad. Sandy's father was a big-time promoter and occasionally helped musicians find other musicians. Seemed he'd played no small part in helping Jimmy (*sic*) find the Flames in 1965. Sandy's dad was rich. Had an office on Broadway, just along from the Brill building, and he was bankrolling his son's own musical aspirations to the tune of equipment and rehearsal space. Sandy had a band called The Fever. The couple of buddies sitting with them on the steps of the derelict brownstone were members. Jim, tall and twitchy, played sax. Vito, small and squat, played keyboards.

Jim said that heroin was where it was at. The West Village was dead and heroin was where it was at. 'You ever tried heroin, Keith?' he asked. 'You should. It's the cure for the common cold.' Later, when he heard Jim play the sax, Keith Gear concluded that it was a cure for talent and technique too – and so began a lifelong aversion to smack addicts. It began right there and then in a cold drafty rehearsal room in an old meat-packing plant, somewhere between the fluffed intro to 'Soul Finger' and the missed bridge on whichever James Brown number he was mangling. Fever played rock and soul music in a style that was very popular among the Italian-American New York bands of the time. Tough raw cover versions of R & B and pop tunes, slowed down to sixteen rpm to tease out their seedy side, their Lower East Side. Later Sandy would claim that Vanilla Fudge had ripped him off, stolen his idea. But as far as Keith Gear could see, and hear, every bar band in New York was trying to sound like that. And, jealousy and resentment aside, Vanilla Fudge had better cover versions anyway. They knew which tracks to cut, which tracks worked. They slowed down 'You Keep Me Hanging On', 'Shotgun', 'Ticket To Ride', 'If You Gotta Make A Fool Of Somebody', and made them dark and gothic and mysterious. Fever slowed down 'Baby Love', 'She Loves You', 'Who Wears Short Shorts'. It wasn't the same. The only thing that was good about Fever was Vito. His Hammond B3 had this big muscular churchy sound that made Keith Gear think he'd want him for a keyboard player if he ever formed a band. The rest was a drag. Sandy fancied himself as a singer but was all cliché and mannerisms. His girlfriend Sandy fancied herself as a backing singer but she couldn't even beat time with a tambourine, let alone do the 'Sweet Inspirations' bit. Keith Gear was only glad there wasn't a guitar 'strung up leftie' that night.

Later, when he got back to England, he discovered that Sandy wasn't even called Sandy. Kay had called him 'Randy Sandy', and he'd assumed that was some sort of nickname based on his prowess. But Kay said no, Jimi said he was called Randy when his dad introduced 'Jimmy' to his son in New York in 1966. And later still he found out that Randy was an anglicised version of his real name, Antonio Randiozi. And even later still he found out that Sandy's dad had disowned and disinherited him, when he'd discovered that Sandy too, like Jim, had opted for smack as a cure for the common cold. It certainly cured Fever of ambition. They disbanded without ever making a record. Around Christmas time 1967 Sandy's dad got them a recording contract and a publishing deal but Jim and Sandy stuck the advance in their veins. Keith Gear didn't know that until he turned up in New York early in 1968. He'd found Jim and Sandy living in squalor. There was nothing on the walls but blood, and still nothing in the fridge but orange juice. Meanwhile Sandy's girl Sandy washed pots at a local bar most evenings while Jim and Sandy sat in blissful oblivion staring at a flickering mute TV, pupils like pinpricks. The neon across the road still said EAT.

Keith Gear stuck one night of it. Returning to the apartment the next day, he found that his guitar had 'disappeared'. Boy Sandy said somebody had broken in while they were sleeping. Girl Sandy stopped him on the threadbare stairs as he made his way out, in search of a cheap hotel. 'Check the pawn shop on the corner of 3rd and Bleeker in the Village.'

And that's where he was when Hendrix walked up to him and said, 'Hey, it's that other cat who plays left-handed.'

* * *

That first time in New York seemed an age ago now. The days as cauldron hot as this one was cold. And in the time that spanned the two visits Hendrix had become the biggest rock star on the planet. Keith Gear had conflicting emotions about that. Jimi attracted illusion and myth from the word go. Bullshitters were drawn to him like begging letters to a pools winner. Everyone projected onto him what they wanted to see. The blues guys claimed him for the blues. The rock guys pledged him to the riff. Musicians praised him to his face and called him 'Superspade' behind his back. Keith Gear hated the way they acted all cool around him and blackened their baby's eyes if she as much as fluttered them in his presence. And most of them did.

Hendrix the master craftsman he loved. He went from watching his hands to watching the way he worked his effects pedals. Hendrix the showman he didn't much care for. Playing the guitar behind his head, pretending to play with his teeth. Dousing it in lighter fuel and basking in the flames, relishing the infamy. The cage door closing. The image trap. He despised all that. He remembered Jimi coming on all-pitiful about it later on. They were backstage at the Albert Hall.

'Oh, man, they always expect me to do that stuff,' said Jimi.

'Then don't fucking do it,' said Clapton.

Fucking right on, Slowhand, thought Keith Gear. Write your symphonies on the astral plane, Jimi. Join the sky dots with your music of the spheres. And stop being the court jester. Clown prince of the underground. There are already too many contenders queuing up for that role.

What happened to Hendrix, or what Hendrix allowed to happen to Hendrix, put Keith Gear off joining a band for the best part of ages.

That night after they all got back from the Fever rehearsal everyone else crashed out but Keith Gear sat up for hours, drinking in the New York nightscape, watching the neon dance on the bare white walls. He listened to a DJ called Charlie Greer on the midnight-till-six show on WABC. Greer read out commercials in iambic pentameters and everything he did seemed effortless and sophisticated and slick. The way he segued jingles. The way he paced the tracks he played. The way he made every song seem like the most significant thing you ever heard. The way he said 'two fifty-three in the a.m.' and made seven minutes to three sound like the most bewitching minute there ever was.

The way Charlie Greer paced his show was how Keith Gear felt about New York that first time. The momentum and sway of WABC was the momentum and sway of the city itself. No stop. All go. That was the trouble with London. It was all stop-go-stop-go. Like it couldn't make up its mind. London lurched and staggered. New York acted like a city should.

'You've got school in the morning,' said his mother absently, like she was doodling on the phone pad, which she was. She didn't sound too concerned on the phone. Her side of the family were showbiz. They'd understand.

'It's only double art,' he said, shuddering at the mundane reality of his Friday timetable. Mr Samuels and his tedious life-drawing class. He could afford to miss that. Mr Samuels had already told him that he'd sail through the O level.

'Your father won't be best pleased if he's got to come and fetch you,' said his mother, a little less absently this time.

The next voice he heard was his father's. 'Where are you?'

'I'm not sure.'

'You must have some idea.'

'Battersea, she said.' She. Bit of a mistake.

A long sad sigh echoed in his ear. That all-encompassing parental 'what are you doing with your life?' sigh.

'Are you anywhere near the river?'

'No. Not really.' Meaning *I haven't a clue, Dad.*

'Can you see the power station?'

'What power station?'

'Oh, for Christ's sake, boy. Battersea. Battersea Power Station.'

'Oh, yeah. Yeah I did. It was over there. I mean left. Left of some houses. The houses were in front of . . . I think it's a railway arch but I haven't seen any trains.'

And so on till the money ran out, when he had to call the operator and reverse the charges.

'If there's a railway arch,' resumed his father, as if he'd been standing there all that time pondering the geography, which he had. 'If there's a railway arch you're not far from Clapham Junction. Walk up the hill to Clapham Junction. And wait there. Wait outside Arding & Hobbs. It's a department store.' He was going to add, 'You can't miss it,' but thought better of it.

Keith Gear followed the Great Bear and the full moon past scrap yards and goods yards and junk shops and lock ups until he came to Lavender Hill. He stood opposite the huge department store kicking his heels until he saw a familiar light green Wolseley execute an extravagant U-turn in the deserted street. He crept into the back seat and slunk down into the comfortable leather upholstery. An all-consuming silence descended. Wandsworth Common hurtled by in the dark. Tree shapes and telegraph poles and Esso pumps and house rows and lamp lights and London all receding in the rear view where his father's eyes – one part weary tolerance, three parts bristling annoyance – met his own. One part pop dreams. Three parts brain feathers.

Some night. Hendrix reflected in the chemist shop window. The friendliness of Kay. The promise of Sonya. And subterfuge and shadows and soaking wet and hot dogs and Hendrix and centre stage and Hendrix and Hendrix and both of them on that stage with the whole room watching both of them, bathed in a halo of light.

'Have you been to another one of those sessions?'

A depot full of tankers flashed by in a rain-splattered blur.

'Yeah, it was really good.'

His profile silhouetted in the window. Sixteen going on fireproof.

'There's no money in jazz you know.'

'It wasn't jazz.'

Crystal Palace twinkling in the distance.

'I don't know why you're wasting your time on that stuff. Mr Fosdyke says you will make a splendid classical guitarist.'

Fozzy said lots of things. He spent a year trying to correct his posture. He said *you'll never make a guitarist if you slouch over the instrument like that. You must execute the Classic Stance.* Correct posture and the Classic Stance were very important to Mr Fosdyke.

'Have you got music in the morning?'

'No, Dad. Art. Mr Samuels and his beloved golden section.'

The golden section was very important to Mr Samuels. Classical harmony and good posture between them constituted the bedrock of a sound education.

Keith Gear was already lost to such things.

His dad glanced at him in the rear-view mirror, head lolling, dozing off in the back seat. 'It's about time you bucked your ideas up.'

FREEFROM

1995

Keith Gear trudged along the Thamesway, guitar case heavy in his grip. It was four thirty on a winter's afternoon, and it had taken him all day to get back from a sparsely attended FreeFrom Music benefit that had taken place in Sunderland the night before. He ached all down his left side and his stomach felt empty. Rain turned to hail as he hurried on past the fast-food joints: Mr Chicken, Leggy Leghorns, Buffalo Boy. He had only small change in his pocket, barely enough for a bag of chips, and nowhere near enough for a box of Mr Chicken's sawdust sautéed deadbird. Not that he would have wanted a box of Mr Chicken's sawdust sautéed deadbird. The last time he'd bought some he estimated that each peanut-sized morsel of battered hen had cost 52p a bite and he felt that he had been ripped off enough for one day. And night.

The Sunderland gig had been a benefit for the jazz trombone player, gig promoter and general all-round chancer Guy Truelove. Having fallen on hard times, Guy had devised a get-rich-quick scheme which entirely bypassed the need to perform or promote jazz music. Unfortunately, this scheme involved convincing several Wearside businesses to part with their pension funds. As a result, Guy Truelove was now on remand awaiting psychiatric reports regarding his suitability to stand trial.

There were thirty-two people at the gig. Like a substantial proportion of the benefits that Keith Gear had played down the years, it made a loss. All he got out of the deal was the chance to play his ferociously uncompromising music to a room full of strangers and the offer of a stained fusty mattress on the floor of the woman who ran the community centre and had organised the gig. The same woman who in the middle of the night had joined Keith Gear on the stained fusty mattress in order to engage him in a few minutes of inelegant foreplay and inconclusive sex. His balls still ached because of her incautious nocturnal fumbling.

He inserted his front-door key into the lock, turned it the requisite one and a half times clockwise, and stepped over a carpet of junk mail, flyers and free sheets. He then pressed the timer switch in the hall and attempted unsuccessfully to drag his tired carcass up the three steep flights of stairs to his attic flat before the light went out again. Groping in the dark for the second time that day he felt his way along the upstairs landing to his door and scraped a second key along the flaking green paint until it slid into its lock. Finally, with weary relief, he shouldered his way into his freezing cold flat. He sank exhaustedly to his knees in front of the gas heater in his living room, lit it with a match, warmed his hail-bitten hands, and thought about dinner. Not the dinner he was going to eat, a solitary tin of soup, but a big dinner, a filling dinner, an unfeasibly gluttonous banquet. His stomach started to rumble.

Keith Gear went to the food cupboard in his tiny kitchenette, took the lonely tin of vegetable broth from a bare top shelf and began hacking at the lid with the only utensil available to him, a blunt and rusty tin opener. He made two crude indents in the soup tin, and then turned clockwise towards the cooker where an empty saucepan sat waiting on the one working gas ring. That ninety-degree swivel from shelf to saucepan, unthinkingly perfected during five years of cooking in the same cramped space, took half a second. During the second half of that eventful second, he noticed that despite initial visual evidence to the contrary, the pan was full of dirty water. It was during the perilous milliseconds before he jettisoned the contents of the soup tin into the dirty water, somewhere between cognition kicking in and preventive action failing to keep its appointment, that he remembered he'd burnt a pan of scrambled eggs the previous morning before setting off on his long haul to the North. Already late for his train he'd hastily squirted the pan with washing up liquid, run it under the cold tap and left it to soak. Now he watched helplessly as the red-brown vegetable broth separated into its constituent molecular particles in the scummy water. For a few futile moments, he pondered the possibility that he might save his soup, but that particular microscopic spark of optimism was soon extinguished. He tentatively prodded at a couple of lumps and watched as each in turn slipped slowly under the murky surface and evaporated in the forty-watt gloom, leaving two smears of red-brown residue to drift in sad isolation around a blue-black film of fairy liquid. Outside bullets of hail played rim-shots on the window.

More in desperation than hope, he reached up to the shelf again and made a sweeping motion with his left hand. To his surprise, his fingertips felt a rock-hard shard of stock cube. Judging by its granite-like constituency it had been there for some time. For all he knew, or cared, the previous tenant may have left it there. But as far as he was concerned, it was no longer a rock-hard shard of stock cube. Technically, it was now a meal. He boiled a kettle, dropped the stock cube into a cup, and poured the water. The cube bobbed to the surface and resolutely failed to crumble. Even after being prodded and stabbed several times by his all-purpose tin opener, the cube retained its rock-hard consistency. He stared morosely at the orangey-yellow beverage that was going to be his only sustenance until the morning and sighed. The pathos deafened him. Cradling the cup for warmth he slumped into an armchair that he had recently rescued from a skip and stared at his reflection in the unlit screen of his black and white portable TV. After a few moments of numbed contemplation, he got up and turned the TV on, adjusted its coat-hanger aerial slightly and stared through snowy static at the evening news bulletin. War. Famine. Global greed. Domestic squalor. Celebrity married. Celebrity murdered. The usual shit. In an effort to get warmer, he dragged the armchair closer to the gas fire. After half an hour, he almost felt like taking his coat off.

The newsreader was about to reveal which celebrity had been murdered when the electricity went off. Lacking both the coinage necessary to restore power, and the willpower to go and disturb anyone in the house for change, he fumbled his way into his bedroom and stumbled fully clothed into bed. Once his eyes had adjusted to the darkness he noticed a half-smoked joint sitting in his bedside ashtray. Striking a match on the cracked and flaking plaster of a bedside wall that was etched with the sulphurous hieroglyphics of many previous nightcap spliffs, he relit the joint, then lay flat on his back inhaling deep and exhaling slow. Red embers glowed and diminished in the dark. Stubbing out the roach in the ashtray he curled up in a crouch, put his hand down his trousers to feel if the amorous gig promoter had done permanent damage to his testicles, then slept for fourteen hours.

He had that dream again. The one he kept having. The one about an art-life inverted. The one where the world goes freeform and the artist is left clinging to stability in the midst of chaos.

It was raining when he awoke. He could hear water gushing from the leaf-blocked gutter directly above his bedroom window and drumming loudly on the corrugated plastic of next door's garage. He turned on the radio where the DJ on Radio Moron confirmed the meteorological conditions. Said it was persisting down outside. Mentioned cats and dogs and something about stepping in a poodle. Keith Gear still had no electricity. It was warm under the blanket. He would have gladly lain there for hours, warding off the day, but his bladder was ready to burst.

He thought he heard footsteps on the landing below, followed by a creak and a closing door. Must be the tenant on the second floor. Bit of a mystery man. Rarely seen or heard. Seldom spoken to or of. Keith Gear would occasionally hear him come in late at night. He'd learned to listen out for his routine. First, the slamming front door and the noisy stumble up the stairs. Then the clumsy dropping of keys on the landing. Once. Twice. Three times or more if he was pissed. Then the difficult negotiations of key and lock. Then the crashing around. Then the TV being switched on followed by an erratic blast of volume, then turned down again, followed by a bit more crashing around, before fading to muffled thuds and pipe work rattling with flushed toilets and taps left running. Finally, silence.

Keith Gear had once seen the mystery tenant scuttling across the landing to the shared bathroom on the second floor. All he knew of him was the back of a balding head, a tall thin slightly stooped man clutching a towel or toilet roll, hurrying. Debbie and Jonathon, the young nearly weds who had until recently lived in the flat opposite on the first floor, thought their reclusive neighbour was some sort of civil servant and that his name might possibly be Stanley.

Keith Gear would rather have knocked on Debbie and Jonathon's door for 50p, but they'd married and moved on now and their flat was currently unoccupied, so reluctantly he got up, got dressed and went and tapped lightly at the mystery man's door. There was no answer so he knocked again a little louder. He was about to give up when a faint voice said, 'Who is it?'

'It's the man upstairs.'

No response.

'Keith. From the flat upstairs.'

'Come in.'

He eased the door open and peered into a cold unlit room that smelt strongly of alcohol and mouthwash. Thick black drapes hung from ceiling to floor, dominating one wall and obliterating all light, the only source of which crept in from the landing as Keith Gear stood there, door intrusively ajar. A radio was on but barely audible. He noted how sparsely furnished the room was. Bare unvarnished boards. No carpet. Just a faded red rug, a single high-backed dining chair stacked with clothes, ironed and neatly folded, a mahogany chest of drawers, a mirror-less dressing table adorned with ornaments, a small bedside cabinet and a bed, single, narrow and occupied. Keith Gear hadn't initially seen its occupant as his eyes hesitantly scanned the room and adjusted to the lack of light but there he was lying on his back, long, thin, rigid and tightly tucked in. Nine tenths shrouded by a starched white sheet, small bald head poking out like a bare light bulb, he looked like a corpse laid out in a chapel of rest. Keith Gear noticed his silver-white pallor. The way his eyes stayed fixed on the ceiling.

'I'm sorry to disturb you.'

'I thought it was the landlord.' Quiet panic in that frail croak. The faintest flicker of alarm in the eyes.

'Only I need 50p for the meter and I can't get any change until I go to the shops. I hope I haven't woken you up. I wouldn't have asked but it's raining hard and . . .'

'It's quite all right. Take one from the piles.' Calmer now. An educated voice. A hint of befuddlement in the tone. But well bred. Definitely well bred.

Keith Gear began to focus. What he had assumed to be ornaments on the dressing table were in fact rows of upturned glass tumblers. There must have been fifteen or twenty of them. Under each tumbler was a small stack of 50p coins. The bedridden host offered no explanation. The puzzled visitor, feeling it impolite to ask, speculated instead. It obviously had something to do with stumbling back from the pub half cut, some sort of retrieval system, presumably, in case the electricity went off and he needed money for the meter. Or maybe he was a compulsive hoarder, just another creature of neurotic habit quietly going mad in his shrunken bed-sit world.

Keith Gear lifted one of the tumblers and carefully took a 50p from the top of the pile.

'Thanks very much. I'll repay you as soon as I've been out. Foul out there,' he added, over-compensating for his imposition, which after barely a minute in the room he felt his continued presence clearly constituted. As he was backing politely towards the door, the tenant spoke.

'Murderer's been at it again.'

Pause.

'It was on the news.'

Keith Gear vaguely remembered something from the night before. Just before the electric went off. Just before his fourteen-hour slumber. He nodded assent.

'Not the vigilantes,' clarified the tenant. 'The other one. The celebrity one.'

Keith Gear nodded again. A cluster of clichéd responses entered his head, auditioned, and were all rejected as unsuitable for speaking parts. Nowhere's safe these days is it? Where's it all going to end? Someone must know something. Let's hope they get him soon.

He went back upstairs, fed the meter, boiled a kettle and listened to the news on Radio Normal.

The old bed bug was right. The celebrity killer had struck again. This was his or her fourth victim and indisputably the most famous yet. The first casualty was Maurice Went, a leading showbiz agent, who was shot dead in the car park of Wessex TV while heroically shielding popular local weathergirl, Penny Tite, twenty-three, with his monumental corpulence. It was widely assumed that Penny Tite was the killer's real target but as she was being suffocated by her agent's protective gut at the time she didn't get a good look at her would-be assassin. In fact, so traumatised was she by the brutal slaying that she had been in protective police custody ever since. The second and possibly most bizarre death was that of pools winner Sidney Dunne, forty-eight, who keeled over and died, huge cheque in hand, at his own presentation ceremony. He had drunk poisoned champagne, leading the police to conclude initially that the killer was in that very function suite when it happened – an aggrieved member of the family perhaps or an extremely discontented hotel employee. Things took a twist when an anonymous phone call was made to the police, apologising for the pools winner's death. No further details were given in the short contrite call but it led police to believe that the suspect's real target was the comedian Kenny Cash who had presented Mr Dunne with his cheque and had taken a champagne flute from the same tray. The third unexplained celebrity killing was that of Jermaine Shaft, half of the veteran husband-and-wife dynasty of showbiz impresarios Jermaine and Gizelle Shaft. Again, as with Maurice Went's demise, there was a suspicion that the killer's real target was the female of the partnership. While Jermaine was a much-loved man, a show business philanthropist and patron of several children's charities, Gizelle ran a travelling circus and had recently featured in a high-profile court case concerning the alleged mistreatment of animals in her care. To the fury of many pet lovers and despite overwhelming secretly filmed evidence against her, she had been found not guilty on a technicality. Gizelle Shaft blithely stoked further outrage by making a less-than-repentant speech on the steps outside the courtroom. Three days later, a single sniper bullet to the head from a semi-automatic weapon killed her husband as he walked arm in arm with his wife across the gravel drive of their mock Tudor mansion. Again, the motive seemed uncertain but this time there was no apologetic phone call.

The killer's fourth victim was Kenny Cash.

The media punditry went into overdrive and the psychological profilers came out in force. 'Someone with a grudge against celebrities,' claimed the sleuths. 'Possibly an obsessed fan with a severe character disorder,' ventured the profilers, narrowing the field of enquiry down to thousands. Keith Gear listened to the speculation for a few minutes then turned off his radio as soon as the phone-in started and the real character disorders started calling in.

The doorbell rang. Keith Gear removed a thick slice of cardboard from the warped and worn window frame, prized open the window and gazed down at the front doorstep. There, looking twitchy and bedraggled in the pouring rain, was his friend of twenty odd years, twenty very odd years, Malcolm Drummond. Scrawny, poker-faced and dishevelled in his ever-present shabby grey overcoat, he was pacing impatiently back and forth in the yard, diffidence oozing from every pore. Even from three floors up Keith Gear could spot the diffidence.

Nicknamed 'Drum' by all who knew him, Malcolm Drummond was a trumpeter, prankster, conceptualist and part-time polymath. It was Drum who had formed the FreeFrom Music Co-operative in 1972. He'd named the organisation after a typing error. The one he kept typing whenever he typed FreeForm. Drum was big on gestures like that. He also referred to himself as an 'avant-grade' artist. He'd even named one of his albums *Avant-Grade*. It was his way of saying screw you to categorisation, his little political statement that hid bigger intentions. The joke ran so deep he wondered whether anyone apart from himself fully understood the profundity of it. Being a FreeFrom musician Drum thought that about a lot of things.

Although he'd never formally joined any of Drum's jazz or freeform ensembles Keith Gear had performed live with him many times in the early 1970s and had guested, sometimes incognito, on numerous FreeFrom albums. In more recent years their musical relationship had ebbed, and lately he found himself on Drum's regular rota of people to call on whenever the trumpeter was feeling depressed and needed to be talked down from his metaphorical window ledge. Keith Gear hurled his keys down into the yard and searched for another cup.

Drum let himself in, slumped into an armchair and sucked the oxygen right out of the room.

'Kim's left me,' he said. 'Eight years up the swannee, Keith. Eight fucking years.'

Keith Gear was surprised it had lasted that long. No musician's relationship ever lasted that long. None of his had.

'Do you know what she told me, Keith? She never really liked jazz. After eight years she tells me that. Faked it all that time. I wonder what else she faked.'

Keith Gear had slept with Kim so he knew the answer to that one.

Drum sat there emitting misery like trapped wind. Keith Gear thought it best to manoeuvre him away from his relationship problems and back to his *raison d'être*.

'Working on anything at the moment, Drum?'

'Yeah, an oratorio,' drawled Drum. 'It's a whodunit in which no one knows who dunit.'

Pause.

'Or cares.'

Pause.

'Or even knows if anyone had done anything in the first place.'

This was what had passed for communication between the two of them for some time now.

'Heard about the latest murder, Drum?'

'What? The vigilantes. Good fucking luck to them. Some arsehole stole my car radio aerial yesterday. Just snapped it off.'

'Never rains but it pours, eh, Drum?'

Drum almost smiled. He appreciated the humour. He liked his irony black with no sugar.

'No. The celebrity one. He's struck again. I assume it's a he. It usually is,' said Keith Gear.

'Who's he got now?' muttered Drum through ventriloquist lips.

'Kenny Cash. It was on the news.'

It was all Drum could do to suppress a sardonic grin, but then Drum knew no other way of grinning anymore. They all came out sardonic these days, whatever the impulse.

Kenny Cash had ridden the alternative comedy boom of the early 80s all the way to the bank. His easy estuary charm and cheeky demeanour, coupled with his full-throttle double-speed delivery of ever-so-slightly radical material aimed at the ever-so-slightly politicised punter, accorded him success out of all proportion to his talent. He was fastidiously correct when addressing matters of sex, race and class in his act, and successfully managed to pass himself off as classless and 'of the people', until some newshound with friends in low places and a nose for a story revealed that the comic's father was in fact a high-ranking civil servant with the Foreign Office and that Kenny Cash, aka Kenneth Carter-Sewell, was to the manner and manor born in every respect. The snoop also revealed that despite holding all of his interviews in a run-down Battersea council flat, which he claimed was his home, Cash actually owned a five-bedroom house in Hampstead. The council flat was just a front, paid for by his agent. Good for the image.

Being outed by the press like that brought about a radical image rethink in the upper-middle-class gagster. His first reaction was to subtly modify his mockney vowels and his rapid-fire patter. With all the missionary zeal of the born again he reinvented himself as the conscience of comedy and began railing against what he considered puerile and demeaning mainstream acts. To this end, he broke one of the sacred unwritten rules of showbiz protocol by naming comedians that he felt did not shape up to the new orthodoxy. Cash vented most of his newfound self-righteous spleen on Lenny Lyons, a cheerfully rotund red-faced sandy-haired comic of the old school, whose stock-in-trade was bawdy songs, corny capers and single-entendre stand up. Indeed Lenny Lyons could get a lot of mileage out of a phrase like 'stand up'.

Kenny Cash took to his moral crusade with aplomb, appearing in every media window display available to him in order to condemn his *bête noire* for racial stereotyping, misogyny and other alleged crimes against quality comic material. He reserved his biggest tirade for a sequence in one of Lyons' sketches where, armed with a lion tamer's whip, he chased buxom scantily clad women around a circus cage. It was only when Lenny Lyons had a severe heart attack, brought on it was said by the constant vilification, that Cash eased off on the slurs. He even claimed at one point that he had never meant to single out Lyons by name and that he was just making a general point about all comedians who victimise and patronise women by putting them in lion's cages and subjecting them to involuntary flagellation.

At the time of his assassination, Cash was a millionaire. Keith Gear had last seen Lenny Lyons being wheeled onto an afternoon chat show on regional TV. Partially paralysed and rendered semi-incomprehensible by his latest stroke, his interlocuter had to slowly repeat everything he said to the chat-show host and studio audience.

Keith Gear had always found Lenny Lyons to be a gentle spirit, whose comedy never harmed anyone. When he thought of Lenny Lyons he always thought of his Aunt Elsie. It was well known that Elsie, town Mayor and pillar of her community, was prepared to interrupt any official function or social gathering, no matter how important or distinguished the guests, in order to watch Lenny's prime-time TV show. Stories of Elsie's devotion were legion. She would arrange her entire social calendar around *Life With Lenny*. She even insisted on watching his show as she lay dying in hospital. Keith Gear's abiding memory of what would turn out to be his last visit to see his ailing Aunt was of walking into a hospital ward to be greeted by a circle of nurses, porters and patients seated in a circle around Elsie's bed laughing at the TV screen in the corner. Elsie, plumped up, dripped up and drowning in flowers was laughing the heartiest laugh of all. On the TV screen a blindfold Lenny Lyons was slowly feeling his way along a table full of prize melons towards a scantily clad woman with enormous breasts.

Drum rolled a cigarette. Keith Gear went into the kitchen

and made tea. Drum turned on the TV. The morning magazine shows were wheeling the psychological profilers in and out as fast as they could, asking each one to expound their theories on the celebrity killer in the seven and a half seconds allotted to them.

'None of us really know shit about each other or anyone or anything,' Drum muttered as he punched the channel buttons so hard that one of them flew from its casting. 'Are you coming to May Grey's album launch?' he shouted, as Keith Gear waited for the kettle to boil.

May Grey was the cross-dressing alter-ego of classically trained pianist Tony Maggs. After many years of doubt and procrastination, he was about to release his first album under his revealing new moniker. *Revealing Monica* was the name of the album. The title was Drum's idea and as punning titles went it was one of his better efforts. This was, after all, the man who had named his most recent album *Instant Drum: Just Add Nauseum*, and the one before that *Colly Flower Era*. In 1976 he'd had to be talked out of calling an album *Flash The Gash*. Keith Gear remembered contributing a track to that same LP, a frenetic guitar improvisation.

As he left the studio, Drum said, 'What's it called, Keith?'

Keith Gear said, 'Dunno. Sounds a bit frantic, doesn't it?'

Knowing Drum's penchant for the unstunning pun he half expected him to call it 'Sounds A Bit Frantic' or 'Frantic Antics' or something like that. The previous time this had happened the track ended up being called 'Wot U Like'. This time when the album came out Keith Gear was surprised to see his contribution credited as 'Hellzapoppin Goonery'. He didn't return Drum's calls for weeks. This was during a period when Drum appeared to be adopting a scorched-earth approach to language that was totally at odds with his genuine linguistic dexterity. Untitled track by bass player Mick? Drum called it 'Mick's Thing'. That tricky piece in 13/8 time? Drum called it 'Thing in 13/8'. That soundtrack sessions for some underfunded never-to-be-distributed art film? Drum called it *Art*

Thing. Incidental music for that scene in the park? Drum called it 'Park Thing'. That scene by the river? Drum called it 'River Thing'. This was when he was deep into his Thing period. And when the Thing thing was all used up, he moved rapidly back to puns. Drum had a degree in punology.

This was a man who could play trumpet as beautifully and as tenderly as Miles. Indeed he'd once called a track 'Miles Weeps The Night' in homage to his hero. So, try as he may, Keith Gear couldn't put Drum's compulsive punning down to a simple lack of quality control. At times he assumed that it was all part of Drum's self-destruct mechanism, his willingness to throw a spanner in the words when methodology and *raison d'être* became too polished and predictable. At other times, he harboured a suspicion that the entire object of the exercise was to wind him up.

As if to confirm his suspicions Drum called out from the living room. 'Hopefully there'll be a bit of a jam afterwards. Bring your axe,' he added sarcastically, knowing that Keith Gear hated the term.

'I don't have an axe,' muttered Keith Gear, rising to the bait. 'I don't spank the plank. I don't wield an axe. I'm not a fucking lumberjack.'

Keith Gear methodically dunked a tea bag whilst his brain searched for an excuse as to why he wouldn't be able to make May Grey's album launch. The most honest reason, usurped and used up long ago, was that he loathed jamming. He lived for performance. Performance was all. Everything else was record industry bullshit and trapping the moment. People were always asking him if he fancied a jam; even now after a quarter of a century of hostility to the question, no one had really got the message. He'd had some of the most inspiring nights of his creative life ruined by some jerk wanting to have a jam. That hippie guy who sat down next to him at a St Tropez party and started bashing the bongos, dismantling his delicate fretwork, and dissipating the reverence of the room in seconds. That young Puerto Rican kid presented to him in the New Mexico desert by a dollar-hungry promoter, along with an offer to duel in the midday sun, an offer that Keith Gear instinctively felt he shouldn't refuse if he valued the future use of his hands. So he duly obliged and sat with his would-be nemesis on creaky bar stools in a deserted bodega somewhere off the Santa Fe trail, all under the watchful eye of the promoter and a couple of his 'associates'. So what does the Puerto Rican kid do? He starts with a few ham-fisted Carlos Santana riffs and then resorts to chopping out cheesy funk lines to order. The only lick he's got. The dollar-hungry promoter looks like he wants to kill his protégé. His 'associates' look like they want to kill Keith Gear. And they probably would have done if Keith Gear hadn't given an impromptu performance of Manuel de Falla's 'Le Tombeau de Claude Debussy' on his Spanish guitar. A performance that made one of the associates wipe tears from his eyes with the back of his huge dirty fist.

Jamming wasn't what Keith Gear was about. Jamming wasn't what he did. He'd even famously walked out on a jam with Jimi Hendrix once. It was one of the two things that everyone knew about Keith Gear. OK, he was seventeen and headstrong but there was a time when Keith Gear's reputation went before him; now it just trailed after him like a long evening shadow.

The other thing that everyone knew about Keith Gear was what he'd done on that night in September 1970 at the Damask Hotel when the lover panicked and the guitarist stopped breathing and the other guests fled and the last guest left saved his idol's life. Jimi had started to choke on his own vomit when Keith Gear had the presence of a very stoned mind to gently ease him onto his side and put his fingers down his hero's throat in an attempt to clear his airways. When that appeared to have failed and Hendrix started to turn blue Keith Gear placed his own lips gently onto those of the overdoser and gave him the kiss of life.

As Keith Gear reached for the sugar Drum came into the

kitchenette and ran his finger along the top shelf of the food cupboard. 'Don't suppose you found a lump of hash up here?'

Keith Gear looked quizzical.

'Remember? Last time I was here? Couple of months ago? We were having a smoke and your landlord turned up for the rent.'

'Oh yeah, I remember,' said Keith Gear, reluctance in his voice, a penny dropping in a padded cell.

'Only I stashed it here,' said Drum. 'Rock-hard piece of Moroccan. About this big.'

'About the size of an Oxo cube?'

'HELLO,' HE LIED

1983

Helena Kirsch opened the red velvet curtains and flooded the bedroom with sunlight. She put the window on the latch and apple blossom blew in, making a pink-white blanket on the bed. In the garden juvenile sparrows and gauche starlings bustled for space in the birdbath. She brought her boyfriend breakfast in bed – lightly grilled kippers on toast – then busied herself in the kitchen, getting ready for work. Keith Gear could hear her heels echoing on the stone floor as she executed her well-rehearsed morning routine from pantry to bread bin to Aga. She turned on the radio. Radio Moron. Pop platters from yesteryear. That's what the DJ called them. Pop platters. From yesteryear.

Keith Gear heard a familiar ringing intro, a riff that had launched a thousand trips. Helena called out from the kitchen. 'Keith, they're playing your hit.' He liked the singularity of that. Your hit. Keith Gear was only ever tainted once with a top-ten record and now the noise was filling the kitchen. He turned on the bedside clock radio. He loved the way that its crappy little speaker mashed everything into tinny particles. '*That's Dominion there from 1969. Brings back so many memories, doesn't it? Ten past nine and . . .*'

'They never say what the memories are, do they?'

'I'm sorry, dear, I . . .'

Helena was fixing her hair and not really listening. Her head had already left for work.

'I said they never say what the memories are, do they?

They say, "Brings back so many memories, doesn't it?" but they never . . .'

'Don't forget to take the bin out, will you?'

Helena checked herself once more in the mirror, turned sharply on her heels and left her man to his musing.

'And the way he says, "That's Dominion there. THAT'S Dominion THERE." Like the location of the record is . . . it's like he's startled or something. You can imagine him pointing at it.'

'Bye.'

Keith Gear heard the front door slam and the car start first time.

'And it was 1970, you retard,' he muttered.

A Bach fugue drifted in from next door. Keith Gear measured out his mornings with the music that emanated from his elderly neighbour's drawing room. On Monday, Wednesday and Friday mornings from nine thirty to midday, Julia offered piano tuition to Grade Five at reasonable rates. On Tuesday and Thursday mornings Julia played Bach on her gramophone. To him Bach's music either sounded transcendental or like listening to maths. He had long since learned that this response had nothing to do with interpretation or arrangement and everything to do with his prevailing mood. Some days he shivered in awe as Bach made union of the sacred and the secular, counterpoint spiralling skyward with endless variants and inversions. Other days he just heard that charmless Lutheran sensibility grinding out ecclesiastical cant and unmelodious logic. This morning he heard the best of all worlds. The square root of music.

On Mondays, Wednesdays and Fridays he heard students of widely varying competence wading through sickly layers of Liszt, cakewalking all over Debussy, hamfisting Chopin, pummelling Rachmaninov into sequined Liberace shapes. Julia's tutees were mostly teenage girls. He sometimes saw them standing on her porch when he went for a morning paper. Arriving early and smoking their nerves away. On

Wednesdays three French girls filled the air with Gaulliose fumes, excited chatter and abysmal counterpoint.

He lay there listening as 'The Art Of Fugue' unfolded in all its perfection. He could hear the acoustics of Julia's drawing room. Sparsely furnished. Hardwood floor. A Bechstein Baby Grand. A valuable vase trembling on a precarious wicker stand. Still lifes littering the walls. A selection of her late husband's daubs expensively framed and lovingly hung. She'd once shown Keith a yellowing cutting from a local newspaper, a faded grey and white photo of a young man with broad shoulders and a small skull accepting a prize. 'Painter shows promise,' said the headline. *Doesn't everyone?* thought Keith Gear, flushing a turd and going to his creativity.

He surveyed the clutter of his music room, smelled the staleness of last night's endeavour, I-spied an inventory of all that he was: a black Fender Telecaster; a Simms Watts Gibson SG copy – acquired for £30 and customised beyond recognition; an EKO Jumbo semi-acoustic and a battered old Spanish guitar, currently unstrung; a Vox AC30 amp; a Revox four-track tape machine; a stack of Revox tape boxes; a scattering of cassette cases; sleeveless albums; sheet music covered in coffee stains; cup circles and cryptic annotation; an overflowing ashtray; a jam jar full of dead forget-me-nots; a wah-wah pedal, fuzz pedal, echo unit, trailing leads, tangled wires; and, the pre-requisite of all musicians, a stereo system of incompatible separates that had to be kick-started in order to work. Drug dealers and hi-fi fanatics have good stereos and dependable circuitry. Musicians don't. Keith Gear risked electrocution from his array of fizzing, crackling, overloaded plugboards every time he changed sockets.

The downstairs phone rang. He went to answer, thinking it might be Helena. She often phoned as soon as she arrived at the photographers' co-operative, usually to impart some important domestic duty that he may have overlooked. *There's a letter on the mantelpiece. Will you post it? We're out of mung beans. Will you get some? Don't forget to put the bin out. Since they were privatised, the bin men don't come round the back yard anymore so please make sure you put it out. OK, Keith? Are you listening, Keith?* He hesitated before picking up the phone.

'Wye aye.'

It was the unmistakable Wearside baritone of Guy Truelove.

'Aven't got you out of bed, 'av I?'

'No, Guy. You've got me out of working.'

'That's no good, man. All good boys should be practising their scales by now. Any of those French lasses in today?'

'What can I do for you, Guy?'

At least Guy had the courtesy to phone first these days. When Keith and Helena first shacked up together, he would turn up uninvited regardless of the hour. A loud hammering on the door at two in the morning? That will be Guy, just back from a gig or a pub lock-in, or a party throw-out. A loud hammering on the door at six in the morning? That will be Guy, having driven all night from halfway across Spain or France or Scotland or the all-night poker school he'd just lost the rent to, or the shed he'd been sleeping in after his girlfriend kicked him out for losing the rent at an all-night poker school.

'You'll have to tell him.'

'I know.'

Keith and Helena lay in bed listening to the persistent hammering. The 'I know you're in there' knock. The 'I'm not going away until you answer' knock.

That was the time he stormed to the door and opened it in a temper to find a dribbling drunk Truelove gurgling nothing but air bubbles through the mouthpiece of his beat-up trombone.

'What kept you?' slurred Guy. Same old pissed-up, piss-taking Guy. Long thick ginger hair parted in the middle. Naturally crimped like something out of Tudor times. Huge beak of a nose that played host to a prominent mole. Fine downy goatee beard. The mark of a red-skinned man who had made it to thirty without ever having shaved properly.

Guy steadied himself against the door, belched loudly and asked Keith if he was 'Going to let me in or what?' He then lurched past his unwilling host into the kitchen, swigged the dregs from an empty wine bottle and asked if he could open another. When Helena came in to check out the commotion her guitar-legend bedmate and Guy Truelove were thrashing around on the floor, mistiming their punches and cursing loudly. They rolled comically to a halt at Helena's slippered feet. During the ensuing domestic argument between unwilling host and even-less-willing hostess, Guy Truelove slipped away with one of Helena's cheapest cameras. He hadn't turned up without invitation since. These days he at least made a courtesy phone call, usually from the box around the corner. Progress of sorts. The camera was never mentioned again.

This morning Guy was sober, smartly dressed, and eager to talk about his latest venture. Guy always had a venture to talk about. Five years earlier he'd run a Music Against Racism night, hiring inadequate PA systems and regularly ripping off the eager unsuspecting bands, a practice that came spectacularly unstuck when he burned one militant reggae group too many. The phone call came at four in the morning.

'Keith. It's Guy . . . Guy . . . I know, man. That's cos I'm gagged and can hardly speak. I'm tied to a foking chair, mun. It's pitch dark in here. You try dialling with your foking nose. Hey. It's no laffing matter.'

But it was.

Another time he turned up on Keith Gear's doorstep, adorned in an African print T-shirt and ju-ju beads, a vision in violent purple and luminous green, and announced that he was renouncing all 'Offay free jazz and imperialist rock and the decadent bourgeoisie avant-garde' to devote himself to what he called 'Third World Music'. He was carrying a copy of the Koran and thinking of changing his name to Gi Truth. The next time Keith bumped into him he had a chorus girl on each arm and was playing in the back line of a rock-and-roll revival show at the London Palladium.

'I'm starting a comedy club, man. Whaddya think aboot that?'

'You mean like a workingmen's club? Cabaret and a scampi supper?'

'Noo. Young comedians, man. Fresh talent. There's a real underground scene developing.'

Keith Gear frowned. Comedy? Underground?

'It's going to be big, Keith. You watch.' He handed Keith an invite to the opening night.

The Party Palace
(Upstairs, Seven Bells Pub, Covent Garden)
Eight Till Late

Keith Gear took the card and mentally filed it away with all the other opening (and, as often as not, closing on the same night) nights that Guy Truelove had invited him to. The last one had been a dodgy benefit for the ANC out in Leytonstone, East London, near to where Guy was living at the time. Booking gigs near to where he was living at the time had always been a characteristic of Guy's promotional activities so Keith Gear assumed that he was currently shacked up in Covent Garden. The suit and aftershave indicated that Guy had landed on his feet again. He'd been lucky not to have had his legs broken in Leytonstone. That gig had been at a Party Palace too. It was Guy's all-purpose name for events. This particular Party Palace had formerly been the Esolda Bingo Hall, a cavernous dank pit of a venue that held two thousand with ease. Unfortunately Guy Truelove had only sold seventeen tickets and until that night had not realised that armchair radicals would not venture out from NW3 to E17. The intrepid never-say-die Guy attempted to get round this minor obstacle by going out onto the drizzly streets of

Leytonstone to drum up a crowd. When this failed, he went into a couple of local pubs and handed out free tickets. Which is how South Africa's finest township band found itself playing to a room full of rioting racist skinheads. The pub names, The King Billy and The Coronation, would perhaps have alerted a less impulsive man.

'You couldn't just give us a lift down there could you, Keith? I've got Health and Safety coming at eleven thirty to give the place the once over.' Same old Guy. He looked a million dollars, smelt of Listerine and scent rather than tobacco and brewery tap, but he didn't even have the bus fare to the West End in his pocket. Keith Gear hesitated. The traffic would be bad at this time of the morning and all he wanted to do was go into his music room and make some noise. Unfortunately, he still hadn't reached the stage of his life where he could summon up the sincerity to tell Guy unequivocally, finally, to fuck off. He doubted if he ever would. The man was one of life's perennial chancers. He wasn't even that good a trombone player but no one had yet plucked up the courage or sheer bloody-mindedness to tell him. And, as Drum once said, if none of your peers have told you that by the time you're thirty, you can probably get by on not being very good indefinitely. Drum referred to Guy's lack of talent as his bluffer's commission.

Keith Gear drove Guy to Covent Garden. There were road works and tailbacks all the way there and he had to sit and listen to Guy banging on about how this whole comedy scene was going to be massive while his own early morning creative impulses ebbed away. When they reached the club, half an hour late, a pissed-off-looking Health-and-Safety man was impatiently pacing the pavement outside.

'Come on in and have a look,' said Guy.

'I want to get back to my music,' said Keith Gear. He seemed to spend his life saying this to Guy Truelove.

During the slow crawl home he turned on Radio Clever. A well-spoken woman was reading from a twee novella. The first words Keith Gear heard were 'She had a smile that lit up her face'. This sent him into paroxysms of derision. It was the kind of writing that utterly vindicated his decision to give up writing lyrics. Radio Clever was awash with the stuff. Writing that was about writing. Writing in order to sound like a writer. He hated that cosy world of middlebrow discourse with its 'imagine my surprise when' and its 'unaccustomed as I am to' and its 'contrary to my husband's expectations', that world where breath is always baited, pauses always pregnant, anticipation always eager, and the angle by which tragedy is averted always narrow.

Where was Drum now he needed him? They could have sport with this. He remembered that time (or 'cast his mind back to that time' as Radio Clever would have put it) when they were driving back from a FreeFrom gig in Scotland, listening to Radio Serious. The announcer had just introduced a piece of African music by saying 'The sound the native musicians made was literally indescribable,' and had followed this up with a flurry of dismal similes which irrefutably confirmed his initial utterance. But you had to talk like that on Radio Serious. Just like you had to talk like THAT on Radio Clever. They couldn't just play the music, they had to lead you by the nose. Always recommending that you listen out for the subtle understatement of the opening passages which would give way to an almost unbearable haunting tension, which in turn would be resolved in the jaunty confidence of the concluding passages. That was usually all the encouragement that Gear and Drum needed. Riffing away as the van roared through the night. Sparks flying from an ever-present spliff.

What did you think of the performance, Drummondo, old boy?

Oh, I particularly enjoyed the skittish flavour of the bassoon, while the libretto, I thought, advanced from gentle lullaby to violent bombast.

What about the assertive notation? Did you not think the parlante passage unconventional in its declamatory intensity?

Well, yes, I did, but I also felt that it explored the rhythmic and semantic possibilities of operatic orchestration with verve and gusto.

Verve AND Gusto?

Well verve most definitely. The gusto was perhaps, on reflection, somewhat underdeveloped

And did you notice the way that the exquisitely brief staccato utterances of the oboe somehow evoked both the frustration of adolescence and the poignancy of approaching death?

Do you mean the exquisitely brief staccato utterances that occurred before the highly dramatic complexity unfolded or the ones that interrupted the lively and vibrant piano interlude?

All the way from Leicester to Leytonstone.

Lit up her face! LIT UP HER FACE! He couldn't imagine writing a line like that without making a wisecrack about immolation. Without Drum to spar with he rehearsed it for his own amusement. Welcome to bad-writing hour on Radio Clever. This morning's novella, *Miranda's Face,* is read by Jemima Horseteeth. Miranda was the life and soul of the party, partly due to her unusual features. She had a smile which lit up her face – the flames engulfed her and soon spread to the curtains.

Or: she had a smile which lit up her face. But when it got too hot she put the fire out with her tears.

Or: she had a smile which lit up her face. Afterwards she looked somewhat ashen.

All the way home. Until: she had a smile which lit up her face. *Oh, shit, the rubbish.*

As he turned into his street he saw the newly privatised dustcart easing past his front gate, where the bin should have been.

Fuck.

Keith Gear screeched to a halt outside his house, left the engine running, ran to his backyard and hauled the overflowing bin into the road. He saw the look of indifference on the dustcart driver's face as he checked his wing mirror and accelerated away down the road.

Keith Gear hurled the bin into the road where it lay all day and the next day too. Pizza boxes, coffee grinds, eggshells, shredded cigarettes and roaches, tomato purée, dark-room debris, sperm-encrusted tissues, Sunday supplements and crumpled sheet music congealed and flattened by tyre tracks. After three days, they received a strongly worded letter from the tenants' association.

A few days later, he drove to his radio session at the Boadicea Broadcasting Corporation's North London studios. The session was for the Earl Raven show, Radio Fun's token late-night sop to difficult music. He couldn't remember if this was the tenth or eleventh session he'd done for the show since 1970. In the early days he used to get regular work on other shows too but down the years all the Raven clones had dropped off or drifted into careers closer to their hearts, like presenting children's TV programmes or advertising carpet warehouse sales on local radio. Now, in England at least, there was just Earl Raven, an unlikely underground hero, a tall elegant aloof man with a goatee beard and a mane of jet-black hair. The Earl had an encyclopaedic knowledge of music and an overly scholastic broadcasting style, leavened with wit as dry as a dustbowl. He also possessed a bullshit detector that could sniff a bad odour at fifty paces. The Earl had always been good to Keith Gear, indeed there was a time when they seemed to hook up at every festival, but these days, the guitarist had noticed, he always seemed to be too busy to attend the sessions in person.

Down the years Keith Gear had been 'meeted and greeted' by music industry caricatures of every persuasion. Kipper-tied flare-wearing pot-bellied dedicated victims of fashion in the late 60s. Denim-shirted Brute-oozing medallion-swinging hairy-chested smoothies in the 70s. He'd been glad-handed and bullshitted by them all. Today he was welcomed by a Filofax-totting red-spec-clad yup called Grub Foster. Grub oozed insincerity from every orifice. 'Hello,' he lied, shaking Keith Gear's hand. 'Great,' he said to everything Keith Gear said.

'How was your journey?' he asked.

'I've lost my contacts book,' observed Keith Gear. 'Must have fallen out of my pocket.'

'Great.'

Keith Gear performed six improvised pieces, 'Ullulations #1–6'. These would later be included on *The Wilderness Tapes*, a compilation of his outtakes, radio broadcasts, incidental music and miscellany, 1979–85. When he asked if he could participate in the mixing process a brusque female PA in a green check trouser suit and downy facial hair screeched, 'No. We have an engineer chappie who does all that.' Nothing much had changed at the Boadicea. They'd been saying that to him since 1969.

During a break in the session, Keith Gear wandered the corridors looking for somewhere to discreetly smoke his stuff. He passed a cavernous studio where a classical concert rehearsal was in progress, dog-legged right and continued along a long passageway and out through a fire exit into a small paved garden area, decked out with a few desultory shrubs in tubs and a sand bucket full of stubbed-out fags. The area was bordered on three sides by a bare trellis and faced an office that had its blinds drawn shut. Keith Gear soaked up the overhead sun and the welcome seclusion and lit one of his pre-rolled joints. He was deep in spliff-fuelled reverie when the window blind suddenly flickered and opened to reveal a roomful of executives chatting and gathering up paperwork at the end of their conference session. A woman at the front of the room switched off an overhead projector and everyone turned and stared at the man in the yard having his illegal smoke.

Retracing his steps through the convoluted innards of

Boadicea House, Keith Gear passed the concert studio again. The session had ended and the huge studio double doors were wide open, revealing five of the younger male orchestra members who had stayed behind to have a jam. A drummer, a guitar player, a pianist, a sax player and a string bass player were rocking stiffly, their body language betraying a life spent interpreting the classical canon in formal clothes. A smattering of female orchestra members sat in a semi-circle of chairs in front of them, hands in laps, heads cocked, a cameo of adoration. Keith Gear leaned against the corridor wall and listened with a mixture of amusement and contempt. He couldn't work out whether the noise they were making sounded like classical musicians trying to perform some hitherto unrealised form of progressive rock or progressive rock musicians groping their way around the classics. He lingered for a few moments, grimly fascinated by this scratch ensemble and its unholy hybrid. The guitarist affecting changes for changes' sake, lurching from 5/4 to 13/8 at inappropriate moments; the pianist making tricky clusters for no other reason than the fact that he could; the sax player parping atonally in a parody of modern jazz; the drummer doing what all classical percussionists do when they get to play a full kit, lying irritatingly behind the beat and sucking the swing out of the thing. He watched the academy straitjacket being pulled tighter with every virtuoso act and thought, *There but for the grace of God, Gear*. The music echoed down the corridor. Conservatoire training reverberating in every paradiddle and diminished seventh. Keith Gear had never heard a seventh sound so diminished.

As he drove home, it began to rain. He turned on the radio. Bach sounded like maths.

NICE SHAME

1983

'That Home Secretary! What a cunt, eh?'

The comedian paused for effect, letting his utterance work the room. The crowd united as one on this matter and loudly voiced its empathy with the sentiment. The Home Secretary was indeed a cunt and audience members turned to one another as if they were about to discuss the myriad ways in which he had proved himself to be a cunt during his four years in office. The comedian basked in warm rays of approval as the audience gathered itself for the punchline. 'We like the set up,' they seemed to be saying. 'The Home Secretary is indeed a cunt. Now furbish us with details of his cuntitude.'

It was the opening night of Guy Truelove's comedy club. The Party Palace was a small room above the Seven Bells Pub in Covent Garden, reached via a set of steep narrow stairs and comfortably holding about one hundred people. By the time Keith Gear and Malcolm Drummond arrived, it was uncomfortably holding two hundred and fifty. This clearly wasn't one of Guy's usual dives or disasters, and he was in his element, meeting and greeting, making sure that the bar was well stocked and that the right people got the right stage-side seats. 'Pretty hierarchical for an alternative night,' grumbled Drum as he elbowed his way towards what remained of the free food.

That was the night when everyone got to meet Tony Maggs' wider circle of friends for the first time. Everyone knew that

Tony had this whole other social scene outside of music but on that opening night he brought his entire entourage with him. Artists, filmmakers and fashion designers from the dockland squats. Photographers and furniture makers from the inner-city squats. DJs, models, club runners and cloakroom attendants from the frontline squats. Every creative person known to Tony Maggs at that time seemed to live in a squat. Tony made his entrance in a Nefertiti head wrap and a glitzy blue silk two-piece. He looked positively underdressed compared with some of his company.

The metropolitan media were also out in force. Prominent among the ringsiders was Sparks Aston, the chief commissioning editor from the new youth TV channel, Channel Raw. He'd already staked out his territory before the first act came on stage, flitting from clique to clique, glad-handing everyone in his path, blank cheques at the ready.

The opening act, billed as 'Mike Davis: Marxist–Leninist Punch & Judy Show', came on with his puppets and props and performed a show of spectacularly random violence, all seamlessly linked with a quietly spoken surreal narrative that had the audience convulsed from the off. From his position at the bar, Keith Gear saw a man displace the contents of a large ashtray with a single involuntary explosive guffaw. Similar scenes of incapacitation were being enacted all around him. One man was trying to offer his friend peanuts from a newly opened packet but seemed to be stuck in suspended animation as he sat quivering helplessly. The friend eventually had to prise the packet from his colleague's trembling hand. Another man headbutted the bar. The woman seated next to him went into incontinence mode, twisting herself into intestinal knots as she attempted to stem the flow of hysterics.

'My greatest ambition, that,' said Drum.

'What?' shouted Keith Gear, above the noise.

'To make a woman physically piss herself with laughter,' said Drum.

The entire room seemed to be engaged in grotesque travesties of posture and it was all due to a sanguine-faced man with a fake bandito moustache making jokes about materialism, collectivism, purges and pogroms with the aid of two wooden hand puppets and a makeshift wooden set, which he gleefully demolished to tumultuous applause during a spoof rock-and-roll finale.

Next up was Archie Studamuir, a walnut-skinned American comic of the old school. Archie was slick, quick and so Las Vegas that everyone wondered what he was doing there. At first, the crowd gave him the benefit of the doubt and laughed out of politeness, but soon his lame jokes about aeroplane food and TWA stewardesses and 'those crazy sports you guys play' were going down like the Hindenburg. Sensing that he was losing the room, he embarked upon a spot of audience participation and attempted to get pally with Tony Maggs and his glittering entourage in the front row.

'And what do you do, honey?' he said, mistaking the immaculately dragged-up Maggs for a woman.

'I'm a musician,' replied his foil archly, adding with perfect timing, 'and what it is that you do, my dear?' Archie Studamuir never really recovered after that.

Next on was Rick Hanley, a fresh-faced kid in his early twenties with a pageboy crop and a little-boy-lost manner. He had already done a bit of late-night TV and had shrewdly made sure that his entourage of rent-a-fans was ensconced down at the front. After Archie Studamuir's stale Copacabana schtick, Rick Hanley went down a storm. His material dealt in basic adolescent staples: buying King Size Rizlas from the tobacconists, fondly remembered TV programmes from infancy, your mum finding your porn mags, zit-jokes. The rent-a-fans lapped it up. After ten minutes of girlfriend stuff he launched into a bit about inappropriately named articles of clothing. Drum began to eat his own fist.

'Windcheater? Windcheater! How does that work then? I mean precisely how does it cheat the wind? . . . And a sweater? A sweater! Is that what it's for? To make you sweat? What's that all about then?'

When he started jumping up and down to demonstrate a jumper, Drum began flicking peanuts at the stage. The set concluded with an over-cooked and convoluted tale about a woman, a necklace, a fish and a bicycle which at one point contained the line, 'Ignore the fish. The fish is a red herring.' This brought the house down. Drum went to the toilet.

After Rick Hanley had done his turn Guy Truelove took to the stage, wet the ringsiders with holy water from his champagne glass, blessed the rest with his microphone and thanked everyone for coming. 'Next week, ladies and gents, we have Ivan the Engineer, Spotty and Socks, Kenny Cash and A.N. Other. But finally too-night. Would you please welcome, all the way from the other side of the room, Del Rees.'

'That Home Secretary! What a cunt, eh?'

Del Rees paused for a moment in order to milk the applause that he had instigated with the devastatingly satirical device of calling the Home Secretary an expletive deleted. Then he lined up his next carefully selected target.

'That Foreign Secretary, eh? What a cunt!'

It didn't take Drum long to realise that Del Rees didn't have any material as such, merely a string of insults and expletives with the occasional 'insert MP's name here'.

Like that.

'That Prime Minister. Boadicea. Now she really is a cunt.'

The room cracked up at that. It was the funniest and most profane thing they had ever heard. Drum turned to Keith Gear and said, 'I wouldn't have been so hard on Rick Hanley if I'd known what was coming. Jeez!'

At the end of the night Guy Truelove was beaming. The hacks, agents and commissioning editors all shook his hand warmly and descended upon Del Rees and Rick Hanley with their calling cards and promises of work. Tony Maggs and his entourage departed as they had arrived, en masse, leaving the room a lot less illuminated for their absence. Once they'd gone the place suddenly looked again like the dingy cramped upstairs room of a pub.

Those who remained indulged in an alcohol-fuelled orgy of backslapping and ego massaging until the complimentary bar ran dry. 'Great, wasn't it?' said some ebullient hack to Drum.

'Not really,' glowered Drum, large after-hours whisky in hand. The hack, sensing the onset of belligerence, backed off and went in search of somebody else to swap platitudes with.

Late, very late, when everything was getting slurred, blurred and maudlin, when the worst for wear were comatose and the best were in their cups, Guy Truelove turned to Drum. 'Wasn't that bad, was it, man?'

Drum shifted drunkenly on his bar stool and stubbed out a cigarette. 'First one was all right. The Punch and Judy man. But the rest of them were shit.' He reached for a whisky bottle and poured the dregs. 'And as for the audience. First thing I would have told that smug bunch of fuckers was what a bunch of hypocritical tossers they all are. Laughing at jokes about Boadicea and her government. As far as I can see most of them look like they're doing very nicely out of Boadicea's government. Very nicely indeed.'

'Well, if you reckon you can do any better, Drum,' said Guy, laying down the gauntlet.

And to everyone's surprise, Drum picked it up. Eventually.

Nothing happened immediately. All he did for months was turn up, pick his spot at the bar, and sit watching like a hawk. Impassively scrutinising every act. Meanwhile the club got more successful. One night a week became two. Ticket touts began working the queue. Twice weekly Guy would dutifully put Drum's name on the guest list and twice weekly Drum would turn up wearing his impassive face. He kept his bar-stool vigil for months and watched that first wave of comedy rebels break through. He saw them all when they were still hungry for it, desperate to be loved, the funny stuff flowing uncontrollably. And he saw what happened when they swam from the slipstream into the mainstream, and got cosy, flabby, and flawed. He saw Amateur Hour turn into Pro-Celebrity stand up. He saw what agents did for egos, what money and success did to material, and what cocaine did to timing.

And then suddenly, a year and a half down the line, long after his friends had forgotten Drum's initial boast or dismissed it as drunken Drum talk, Drum went for it. It was the Tuesday night open-floor spot. Guy asked for volunteers as he always did and without warning Drum left his seat, got up on stage and told everyone that they were all doing very nicely out of Boadicea's government. Very nicely indeed.

Having wagged a mildly admonishing finger at the yuppies in the audience, he turned his attention to the comedians themselves. He could have gone the easy route. He could have roasted any one of those public-school-educated slummers who got up on stage and dropped a glottal stop in order to sound less posh than they were. But Drum saw truth in the incidentals.

'So I'm walking into the gig tonight and I see the publicity photos of all the performers on those posters outside. Hey, a year into the comedy revolution and it's being sponsored by Kodak, already.'

Splutters of guilty recognition rippled around the room.

'I'm sorry! But I don't recall seeing publicity photos outside this pub those first few months. The London Palladium. Yeah! All those Cambridge Circus theatres. Sure! Richard Stilgoe? The Two Ronnies? Everytime. But the Party Palace. Hello, operator? Can you get me the Alternative Party Palace? Y'know? The place that has all those photos plastered outside? The place where all the radicals play? Yeah, that's right. The non-star place.'

Drum had seen through all the rebellion rhetoric right from the start. His co-comedians stood shifting awkwardly in the wings as he went for the jugular.

'And I wouldn't mind it if they were just like regular unpretentious snapshots, but they're all so well posed, aren't they?

And so expertly lit! Soft-focus, obedient little puppy dogs. Begging on all fours. Please notice me. Please notice me. Please throw me a bone. And then I flick through *The Stage* – my favourite publication, never miss a copy – and I see the same poses and the same soft-focus snaps for regional TV presenters and jugglers and clowns and every desperate Equity extra seeking work. Gag merchant. Will fellate for money. Is there one photographer who gets all the work cos it's the same fucking pose, man, whether it's Kenny "will fellate for" Cash or Hypno Dan the Hypno Man. And then I'm watching my TV and *Saturday Night Live* comes on – y' know those American alternatives with fire in their bellies and a contract in their pocket – and there's the same fucking poses. Fucking comedy turns in skinny ties and tight sweaters pouting and posing like they're in some CBGB's punk band instead of acknowledging what they truly are. Fucking wise-crack merchants waiting for the whore of Hollywood to spread its legs.'

People were whooping now. The next comedian on the bill had slipped away and sought refuge out of earshot in the toilet. Drum ended the section with his 'what-they-say-what-they-do' bit. Juxtaposing pseudo-radical dialogue and photo poses until the woman with the incontinence posture looked like she had just fulfilled Drum's ambition by filling her knickers.

'I'm a really alternative comedian with red-hot controversial material!'

Drum gave the audience a side-on stare. Mock moody.

'I'm a public-school rebel and I don't compromise!'

Drum flicked his fringe across his face and mimed a cameo of drama-school angst.

'I'm a rad-fem comic with the manners of a pig. Get my good side! Get my good side!'

Drum put a finger in his mouth and pouted like a Page Three stunner. Then he slowly inserted a second figure and pretended to fellate. Then a third and pretended to gag.

'Tear down those Two Ronnies posters. There's a new comedy kid in town!'

Drum turned round and spread his arse cheeks in anticipation of being shafted.

Kenny Cash was top of the bill that night. He didn't stand a chance.

Nobody should have been surprised at Drum's transformation. None of his friends were. Back in 1972, just after he had formed the FreeFrom Music Co-operative, he instigated Jokecon too. The aim of Jokecon was to disseminate jokes as if they were concept art. Drum had served briefly with the British Army but had been discharged in 1970 after trying to form a union. His first job after being booted out of Her Majesty's forces was as a night porter in an East End hospital. What Drum surmised from his army travels and his portering was that fifty per cent of all known jokes originate in institutions: the forces, borstals, prisons, hospitals, etc., while the other fifty per cent are hatched by professional gag writers in smoke-filled offices. To Drum jokes were a folk form and he was a self-appointed curator, an anthropologist, the Cecil Sharp of quips.

Drum began by telling jokes in the hospital canteen and then waited to see how long it took them to reach the wards. He got into the whole Chinese whispers aspect of it, comparing and contrasting variation in set up and punchline, measuring degrees of mutation or distortion. When he let Gear, Maggs and Truelove in on the act things got really abstract. One liners, tall tales, shaggy dog stories and urban myths were invented and imparted to strangers on trains, on planes, at bus stops, taxi ranks, waiting rooms and shop queues. Drum took to reciting them loudly into telephone receivers in public call boxes with no one on the other end of the line and then getting someone to film the event on a cine camera. He accumulated reels and reels of the stuff, startled passers-by all staring at the shouting lunatic in the phone booth. Nobody got rich from the venture, Drum never got round to turning it into an exhibition or a TV show, as the more fiscal-minded might have done. He just did it for the crack. Even now, all these years on, Gear, Maggs or Truelove would occasionally overhear a joke that had been hand-reared and released into the wild in the early 1970s. *Can I use your Dictaphone?* That was one of Drum's. And the one about the architect who had his housemaid backwards. That was Drum's too.

It all took off after that open-mike night at the Party Palace. Drum had always been a good raconteur. When his melancholy wasn't biting he often interjected surreal or bitter-sweet monologues into his freeform music sets, but late in 1985 he suddenly dispensed with the trumpet and the experimental music altogether and became a full-time avant-grade comedian instead. It was as if everything else Drum had ever done was a rehearsal leading up to this moment. He seized it as he seized a microphone, with both hands and a hyperactive larynx.

It was around this time that a campaign was launched to introduce 'non-competitive' sports to schools. Drum homed in on the unspoken truth.

'Yeah. I'm all in favour. Let's eliminate the one thing that poor kids might be good at. Let's deprive the already deprived of the one thing they've got. Little Leroy may be able to run like the wind. Little Gary may be able to dribble blindfold for fifty yards with a football on the end of his big toe, but little Jennifer and sensitive Jason feel left out so let's ban it now. And while we're at it, let's introduce non-competitive maths and non-competitive English too. Any English teachers in tonight?'

A nervous murmur went round the room.

'I order you to go back to school tomorrow and rip those essays up! You take little Jennifer's gold-star poem about catkins and butterflies off the classroom wall and you burn it in front of her eyes. Yeah! And when little Jennifer's mummy and daddy come up the school demanding to know why little

Jennifer hasn't had an essay marked in over three months you tell them its all due to non-competitive English. New regime! Spread the word, daddy-o. And don't forget to mention the non-competitive piano class too. And the non-competitive speech day.'

On another occasion the American crime writer Hanny Duvant was in the Party Palace audience. Drum had heard him on the radio, professing his admiration for the comedy of Lenny Lyons, who although now verboten by the alt-com police was beginning to attract a cult following in the USA thanks to his old shows being re-run on late-night cable TV. Drum launched into a perfect parody of Duvant's sub-Damon Runyan prose style.

'I identified my contact and greeted him with a grunt. We rendezvoused as arranged at rush hour, in the crowded smoker's compartment of a cross-town cable car. The grizzled gradients and rattling axels made conversation hard and body language child's play. I sipped hot coffee, tipped my homburg and pulled in my gut to allow a shapely dame to pass. "You don't get many of those to the pound," I guffawed, digging his ribs and blowing my cool.

'Later she took me in hand and tugged at my purse strings. "Johnny," she said, as she counted dollar bills and lightened my load, "you have the look of a man who votes to the right, dresses to the left and always looks behind him before crossing a busy road." I beat out a bongo rhythm on her breasts, shouted way-hey, and rotated my bow tie. "Stop that," she said, "I've had it up to here with jerks." I could barely contain myself as the next innuendo took shape on my bruised and battered lips.'

Some nights Drum's material was beyond the pale. When the newspapers reported that thieves had burgled the home of Kenny Cash and left the comedian's old English sheepdog tethered to the nearby railway line, where it was subsequently decapitated, Drum incorporated the incident into his act. One night it might take the form of a maths question. 'If a train leaves Waterloo at six fifteen, travelling at an average speed of 50 mph, how long has Kenny Cash's dog . . .' Another night it might be a sing-a-long. 'Dog on the line it's all mine all mine, Dog on the line it's all . . . c'mon. Second verse.'

One night Drum introduced a song into his set. Called 'Nice Shame: Legs About The Face', it was a manic parody of a novelty punk record called Nice Legs (Shame About The Face) that had made the pop charts a few years earlier. Drum had conceived his version in the back of a transit while travelling back from a gig one night high on bathtub sulphate. At first he performed it as he had done that night in the van, as a speed-rant a cappella. It quickly became an established part of his act. In fact, it became so popular he had to start saving it for an encore. Eventually it would become an albatross, but before that, to everyone's surprise, it became a top thirty hit.

In April 1986, Keith Gear turned on his telly and there was Drum performing his amphetamino antics on *Top Of The Pops*.

> Nice shame/legs about the face
> Nice shame/legs about the face
> shame face/legs about the face/legs about the face

A hastily convened deposition from the alternative comedy police led by Kenny Cash put pressure on the record company and managed to get the extended twelve-inch version withdrawn from the shops.

Guy Truelove had originally suggested that the gang should all appear on the record, which he was prepared to put out on his own Import Ant label. Guy would play trombone, Tony Maggs keyboards, Keith Gear guitar, with Mick 'n' Dick, a couple of stalwarts from the FreeFrom Co-operative, on bass and drums. Everyone was up for it. Tony Maggs worked out an arrangement for the track, scoring brass parts for Drum and Guy, an *Addam's Family*-style mock-goth middle eight for himself, and a killer melodic hook for Keith Gear.

Everyone was looking forward to filling a Trojan horse full of avant-grade artists and wheeling it into the hallowed fortress of light entertainment TV.

Initially Drum said yes, but then Empire Records came sailing in with a lucrative contract and five-figure inducement. Instead of telling Empire where they could get off, Drum said, 'Where do I sign?' He even acquiesced to Empire's 'request' to use their own session musicians and 'more commercial arrangement'. The session guys did a competent enough job. They even got to appear on *Top Of The Pops* in ersatz-punky threads and blow-dried new-wave haircuts. But behind the scenes, Drum's friends were both amazed and appalled at the speed with which he turned into a showbiz lacky. In exchange for all this hassle, compromise, betrayal and back-biting Drum got a week at number twenty-nine, a week at number twenty-eight, and the belated realisation from one of Radio Fun's prime-time DJs that the record could be interpreted as a thinly coded paean to oral sex. This was followed by an eternity where nobody ever wanted to hear this irritating novelty record again and wasn't it a bit disturbing when you thought about it anyway? 'Nice Shame'? 'Legs About The Face'?

It took Drum six weeks to blow a decade and a half of credibility with the jazzers and the FreeFromers. Six weeks to go from respected renegade to washed-up wisecracker with a novelty hit.

Drum's reaction was a resolute 'so fucking what?' The rejection from his peers merely spurred him on. He began to critique everything with renewed vigour: every cosy notion, phoney assumption, bigoted belief, flimsy edifice, moral stand, ethical certainty, taken-for-granted definition of what it meant to act alternative and think for free. Every gig he did, Drum played 'Top the Topper'. He'd steal punchlines from every other comedian on the bill and there right in front of their unbelieving eyes he would take it to the next level. Everyone was there the night he stole the show at Cinderella's

Ball, the big Gay Pride Benefit. He'd only got the gig because Tony Maggs had influential friends in glittering places, and when he first staggered out on stage, all beery and bleary, even Tony wondered if he'd made a fatal error of judgement. Within seconds of the maître d's intro, he was convinced that Drum was going to get killed.

'Good evening, arse bandits!'

Silence. Drum gazed at hundreds of gay faces all fixed with shock, hate, dismay, all staring at this guy on stage who had delivered those opening lines and who's next words were 'Good evening, shovellers, gardeners, diggers and wearers of the brown felt hat.'

Someone threw an Aids ribbon onto the stage. Drum held his nerve. 'That was a very gay heckle wasn't it? What next, balloons?' But before the 'what nexts' could compose themselves Drum got his onslaught in double quick.

'The point I'm making is you haven't gone far enough yet. Semantically you've only just begun, as Karen the queen of anorexia once sang. OK, so you've re-appropriated the "queer" word. Good. Excellent. One less gorilla-brain in the street growling "fucking queer" at you. Now can we have gay back. Only joking . . . chums. If you really had balls you'd go for the big ones. How about reclaiming "arse bandit". Think about it! Some repressed fucker shouts "arse bandit" at you in the streets. And you turn round and say, "Yes, I am the premier arse bandit of old Compton town. Now stand and deliver. Your rectum or your life." Get it printed up on a T-shirt. Let them see the slogan. *Primo arso bandito*!'

The first whoop went up. The first converted corner table shushed their noisy neighbours.

'What have they got left? What can they fight you with if you reclaim all the hate words and sprinkle a little fairy dust on them? Hey, bum chum? I'm talking to you. Yeah you, the one serving drinks in the pinny. Anyone ever call you that? Bum chum? Yeah? Well next time you respond like this. "Yes, I weel be your bum companion anytime, my leetle bum buddy." I'm sorry, I don't know why so many of my gay characters are Mexican tonight, it's just . . .'

The rest was drowned in laughter.

And then having got them eating out of his hand Drum did something that no one would have thought possible. He turned the whole joke on its head.

'But not faggot,' he concluded. 'You can't reclaim burning at the stake. It would be like the Jews reclaiming the Holocaust. There's only so much you can appropriate. There's only so much that you'd want back.'

For the rest of the night the whole room wore a collective face that said, 'How did he get away with that?' The reviews said the same thing. That's how he liked it. That's where he preferred to be. Preaching to the unconverted. Fearless and unbowed beneath the glitter ball. Not making Boadicea jokes to the ever slightly liberal or buttering-up yuppie TV execs from Channel Raw.

Which is why he was invited back the next year. This time Drum pushed the empathy button straight away.

'I was in New York. This was 1980/81 and this guy says to me, "Man, people are dying and no one knows why. Gay people are just getting the flu and dying." I thought he was a crank you know. Real *Invasion of the Body Snatchers* stuff.'

Pause.

'The remake. With Donald Sutherland and Leonard Nimoy. That's where it started for me. That's where it began. In Greenwich Village with that scared and feverish man. How little he knew. How little we all knew, right?'

Murmurs of sympathy went around the room. Heads nodded poignantly.

'And now I see everyone wearing ribbons and more and more people are getting gaunt and sick and I'm thinking this. Why aren't we wearing ribbons for flu victims too? I mean, is there a pain hierarchy now? Is there a cause célèbre waiting list? Do you know how many old people die of flu every winter? Or bronchial pneumonia? Or hypothermia? Do we have enough ribbon for them too? Do you know how many . . .'

A champagne glass arced through the air, undetected by the spotlights and Drum's comic radar. 'Another very gay heckle,' as Drum would have put it if he'd thought of it then, and not later as he sat abandoned and ignored in a drab back-stage dressing room, blood still seeping from an open head wound, trickling down his supporting arm, running off his elbow into the wash basin and encrusted in crumpled tissues at his feet.

ARTFIST

1999

On 24 December 1999, Keith Gear wrote a letter to *ArtFist* magazine, the self-styled bible of 'maverick music and outsider sensibilities', in reply to a four-page feature about him in their latest edition. The feature, included in a special supplement entitled '100 Important Artists of the 20th Century', was almost wholly complimentary.

Dear ArtFist,

Would you please stop referring to me as a 'sonic terrorist'? Despite my best-laid plans, I have so far been unable to take out a single corrupt politician or city financier by pointing a loaded Telecaster at them. Unlike Woody Guthrie, my machine appears singularly ill-equipped to kill fascists. Likewise these 'incendiary guitar notes' to which you refer. I am not aware of any instance where a judiciously positioned flattened fifth has stirred up strife or sedition, or eliminated a corrupt Member of Parliament.

Keith Gear had an on-going love-hate relationship with *ArtFist*. On the one hand, its writers had always given him generous and largely uncritical coverage. On the other, he hated the magazine's earnestness, its elitism, and its dense convoluted prose. In the twenty years of its existence, *ArtFist* had made a fine art out of tautology and mixed metaphor, while some of its analogies were so tortuous that, as Drum once suggested, someone should have photographed them and sent them to Amnesty International as evidence of abuse. In its inaugural issue, *ArtFist* referred to Keith Gear as one of the 'leading avant-garde pioneers'.

'So far ahead we can barely see you,' scoffed Drum.

Keith Gear took his scissors to the appropriate sections of the '100 Important Artists' article, pasted them on to a sheet of plain A4 and typed his comments underneath.

> Gear arrived on the burgeoning Underground scene in the autumn of 1966, already a fully fledged auto-dictact and guitar hero.

No I didn't. I was an inquisitive sixteen-year-old kid with a lot of front. I didn't know what the rules were or whom I was upsetting. There wasn't a 'scene', burgeoning or otherwise. There were just venues and curious people. Some more curious than others.

> Hendrix had arrived in town around the same time and the two soon hooked up, kindred spirits in sonic exploration.

Although it is true that I shared a stage or two with Jimi Hendrix in late 1966 – always in the company of other musicians, I should add – I didn't really get to know him until a year or two later. He remembered me not as 'a kindred spirit in sonic exploration' but as 'that other cat who plays left-handed'.

> Gear's early confidence and purist sensibilities were clearly manifested in his initial refusal to join a group or sign to a record company. However, he quickly grew disillusioned with hippie hype and phoney guitar heroes. Famously he even walked out on a jam session with Jimi Hendrix, an early reminder of his restless creative spirit and extraordinarily high standards.

I had the time of my life hanging out with Jimi Hendrix (particularly during the recording of Electric Ladyland*). It was* *his hangers on I couldn't handle, not Jimi. I was not 'indifferent to the machinations of the music industry', as you put it later in the article. I was only too aware of the vultures hovering, contracts in claw.*

In 1969, Gear took the industry shilling, swallowed his purity and joined Dominion, one of the earliest British supergroups. They made one album, *Garlands For Godhead*, and split acrimoniously in the autumn of 1970. Gear's subsequent musical path, recalcitrant diffidence, and distrust of the record industry were cemented during these turbulent times.

Cement that musical path now! (Then go and clip the hedge.) You have considerably understated the case. Everything I have done since Dominion has in some way been a response to my fleeting encounter with stardom. I saw what it did to friendships. I saw what it could do to a young man's ego. I can still hear the screams. I am still fleeing from the burning house. I am still wading through the not-yet-set cement.

Becoming increasingly withdrawn and reclusive over the next two years, Gear released his first solo LP, *Doyen*, in 1972. The album boldly contained just four lengthy tracks, 'Doyen Parts 1–4', a symphonicly crafted quartet of teasing fretwork and multi-tracked mosaics. The softly lit cover shot of Gear revealed a beautifully sculpted face partially hidden by a tangle of black hair, and a hint of a halo in the back lighting. Doyen announced the arrival of a guitar supernova.

I did not live like a recluse. I was part of FreeFrom, a socio-pataphysical music co-operative set up by my friend Malcolm Drummond. I guested, twice anonymously (but not that anonymously), on all three FreeFrom albums. These were Cloud Hill *(1972, Ariel)* Avant-Grade *(1974, Overground) and* 100 Ton Haiku *(1976, Aphrodite). These endeavours have obviously passed you by, due no doubt to reluctance on your part to acknowledge Drum's enormous contribution to modern music. I also made music, similarly incognito, for Polish cartoons that were shown on children's TV. At the time, I was still in dispute with Dominion and their draconian record company overlords over unpaid royalties. The cover shot was the photographer's idea. It was meant to be a parody of a Marc Bolan sleeve (who some said I resembled at that time). I went along with it but thought the results looked rather pompous.*

> Gear increasingly turned his back on his UK audience, performing mostly on the Continent during the mid 70s. One of the more bizarre rumours circulating at the time was that he was providing incidental music for Eastern European children's TV cartoons. Of this period, little more is known. The sonic maelstrom of impressionistic turbulence displayed on side two of Gear's second solo LP, *The Death Of Language*, released in 1976, created a torrential tsunami that sent ripples reverberating through the music industry and anticipated the high tide of punk's new wave by several months. The album's very title announced the end of the old rock order and a call to arms. Divided into two long tracks, side one was called 'Miró', in honour of the Spanish surrealist painter (as was the parodic and knowing cover photo). The title of the second side, 'THDOL', was a corrupted acronym of the LP's title.

I think the key phrase here is 'of this period little more is known'. This is journalistic shorthand for 'little more is known by me' or 'I can't be bothered to do the research'. Why do you people try to contrive charisma out of absence? I did not turn my back on the UK. I got sick of playing for rip-off rock promoters and festivals where it always rained. I preferred to play Communist Party festivals in small villages in France and Italy. These festivals had a sense of community that I found almost completely lacking in England. England has its summer fetes in one place, its rock gigs in another and its brass bands somewhere else. I came to hate this never-the-twain mentality. In Italy and France, in rural villages of no more than a thousand people, I performed what you no doubt would refer to as a 'sonic maelstrom of seismic intensity' to an audience of old and young alike. There was no ageism, sexism or any other ism on these bills. On one occasion, I performed between a Vivaldi string quartet and a fire-eater. On another occasion, I was sandwiched between a septuagenarian accordion player and the local junior school choir. They were some of the most enjoyable gigs of my life. And I got paid.

The Death of Language *may well have preceded the first punk records (I have no idea, the trouble with 'recalcitrant diffidence' is that you aren't paying that much attention to anybody else's 'recalcitrant diffidence') but apart from the fact that some of it is undeniably loud and violent, it has nothing whatsoever to do with the representational politics of punk. On 'THDOL' I was attempting to banish the adjectival, the analogous and similitude from my music. I appreciate that this might be somewhat difficult for an* ArtFist *textpert to grasp, but I wanted to get beyond representation in my art. There is nothing impressionistic about that record, expressionistic maybe, but expressive of music, notes and noise per se, not of anger or punk nihilism, or anything else for that matter.*

The 'garbled incomprehensible message' to which you refer at the end of side two is not a 'telling exposé of the meaningless of communication in contemporary society'. It is my friend Malcolm Drummond reciting the words 'like something? LIKE SOMETHING? A leaf's a leaf. Stop picking on it.' These words are also etched into the run-out grooves of the British release. They were taken verbatim from a heckler, high on LSD, that Drum once heard disrupting an arts-lab event in Cricklewood.

I presume your writer has an American import copy of the album. On the British release the original title of side one was 'The Larks Wing, Encircled With Golden Blue, Rejoins the Heart of the Poppy Sleeping on a Diamond Studded Meadow'. This was the name of a painting that currently hangs in the

Miró Foundation building in Barcelona. I was invited to the opening of the museum and was glad to go, both to meet Joan Miró, an inspirational man, and to celebrate the death of Franco. There were copyright problems with the title in the USA, not caused by Joan Miró but by the Idaho gallery, which was temporarily exhibiting the painting at the time of the LP's release.

The cover art was not parodic or knowing, not in any sense that you would grasp anyway. My girlfriend at that time, the artist and photographer Helena Kirsch, was thirty-five and had just learned that she would be unable to conceive children. The LP cover, the child's balloon floating away, was her poignant depiction of that.

The title 'THDOL' was not an acronym, corrupt or otherwise. It stood obliquely (and bleakly) for 'The Dole'. When I started recording the album early in 1976 I was penniless and for a while homeless. I was signing on when the album was released. Such are the luxuries of the avant-grade artist and FreeFrom musician.

Towards the end of 1976 Gear began performing gigs under the name Idiot Bastard Son. It was a sudden bizarre change even by his idiosyncratic standards. For two years, Gear in his IBS guise confronted live audiences with amplified excesses and full-on agitprop swagger. Equally revelatory was Gear's singing and lyric writing. Although he had co-written and shared vocal duties with Dominion, his unique sense of song narrative now came to the fore with the sparse psychomorphic lyricism of songs like 'Leader Harry', 'Dracula Lives In Bethnal Green', and 'Ghost Code'. In his IBS incarnation, Gear refused to sign to a record label, never recorded a studio album. He survived the punk experience with his purity intact.

For one brief moment I thought that if enough of us made this kind of noise the music industry might crumble. Misguided, I know, but you must allow us leading avant-garde pioneers our naivety once a decade. I found punks to be as career orientated and fame-obsessed as any other rock musicians, perhaps more so, given their supposed antipathy to these things. You should have seen the backstage politics at some of those gigs I played. To see groups that your magazine reveres to this day bickering over billing and contractual riders was sickening. Unfortunately, this attention to detail did not extend to defending me when their imbecilic fans threw bottles and spat at me. The grotesque spectacle of that coupled with Boadicea's election in May 1979 killed Idiot Bastard Son.

Regarding my 'intact purity', it was initially my intention that Dominion should not join the record industry either, but being nineteen and lacking sufficient confidence, I was outmanoeuvred by record-company reptilians. At least Idiot Bastard Son stuck to its guns in this respect. When the Boadicea Broadcasting Company asked me to shorten my new stage name to Idiot for broadcast purposes I offered to shorten it to Bastard instead. Earl Raven was the only DJ brave enough to give me session work at that time. And to call me by my rightful name.

And what is 'agit-prop swagger' when it's at home? Mick Jagger poncing about on the top of a train as it hurtles through the Russian countryside? Was 'Gimme Shelter' a plea for political asylum?

The term 'punk', I found, became synonymous with a rigid musical style very quickly. I came to hate that contrived a-rhythmic slack-stringed style that some say I innovated. I hated seeing people pretending to play their instruments less well than they actually could. I hated people who sang less well than they could. I hated people pretending to be less intelligent than they were. (Granted this stance is almost obligatory in rock-music circles.) I hated the idea of post-punk and 'radical' funk in all their dismal anaemic (lack of) variations. Radical funk was so radical that you couldn't dance to it and, as my friend Drum once said, funk you can't dance to is as pointless as porn you can't fuck to.

After retreating from the punk front line in 1979 to lick his wounds, Gear entered another hermitic period. The sprawling double album of miscellany, 'The Wilderness Tapes', released in 1986, was a bewildering indulgence, part joyful valediction, and part endurance test. The lo-fi quality of the home-recording segments made it sound like an incongruous curio at the dawn of the new age of digitalised sound. The album's rapid withdrawal due to alleged copyright problems with the Boadicea Broadcasting Company has subsequently made it a collectors' item.

And ensured to this day that I have never collected a penny in royalties from it. The problems were not with the Boadicea Broadcasting Company, who were most accommodating, Earl Raven particularly so. The problems were with Depravation Films of Hamburg, a hardcore adult-movie company. With the aid of a session trio I had made incidental music for them in 1980 (side three: 'Labia Franca'; side four: 'Kino 66'). A contractual oversight on my agent's part (a Mr Truelove of Sunderland) led me to believe that I owned these recordings. A letter (and promise of an impending visit) from a Mr Schmidt of Bremen subsequently disabused me of this notion. 'Kino 66' was incidentally a minor hit in Germany and Belgium, and was the opening theme of a film called Love Hotel. *Naturally, I have yet to see a penny of royalties. Or indeed the film, which I am assured, is 'hot'.*

As for 'lo-fi', several of the recordings made for the Earl Raven show (side one: 'Shiver Loops # 1–8'; side two: 'Scapes #1–10'; side four: 'Ullulations #1–8') were, if my memory serves me correctly, done on a four-track Portastudio in my own front room and had far more bite than anything I ever recorded on thirty-two- or sixty-four-track at the Boadicea Broadcasting Corporation's own palatial facilities. A practice that was curbed incidentally when the Boadicea decreed that one of my sessions ('Ullulations #4–8') was not of 'suitable broadcast quality'. The amplified Tibetan finger cymbal featured on 'Ullulations 6', for instance, had more resonance and presence than any lynn drum, syn drum or cheap-bleep toy from Shitatronics of Tokyo that I encountered during that terrible period of digital cleansing. When I think back on those times now I think of those eighty-eight variations on the ding-dong 'Avon Calling' door chimes that you got out of the average state-of-the-art synthesiser.

> Gear's last known recording, *Tree Music*, from 1989, was by far his most extreme album to date. A radical departure even by his restless standards, *Tree Music* sprouted shards of jagged lo-fi minimalism that bloomed into a forest of innovative analogue density, some of which is barely audible to the human ear. The record's poor distribution can only have added to its cult status.

Tree Music from the Early Beech Period *was released in 1987, not 1989. You reviewed it eighteen months after it came out. It was released on Guy Truelove's Import Ant label and was not, as far as I'm aware, 'poorly distributed', although I am grateful to you for pointing out the correlation between bad business practice and cult status. I'm also flattered that my lo-fi went from being incongruous to innovative in such a short space of time.* Tree Music from the Early Beech Period *was almost totally ignored by the music press at the time of its release. The one exception to this, as I recall, was* Music Maker, *who graded it 0/10 and ran a picture of me looking somewhat dishevelled above a caption that read: 'HE TALKS TO THE TREES'.*

Tree Music from the Early Beech Period *is my most fully realised album. I am still proud of it. I wanted to make a record that was literally (should that be non-literally?) indescribable. Your belated review would suggest that I succeeded. A shard of jagged lo-fi minimalism, please, and some prawn crackers to go.*

A few concluding points.

I trod the freeform path out of logical necessity not out of a desire 'to shock'. It was the inevitable next stage of my search, as inevitable as even temperance was to Bach's particular set of circumstances, as inevitable as the twelve-tone system was to Schoenberg.

I live in a constant state of uncertainty. In your world, however, critical hindsight is always 20/20. Records are forever being classified as 'a response to this' or a 'a refutation of that'. Glancing through some of the other 'important artists' in your supplement I note that we are variously on the cusp of this movement or hovering on the fringe of that scene, eclipsing and heralding as we go, as we prepare to be propelled centre stage, or marginalised to the fringes at your editorial whim. No wonder I keep getting these headaches. I'm dizzy all the time! I should have majored in kinetics. We're always extending the parameters of x while subverting the limits of y, infuriating the blahs and consolidating our bleehs while tickling the soft pliant underbelly of whatever holds our attention in any particular week, month, epoch or lifetime.

Meanwhile all we really possess, you and I, is our competing subjectivities. All you have to go on is my vibrating air. All I have in front of me is a half-yearly PRS statement telling me that I am in credit to the sum of £14.37, and should this sum subsequently rise above the magic threshold of £50 they will have no hesitation in paying me. A little more humility is called for all round, wouldn't you say?

I am enclosing a cassette tape containing my latest LP, Dusk Music. *I do not at present have a recording contract.*

Yours sincerely

keith gear

He read through his letter again, omitted a few minor points and repetitions, erased a couple of 'fuck's, changed 'ill-informed asshole' to 'mistaken' and 'hack' to 'journalist'. Then he licked the envelope's foul-tasting animal glue adhesive and walked to the post office.

STILL RAINING, STILL DREAMING

1969 and 1967

'Bo Diddley was an Aztec.'

Jimi fell back into the throne of velvet cushions, laughing.

'Still is,' said Keith Gear, after an eternity of pondering the great imponderable.

'Yeah, with amulets and ju-ju beads,' added Jimi, historical and sartorial accuracy not being his strong point. The acid had seen those off an hour ago.

'Is anyone getting anything?' said Kay, provoking huge volcanic bubbles of mirth among the men.

'Uh-oh, looks like Kay got a dud,' said Jimi. 'No, angel,' he said quickly to console her, 'I'm putting you on.'

Kay looked puzzled. A frown formed on her flushed face. 'No, but is anyone getting anything?' she repeated, eyes dilating wildly.

'Hang on,' said Keith Gear, emerging from the depths of his armchair and levering himself up on his elbows. 'I'll just check the manual.'

They dissolved into giggles again. All of them.

'You haven't got a manual,' said Kay, going all mock dumb on herself.

'Yes I have,' said Keith Gear. 'It's on this ancient parchment that five minutes ago I did place down this gap in the side of the armchair.' He thrust his arm into the gap.

'Oh, man, you speak the Queen's English how it is meant to be spoke,' said Jimi.

'Meant to be spoken,' said Kay, not clocking Jimi's wink.

'Meant to be spoketh,' muttered Keith Gear, preoccupied as he was with extricating his arm from the side of the chair.

'Spoketh the hour. Spiketh the man,' said Jimi. 'Oh, man,' he exhaled as planets orbited very fast and the un-sense dribbled from his lips.

'I think I'm stuck,' said Keith Gear, waggling his arm from side to side to free it from the entrails of the chair.

'Stucketh,' said Kay.

'You're gonna have to, like, walk around with that now,' said Jimi.

'What? With a huge armchair on my arm?' asked Keith Gear.

'I guess that's why they call it an armchair,' said Jimi. This was the funniest thing anyone had ever said and their laughter swelled to a hysterical crescendo again.

'Hey, what's this?' said Keith Gear, freeing his arm and pulling out a lump of hash.

'Wow! How did that get down there?' said Kay.

'I told you to clean up the place when I was on tour,' said Jimi.

'Clean up your own mess,' said Kay, slapping him on the arm.

'Maybe Inspector Pilchard put it down there,' said Keith Gear as Jimi reached for the Rizlas.

It all went quiet for a bit, as paranoia competed with lysergic giggles.

'Anyway. Is anyone getting anything?' asked Kay again.

'Someone's shooting at us.'

Sonya and her loverboy were lying in the tall reeds next to the marshes and they were being shot at. Keith Gear knelt to see who by and where from. Another shot whistled past his ear. There was a rustling across the way. Shapes emerged from the scrub by the gasworks wall. An extended hand executed a sarcastic wave.

'It's OK,' said Sonya. 'I know him.'

'Who is it?'

'It's Billy Gordon I was at school with him. It's OK. It's only an air rifle. Hi, Billy.'

'How old is he?' said Keith Gear as the brawny muscular figure loped towards them, grinning inanely. Seventeen going on Desperate Dan.

'I know. He looks about twenty-nine, don't he? He moved to our street when I was in the third year. He was in my class for the last term. He's not all there.'

As if to prove the point Billy Gordon raised the air rifle and took aim again. The two of them threw themselves into the long reeds. Another shot whistled above their heads.

'Pack it in, you ginger-haired pillock!' shouted Sonya.

It was all starting to remind him of that playground joke. What do you call a gorilla with a machine gun? Sir.

'He's Scottish,' said Sonya, by way of explanation, as they lay face-to-face in the reeds. 'Billy the pillock Gordon of the Gordon clan.'

They waited for another shot.

A minute ago Sonya was hitching up her yellow dress and wriggling out of her knickers. Now a madman was using them for target practice.

Another shot rang out.

'Come on, let's go.'

That summer of 1967 was all about Sonya. Keith Gear ignored the sick-fuck musos at the MQ Club and their sick-fuck limericking. *There was a young girl called Sonya. Who said, have you got any on ya? For the price of a smoke, she'll give you a poke and . . .*

'Kay, you're always doing that,' said Jimi.

'Doing what?'

'Saying oh, you know, I'm not feeling anything and so we all go with that for a while and it's a drag cos it brings you down from your own trip, y'know, and you have to, uh, focus on that for an endless amount of time while you try to figure whether Kay is on a bummer and then something will happen and everything connects in harmony again and I'll look at you and your eyes are like . . .' Jimi searched for the words. 'Witchy, you know.'

Jimi spoke fast and soft. They were two hours into their trip and peaking tumultuously. Jimi always spoke fast and soft. Most stoneheads spoke slow. Not Jimi. He even gabbled his murmurs. The only time he spoke slowly was if he was really drunk or if he had just taken a mandrax to help him sleep. Then he slurred at sixteen rpm.

'Are you going to do that TV show?' said Kay.

'No, man. I'm cutting that scene. Those British TV shows are, like, every time I do one it's mass confusion. It really bugs me. Remember *Top Of The Pops*? We were doing, what song was it? "Burning of the Midnight Lamp". And they expect you to sing to a prerecorded backing track, and I'm all sort of like ready to sing and the record they play instead is . . . What was it?'

'It was "The House That Jack Built", Alan Price,' Keith Gear reminded him. 'I was watching the show at home. It was hilarious. You said something like, "Uh I don't know this one, man." And they had to cut back to the compère, Pete Murray.'

'He was a nice cat,' said Jimi, 'a bit square, but you expect that on a pop show in England and he didn't seem to mind. I mean, it didn't throw him. It threw me more than it threw him. But, nah, that's not where my head's out now, playing that kind of . . . I guess Chas would always want me to play that kind of show, but that's not where you can play outer-space music, is it? I mean, I can't mime outer-space music and they always expect you to mime and even when you can play live they never let you play loud. The engineer cats always turn it down. I spoke to Aretha and she said, "I ain't miming for no one. I'm through with that shit," and, y'know, I thought, if it ain't good enough for Aretha . . .'

'They make everyone mime though, don't they?' said Kay.

'Everyone,' agreed Jimi. 'The Cream. We did that German show with them and they mimed on that. We wouldn't but they did. "Strange Brew", I think it was. Uh, do the Stones mime?'

'Yeah, the Stones mime,' said Keith Gear. 'And The Who.'

'Some people mime better than others,' said Kay. 'Dusty can't mime to save her life. I don't think she even tries.'

'I don't even like singing most of the time,' sighed Jimi. 'I just wanna play. I don't wanna stand there going . . .'

He made with the fish mouth. They all laughed.

'No, man,' said Jimi. 'I'm gonna play live and loud and play whatever I want to play. And if I wanna paint pictures and play my space music I'll play my space music. And if I wanna play the blues I'll do that. And if they don't like it . . .'

'What show is it anyway?' asked Keith Gear.

'It's *The Lulu Show*,' said Kay.

'Lulu?' said Jimi, a disbelieving smile playing across his face. 'Uh, no, man. You're putting me on. Can that be a groovy proposition right now? *The Lulu Show*?'

'It'll be OK,' said Kay. 'What can possibly go wrong?'

Keith Gear's mother knocked politely on the door of her front room and brought in tea and cup cakes for her son and Celia. She used that polite knock, the one that mothers always use, the one that alerts offspring to the impending presence of parents, the one that wards off the possibility that a mother should see her son in flagrante delecto, or near enough, with a member of the opposite species, who although Chelsea bred was clearly no better than she ought to be. Keith Gear genuflected and disengaged himself, hiding his protuberance with a cushion as his mother entered the room. Celia in turn hastily re-buttoned her skirt, although not correctly, and made an unconvincing show of watching the TV, which had gone on the blink without either of them noticing.

His mother put the tray down on the coffee table, went over to the TV and gave it a hard thump. The picture jolted back into life. 'Oh, it's that one you like, isn't it,' she said absently as she absented herself from the room.

He knew that something was amiss the minute he saw Hendrix wince at his out-of-tune guitar and casually retune midway through 'Voodoo Chile'. He'd seen Jimi do that wince before. It wasn't a concerned wince. It was a 'Who gives a fuck?' wince, the wince of a man at the peak of his powers, ready to chop down mountains with the back of his hand. Not even a wince really, more of a mocking smile, a smile that said 'Can I really be getting away with this?' He glanced over at Noel in his Plaster Casters T-shirt, winced his smiling mocking wince, and ploughed on through a rough-and-ready 'Voodoo Chile'. Then he started playing 'Hey Joe'. Then he stopped playing 'Hey Joe'. Just stopped completely. On prime-time Saturday evening TV. 'Uuh,' he went.

It was 4 January 1969. Celia was wearing the beads he had bought her for Christmas from the Chelsea Antique Market. He'd taken the king's shilling and joined Dominion by then. Spencer and Kenny had introduced themselves to him at Antonia Soamesby's party in Chelsea. That's where he first met Celia too. Playing guitar in the corner of a quiet room at a loud crazy party. Playing guitar allowed him to be the centre of attention and warded off conversation. The best of both worlds, the guitar acting both as magnet and barrier. He liked the juxtaposition and being able to dictate the terms like that. That's where he was when Spencer and Kenny loomed up through the hashish haze. Leaning against a cold marble mantelpiece, Pre-Raphaelite paintings on the wall, making drone shapes and mantra modes. Entrancing those who could keep their dilated pupils focused long enough, but entrancing Celia most of all.

Spencer was tall and aloof and plummy. He said, 'Would you like to join my band? I have a recording contract. I play rhythm and lead. Kenny plays bass.'

Kenny was diminutive, cheeky grinned and smiling nicely. 'Nice guitar, man.'

Gear said, 'Thanks. Nice shirt, man.'

'Thanks, man.'

Keith Gear thought, *Why not?* It was about time. Even Jimi had told him it was about time. It had been about time for ages. The Summer of Love had come and gone, autumn and winter with it. Paris had burned. Haight had turned to hate and here he was all preen and promise still strumming at Chelsea parties to Biba waifs and trust-funded dandies. Leaning against a cold marble mantelpiece. Pre-Raphaelite paintings on the wall.

Besides, he'd written all those songs. 'Flowers and Owls', 'Greenwich Dream Time', 'Doyen'. Might as well do something with them.

Spencer couldn't write songs. He'd told him that right from the off. 'I am exceedingly well connected. I have a recording contract. I have good reliable management. I play rhythm and lead. I can arrange. But I can't write lyrics.'

'Uuh,' went Jimi. 'Uuh, we'd like to stop playing this rubbish and dedicate a song to The Cream.' And with that he name-checked Eric, Jack and Ginger and launched into 'Sunshine of Your Love'. As the ramshackle impromptu tribute took shape Keith Gear knew that something monumental was occurring. He had an internal body clock honed to the requirements of light entertainment. He knew instinctively when three minutes were up. It was a skill learned through late nights listening to his radio under the bedclothes, or during daytime at the back of class with earpiece affixed. If a bad record came on, Jim Reeves, say, or Ken Dodd or the Singing Nun, he tuned out or turned off and knew exactly when to turn the radio back on again. He knew the difference between two minutes thirty and two minutes fifty. He knew 'House of the Rising Sun' was long, long, long the first time he heard it, listening awestruck and amazed as it sailed on through that two thirty barrier without showing signs of stopping. Now Jimi was doing the same. Celia was stroking his neck and there was Jimi still playing his Cream tribute and there were the credits rolling and there was Lulu standing at the side of the stage waiting to come on and sing her final number and looking like a spare part at her own party. Fucking far out, man!

'It'll be OK,' said Kay. 'What can possibly go wrong?'

It was Thursday night. The three of them were on Strawberry Fields blotters. Outside in the clear January sky the stars played with Laughing Sam's dice.

'Hey,' said Keith Gear, 'did you know there is an acid called Purple Haze now?'

'Well, about time too,' said Kay, and they all laughed again.

They talked in halting stutter-filled sentences about symphonies composed of ocean waves and the big global note that unified all sound. They conjured a meridian line that ran through Morocco, Algeria, the northern Arab lands, Persia, India, Nepal, Vietnam, forking down to the gamelan of Java and Bali, and up through China and Japan. They imagined a snaking caravan of nomad music undulating across desert sands and Himalayan foothills, coming to rest in some Javanese forest clearing or a rice field by the Yangtze. Each of them on their different trips. Each of them feeling the same vibration.

'What do squirrels eat?' said Kay, as she studied the shimmering brown bark of a pine tree outside the window.

They contemplated this great theological riddle, this pine koan. Distant traffic hummed.

'What are you getting?' said Kay.

'I'm getting fairgrounds,' said Keith Gear.

'Oh, you mean, like the carney?' said Jimi.

Keith Gear had never heard this word. A children's merry-go-round whirled inside his head. The meridian line vanished. *Ptoof!* The caravan dissolved like desert mirage. *Ptoof!* He imagined a new set of grid lines. An aerial view of Purley and the fairground that deposited itself every year on whichever patch of wasteland was available. There, on the bombsite by the fire station. There, in the scrub where they built the new library. There, in the wet willow meadow that got boggy and swamped no matter how much straw they laid. There, amidst the ruins of the old munitions factory. The merry-go-round whirled. Purley whirled.

'Don't records sound great at the fairground?' he said. 'I mean, that's the kind of sound you should try to get on your next LP, Jimi. Make it seem . . .'

He imagined the rest. His proximity to the big booming speaker box. The smell of axle grease rising up through the wooden slates of the Jollity Farm. The gypsy boys duck-walking anti-clockwise to the motion. Devil-may-caring as they edged dangerous inches closer to the grinding cogs that drove the rides and would take a young man's leg off if he slipped. A weather-beaten booth attendant dropping the needle and an inch of fag ash onto the record then resuming his pose. Resting tattooed arms on the counter and scrutinising the girls with inscrutable eyes.

An amplified burst of crackle and static as the needle hit the record. Junior Walker's dirty sax wailing in the warm August air. His teen head whirling it all back to life. The speaker box booming and the greased cogs whirring and the gypsy boys walking and the plastic horses prancing and the dirty sax wailing. All the colours running, all images melting into the oneness of it all.

He got into the fairground thing for some while.

'Anyway, if you don't do it, I will,' he said finally.

They all laughed again. A long, long time.

Kay lit a candle. The acid surged. They stared and stared. Mesmerised by a flame.

'There isn't a squirrel out there,' said Keith Gear, averting his eyes to break the spell and gazing out of the window into the street-lit darkness.

'I didn't say there was,' said Kay, affronted. 'They're hibernating.'

'Like us,' said Jimi.

'Let's go out,' said Keith Gear.

'Let's not,' said Kay.

'Come on, let's go,' said Sonya, gripping his arm and leading him the back way out of the club.

That summer of 1967 was all about Sonya. And some of autumn too. Keith Gear ignored the sick-fuck musos at the MQ Club and their sick-fuck limericking. *There was a young girl called Sonya. Who said have you got any on ya? For the price of a fag, she'd give you a shag, and . . .*

'Come on,' urged Sonya as they stacked up crates and kicked over pop bottles in their haste to scale the back wall of the back yard of the Falcon Club where inside the local greasers were trashing the place.

They frequently did this. Scuttling from shop doorway to alcove to alley to avoid the local bike boys on their Enfields and Nortons and Ducatis, half of whom Sonya knew. They didn't take kindly to strangers. Strangers being anyone from half a mile further up the road.

The band was the inappropriately named Ricky Fontaine and The Invincibles. They were an amalgam of everything they'd ever heard and learned. Sounds Incorporated meets The Shadows meets Booker T. Strictly cover versions but slick with it. And danceable too. Keith Gear was at the bar and Sonya was mod-stepping to 'My Little Red Book' when the biker boys announced their presence with the telltale splintering of a chair. Some girls screamed and some girls laughed to see such fun. The DJ in the record booth thought he could calm things with a disc. Having seen one too many westerns, he cast himself in the role of the saloon-bar piano player who plays on while bottles crash and windows smash and tables turn all around him. Hastily he grabbed a record blind from his box. This turned out to be Cliff Richard's 'Batchelor Boy'. This enhanced the surrealism of the event no end. As the crowd scattered and the room filled with moody boys and malevolent boys, all intent on alchemising the furniture to matchwood, Cliff's inane little ditty continued to drift incongruously across the dancefloor. Before Sonya yanked him away the transfixed and slightly stoned Keith Gear noticed that one leather-clad boy was smashing a chair in time with the music.

Pretty soon they all were.

'Meet you by the swimming baths on Lavender Hill. Eight o'clock,' Sonya had said. Keith Gear darted from doorway to doorway. Killing time. Far too visible and way out of his territory. Sunday clear air with daylight to spare. Sun refusing to cool down or set. Keith Gear moving from doorway to doorway to escape its searchlight glare. And hopefully the attentions of the motorbike boys who own every inch of this. The one good thing about the motorbike boys is you can usually hear them way off. One gang roared by at ten past eight and Keith Gear made a convincing job of looking in the nearest shop window, which belonged to a surgical appliance manufacturers. Had they been more attentive and onto his scent, the Battersea Bikerboys might have paused to wonder why a well-dressed teenage boy from Purley Oaks was studying a windowful of trusses so intensely.

He continued to dart from window to window, from alcove to alley, all the way down Lavender Hill to Arding & Hobbes, the huge department store where his Dad had picked him up that night. One step ahead of his shadow. Five minutes away from getting the next Clapham Junction train out of there. Forget it. She's only a girl. It's only a gig. Plenty more fish in the . . .

'Hey, loverboy.'

Sonya called out across a deserted street. She had her friend Sandra with her.

'What you doing down here? I said the swimming baths.'

'There's grebos everywhere.'

'You scared then?' said Sandra, sullen and sulky. Cracking gum and looking at loverboy like he was shit.

'Is she with you?' he asked.

Another distant roar. Another Enfield rumble. Keith Gear swivelled in search of its echo.

'No, she's off to her aunt's. Ain't yer, Sandra? Me and Sandra have been listening to *Pick Of The Pops*. Ain't we, Sandra? "Whiter Shade of Pale" is still number one. Ain't it, Sandra?'

'S'really dreary that record,' said Sandra in a 's'really dreary' voice. So dreary in fact that Keith Gear didn't notice that she was having a laugh at his expense.

'See ya, Sandra,' said Sonya, waving her across the road.

'See ya, Sandra,' said Keith Gear sarcastically, waving to the space where she'd been.

And the rest of that summer was Sonya but the nights were already getting longer. Keith Gear hadn't noticed that. The darkness was calling out like an omen but he was too wrapped up in Sonya to care.

He took her home to his parents. Just the once. She held up a skimpy yellow dress and said, 'Do you think this is a bit revealing?'

Christ, no, thought Keith Gear. No, Sonya, wear it always. No wonder we get shot at. When they walked past some building works in Battersea Rise one fine day, brickies stopped loading their bricks and scaffolders wolf-whistled from the scaffolding. The summer stood still to look at Sonya in that dress. But later in the reed banks ringed by gasworks, when the yellow dress rode up and loverboy lowered himself in expectation, he saw the fear in Sonya's eyes as she said, 'If I get pregnant you'll run a mile, won't you?'

His mother laid a tablecloth on the lawn and they all had Sunday tea in the July sunshine. His mother went to a lot of effort. Out came the best crockery and the china teapot. And when she offered ham and he said, 'It's all right, Mum, I'm having the cheese,' Sonya was confused because she'd had the ham and the cheese and the cold chicken and the pickled eggs and the home-made piccalilli, and a little bit of everything in fact. She wasn't familiar with middle-class etiquette and he saw that she wasn't familiar with middle-class etiquette and he also saw that his mother had seen that Sonya wasn't familiar with middle-class etiquette and he hated her for making Sonya feel uncomfortable.

'Quite an appetite,' she muttered, sotto voce, as Sonya piled food on her plate. 'Tuck in,' she said sarcastically as Sonya started scoffing without waiting.

In fact, he loved it when Sonya went stomping with hobnailed boots on through the culinary minefield that was high tea with the middle classes. And he loved it even more when Sonya took a sip of her lapsang souchong, made a face and said, 'This tastes like hedge, have you got any proper tea?'

'Certainly,' said his father, who hated China tea too, and went off to the kitchen to boil the kettle. His father didn't mind in the slightest. He liked Sonya in that dress. Thought she looked just fine and dandy.

'I saw Gillian today,' said his mother, when his father was away making proper tea. 'She asked after you.' Gillian was his fifth-form romance. Gillian read him Rupert Brooke and Siegfried Sassoon and tousled his hair as he lay in her lap on the school lawn. Gillian sketched in churchyards and talked of university and of a cloistered life of learning. But Gillian didn't let him put his hand down her pants like Sonya did.

One day, left alone in the house, his father out on call, his mother at the local flower show, he and Gillian had sat on the sofa in the front room listening to dreamy Delius and earthy Animals. Gillian had said, 'What are we going to do all afternoon?'

'Lets go upstairs and make love,' he had replied. He had never been so ready. This was supposed to be the moment. Gillian's face froze and she pulled herself away from him. The room grew colder. They went out for a walk instead and no more was said of going upstairs.

But Gillian must have told her best friend Anna. Because a couple of weeks later in a quiet alcove backstage at the school concert after Keith Gear had just performed 'Suite Española' by Isaac Albéniz to rapturous parental approval, Anna alluded to the event. Said something about Gillian having a 'bad experience' when she was growing up on Daddy's plantation in Malaya. Keith Gear nodded sympathetically. 'She's just not ready yet,' said Anna. Keith Gear nodded sympathetically again. Anna placed a sympathetic hand on his. 'But I am,' she said, wicked eyes all aglow.

Gillian was his mother's kind of girl, not ill-bred Sonya in her yellow dress and no better than she ought to be. Sonya just brought out the petit-bourgeois snob in her. She'd rather have seen her son messing about with any amount of show-girls as long as something of that world rubbed off on him, not this common little tart with her ravenous appetite, unsophisticated palate and crude lipstick-smeared little mouth gawping wide open as she ate.

At five thirty it started to rain. A sudden summer cloudburst brought the outdoor tea to a close. The best tablecloth got sodden and they all made a mad dash for the conservatory. 'We're going upstairs to listen to records,' said Keith Gear to disapproving looks from his mother. And for the rest of the evening she made a great show of bringing them tea and sponge cake even though they'd already eaten their fill, not even knocking politely as she later would for Celia, who although also clearly no better than she ought to be was at least Chelsea bred and not Battersea bred.

He did take Sonya home one more time after that. Not to meet the parents again but to sneak back to the house one wet Wednesday afternoon for one last shag in a comfortable bed before he went to America to stay with Randy Sandy in the East Village.

They spent a rainy afternoon in the front room, listening to The Kinks and Hendrix and Love and Hendrix and John Mayall's Bluesbreakers and Hendrix, watching the French windows steam up with their laughter and kisses and conversation. This is never going to end, thought Keith Gear. Everything will be just the same when I get back from America. He didn't know then that everything ends. Time stood still when he was with Sonya.

'Kay, when are we going to get some furniture?' said Jimi.

Keith Gear took in the room. Bare boards. No curtains. Just a mound of velvet cushions and an armchair in one corner that they'd made their oasis. Crawling across a desert of pinewood floor, clambering over the faded chintz terrain into welcoming crevices and satin valleys as the acid torrents washed over them.

'Give me all your money and I'll go out tomorrow,' said Kay.

'Uuuuuglug,' gurgled Jimi. 'Huuuughlugug,' he gurgled again. They all did.

'I'm seeing space aliens and saucer ships, and you're like flashing on my bank account.' Strychnine ripples tickled his ribs. He laughed again. They all did.

'I'm just being practical,' said Kay.

'Yeah, those space aliens have got to have somewhere to sit,' said Keith Gear.

Having dealt with the furnishing issue they turned their attention to another task. Distilling the essence of all known music (and some unknown, and some that was yet to be) into one three-minute single. It was Jimi's flash. He'd hit upon the notion that you could boil it all down that way, extricate the essence, alchemise the x-factor into one all-encompassing cosmic common denominator of noise.

'Music comes out of the delta and smoky bars and swamp methane and . . .' He paused to consider the myriad options spanning centuries, continents, octaves and oceans.

'What are you getting?' he asked Keith Gear.

'I'm still getting fairgrounds.' He laughed.

'Is that all man?' spluttered Jimi. 'Is there nothing else there?'

'Nope. I'm afraid it's all fairground as far as the eye can see.'

'Oh. OK, I can dig that,' said Jimi, slumping back into his cushions.

'Where did you get that top?' asked Kay, plumping up hers.

'Oh, some side street off Petticoat Lane. I forget.' Keith Gear fingered the green velvet material of his tunic top. 'Eric had one just like it, but he wouldn't tell me where he got it.'

He was wearing that green velvet tunic top when Celia first saw him at Antonia Soamesby's party. He was sitting on a red plastic tractor in the kindergarten room, rolling a joint. His fringe fell across his dreamboat eyes. There was something innocent, absorbed and unselfconscious about the way he sat there, astride a child's toy, spreading out Rizla papers on the tractor's pretend red engine. Celia had asked the same question that Kay asked. They were the first words she said to him. 'Where did you get that top?'

'Eric doesn't give away his trade secrets,' said Jimi, laughing again. 'Jack will, but Eric won't.'

'He doesn't own them,' said Keith Gear. 'They aren't his to own.'

'True,' said Jimi, sinking back into the earth's crust, still seeking the perfect synthesis of delta blues and smoky bars and swamp methane.

'Imagine if you could build a machine that did it for you,' said Keith Gear, connecting once more. 'I mean just process all sound and feed it in and the computer would then . . . I dunno, it would be this perfect platonic universe, I suppose. Like somewhere there's a perfect tree and a perfect chair and . . .'

'A perfect tune,' said Jimi.

'That's it,' said Keith Gear, leaping up and pacing around the room. 'And it would all be based on all the records I heard at Thurston's Fairground in Lime Meadow on whatever day it was when I was fourteen. That summer! Yeah! You'd find it all there.'

'Oh, man, we gotta build you a time machine and get you back there before it's too late.' Jimi giggled.

'I was standing by the dodgems watching the fairground guys. You know the way they swing off the back of the cars when they collect the money. I've always thought that was so cool.' Keith Gear mimed the action. Hanging from an imaginary pole. Showered in sparks.

'And the tune they played was?' asked Jimi.

'"Let's Dance" by Chris Montez.' He was swaying giddily, gormlessly.

'Man, that's so corny,' sighed Jimi, raising his eyes to the sky.

'And the tune they played was?' said Keith Gear, picking up the thread. '"The Price of Love".'

'Oh, I like that one,' said Kay, absently playing with her hair.

'The Everly Brothers,' said Jimi.

'Yeah,' said Keith Gear. 'Electric Everlys. Not corny Everlys. Let's play it now.'

'You could play right now?' enquired Jimi. 'I can't even feel my arms. I don't know where they are. Its like that Hindu cat . . .'

'Shiva,' said Kay.

'Yeah,' said Jimi, 'like Shiva waving. Oh, man, I got into so much trouble last time I tried that. I just can't play when I'm tripping on acid. I can play when I've been smoking hashish or when I've taken a pill but tripping . . . last time I went on stage tripping I just sat on a speaker cabinet waving at the audience. Where was that, Kay?'

'Can't remember,' said Kay, drifting away again. 'Is anyone thirsty? I'm really, really thirsty.'

'And the tune they played was,' Jimi softly sang in lullaby tones. 'And the tune they played was?'

Kay went to find glasses and to see if she could still remember how to operate the taps.

'"She's About a Mover",' said Keith Gear.

'Hey, that's a great record,' said Jimi. 'That was playing the summer before I came to England. It was on the radio all the time.' Now it was his turn to be animated. Getting up to mooch around the room, going 'she's about a mover, she's about a mover'.

'Yeah. That would have been the last time I went to the fairground,' said Keith Gear. '66. She's about a mover and the dodgems.'

'They all got that groovy organ sound,' said Jimi. 'All those records you mention.'

'Yeah, well the organ sounds so good at the fairground,' said Keith Gear. 'Which is why you've got to get that sound on your next record.'

'Who we gonna need?' said Jimi, entertaining the perfect jam session. 'I'll start making a list.'

'Well, Junior Walker for starters,' said Keith Gear.

'And Stevie Winwood,' said Jimi.

'Yeah. And Booker T.'

'And Steve Cropper. Don't forget Steve.'

While the two of them built a supergroup, Kay stared at silver jets of water, a bare kitchen bulb and patterns in the Formica.

'And we've gotta have room for Al Kooper in there too,' said Jimi. 'Those root chords on "Like a Rolling Stone". The way he . . .'

'So if we feed all that into the machine . . .' said Keith Gear. 'We've got the greatest record of all time.'

'Do you think so?'

'Hey, do you remember that chick Sonya?' said Jimi suddenly. 'She used to hang out at the MQ. The guys had a song about her. *There was a girl called Sonya.* A lyric.'

'Yeah, I had a thing with her for a while.'

'Oh, man, I'm sorry. I didn't mean to be . . . actually she was really sweet, I always thought. I remember one time going backstage after a jam and she stood there by the dressing room door and I said, "You want an autograph?" and she said, "No, it's OK, I'm just waiting for someone, you know," and afterwards I thought that was really presumptuous of me, to assume she automatically wanted my attention. Bad ego.' Jimi laughed.

'She was probably waiting for me,' said Keith Gear wistfully.

'Oh, sorry man, I . . .'

'It's OK.'

When he got back from America that first time he didn't hear from Sonya straight away. Days turned into weeks and still no call. Sonya's house didn't have a phone but Sonya and her friends all knew how to make free calls from kiosks by pressing down the receiver bar the requisite number of times. Sometimes she did that three times a day from the call box at the bottom of her road. The same one that he had called his parents from that first night. August turned to September and still no call. He played his guitar in the conservatory and stared at the rain and still no call. He took a train up from Purley Oaks to Clapham Junction via Waterloo and went looking for her. He wandered the streets, too man-proud to knock on her door. Still no sign. He sent her a telegram and went up there again. This time he did go to the house. Her mother came to the door in curlers and shrieked: 'What do you think yer doing sending a bloody telegram? I nearly died. I thought me old man had croaked it! No one round here gets a telegram unless it's bad news, you silly fool. No, Sonya's not here, she's out.'

'Whereabouts is out?' asked a singularly guileless Keith Gear.

'Out,' said Sonya's mum, slamming the door.

He surveyed the narrow terraced street. Curtains twitched. Small children had gathered to watch. Brazen mothers stood on doorsteps. Rolling pin arms folded as if to say, *You tell him, Doreen. Silly fool. Sending her a telegram like that and frightening the life out of her.*

Keith Gear had always got on well with Doreen and Barry, Sonya's dad. Despite the ominous rowing he'd heard that first fruitless night he'd soon swallowed his cosy suburban prejudices and seen that rowing was just part of their routine. Barry drove a bus down at the local depot and was something prominent in the trade union. Campaigned against the colour bar and racial prejudice. That sort of thing. Sonya made him out to be dozy old fool. Took great delight in telling loverboy how she'd brought an airman back from the MQ one Saturday night and had it off under a blanket on the sofa as her dozy old dad lay dozing after a late shift. Keith Gear thought Sonya's dad was sound. Called Sonya a scrubber.

Doreen must have told her daughter he had called, because next day there was a phone call. 'I've had a cold,' was all she said by way of explanation. 'Meet you up the junction. Seven o'clock, Wednesday.'

There she was. On time. White plastic mac buttoned up. Lips likewise. They walk around for a bit talking inconsequential talk. Up Battersea Rise and down the other side. He talks America. She talks bronchitis. He makes some feeble joke about rubbing Vicks on her chest. She steers him back towards the Junction. At the station entrance, she puts her hands on his shoulders like she's positioning him to be still. He thinks they are going to kiss. She looks him straight in the eye and says, 'I. Don't. Want. To. Go. Out. With. You. Anymore.'

Why?

Buried deep down inside his grooviness he hears an empty vessel roar: Why? Why? Why? Why? Why?

'Everything you say is so vague.'

Loverboy was concentrating so much on cultivating his cool and drifting in Jimi's slipstream that he never really stopped to consider that to a Battersea girl, seventeen going on battle hardened, he might conceivably be coming across a little too frequently of late as a tad precious and precocious.

Why? Why? Why? Why? Why?

'I mean plans, ambitions. What do you want to do with your life?'

Plans? Ambitions?

And, anyway, she'd met an apprentice gas fitter called Pete and they were going to get engaged. 'It's time I sorted myself out,' she said.

She couldn't be nasty though and after he'd stood there for five minutes, trance-like and head-numb, she said, 'Do you still want to borrow that Bluesbreakers LP?' She led him moon-legged and glaze-eyed back to her house where her mum obviously knew and her dad obviously didn't. It was written in their faces. She left ex-loverboy hovering awkwardly by the front door while she went inside to get the record. Wait there. New house rules. Out of bounds begins immediately. You. Are. Never. Coming. In. To. This. House. Again. Barry came to the door still in his uniform and struck up blokey conversation while Doreen made indiscreet ushering gestures from the corner of the kitchen, which Barry, full of oblivious bonhomie, didn't twig.

Keith Gear sat in an empty train compartment and stared out of the window. The journey back to Waterloo went by in a blur. Hurt and pride fought for dominance in his head. All his latent snobberies swam to the surface and gasped for air and breathed out bile. How could she? The fucking cow? Me the doyen of the Telecaster. A prince in waiting. A fucking gas fitter called Pete.

'No, wait,' he said. 'I'm going to be really mature about this.'

Just outside Queenstown Road he opened the compartment window and skimmed her John Mayall's Bluesbreakers LP across the tracks.

When he got home his mother was pruning a trellis of unruly roses in the warm evening light. 'You're back early.'

'Yeah. I think I'm getting a cold. I think I'll go to bed and stare at the wall for a while.'

His mother frowned momentarily at the phrasing and went back to pruning roses.

The next morning he felt much better. No one was ever going to hurt him again.

'Hey, Kay, do we have any grass? I want to roll a joint?'

Jimi called out to Kay in the kitchen. There was no answer. Kay was still in deep contemplation. A tap dripped.

'Do you wanna smoke, Keith?' said Jimi, looking at the floor space around him and hoping that marijuana would just manifest itself.

'I don't enjoy smoking when I'm tripping,' said Keith Gear. 'I find it never really cuts through the acid.'

Jimi continued to sweep the floor with his hand. 'Oh, man, I wish I hadn't told Kay to clean up the place now.' He managed to look placid and distressed all at the same time. 'Kay,' he called out again.

Keith Gear got up and went to the kitchen. Kay was looking out of the window into a walled kitchen garden. She was crying silent happy tears. 'That tree,' she said, 'is the tree of life.'

'Jimi asked if there's anything to smoke?' said Keith Gear, trampling on her trip.

'Only cigarettes,' she murmured and went back to her tree of life. 'That tree is every tree that ever existed.'

Keith Gear filled a glass with water from the tap and went back into the living room. 'Kay's studying the tree of life.'

Jimi had re-arranged the cushions into a throne and looked blissfully spaced out. 'Hey, man, I hear you're a pop star now.'

'No. I finally joined a group, that's all.' He told Jimi about Dominion and the Chelsea party and big record-company money and about how Spencer was this rich-kid talented arranger who played lead and rhythm just like Gear did and about how they interlocked harmoniously and about how he could write lyrics but Spencer couldn't and there's this drummer called Richard who used to be in Expression, that Irish band, who toured with you in the package days and the way he said package days made it sound like a century ago, which in a way it was.

'What do squirrels eat?' asked Kay as she re-entered the room, still fixated on her tree.

'Well, nuts of course,' said Keith Gear.

'And apples too?' asked Kay, almost childlike.

'Yeah. Apples too.'

'Oh good,' said Kay, diving into the cushions and demolishing Jimi's velvet throne. 'There's loads of rotting apples on the lawn out there. Do they eat rotting apples?'

'Yeah,' said Keith Gear. 'The rottener the betterer.'

This sent them off again.

'How's the tree of life?' asked Jimi.

'Oh, it doesn't look the same from this window,' said Kay, suddenly indifferent. 'Crappy old tree.'

'It's not the same tree, that's why,' said Keith Gear.

'Of course its the same tree,' said Kay, affronted.

'No it's not, Kay. That's a pine tree. The one out the back is an apple tree.'

'No, silly,' said Kay. 'That's not what I meant. I meant it's all the same tree. Isn't it? In the end.'

'I suppose so.'

'It's all a question of perspective isn't it?' said Jimi.

'No, Jimi,' said Kay, putting on a mock-spooky voice. 'It's all a question of tree.'

They all laughed again. Wheezing out air until it hurt.

'Imagine if your head was a lighthouse,' said Keith Gear. 'And each flash was like the beacon shining from a slightly different angle as it rotated so, like . . .'

'Wait a minute,' said Jimi. 'What became of the fairground?'

'Oh, I've moved on,' said Keith Gear nonchalantly. 'New direction.'

'So lighthouses is the future then?' said Kay.

'I believe so,' said Keith Gear, sinking into the depths of an armchair.

'And not my tree of life?'

'No, Kay. That was an illusion. Lighthouses are where it's at. Rocks and shipwrecks and sirens and searchlights circling very fast and – oh, man!' He paused. 'This acid is so strong.'

'Life is a cycle,' said Jimi sagely. 'And music is a continuum.'

'Is anyone getting anything?' asked Kay. 'I mean, how can we be sure that . . .' She watched her words form cartoon speech bubbles.

'Anyway, I'm due back at the swamp, man,' drawled Jimi, reclining once more and surveying the ceiling. 'Kay, we need to get some furnishings. At least a lampshade. Gotta be able to see what's occurring in this fancy-pants swamp of mine with voodoo and smoke rings and Bo Diddley coming down from the mountains with his sky music that he learned in a previous lifetime.'

'Oh wow! Bo Diddley,' exclaimed Keith Gear. 'How did he get in here?'

'Bo Diddley was an Aztec,' said Jimi.

AVALONIA

1989

Keith Gear drove slowly up narrow winding country lanes to the annual Avalonia festival. It was the only English outdoor event he never missed, the only one that had something of that inclusive European festival vibe about it. Three days and nights of music, dance, theatre, comedy, poetry, puppetry and unforeseeable hybrids thereof. A gathering of the resistors. The unmarketable. And their children, and their children's children. And their dogs. All drawn to Wessex on this hot midsummer's morning.

Birds were bustling in the hedgerows. Backpackers came shuffling through the dust. Canny locals were setting up roadside stalls to sell flat Pepsi, tequila slammers, sun block, bin bags, bog rolls, Rizlas, and other festival essentials at a four hundred per cent mark-up. From all directions, snaking as far as the eye could see, cars and campers, hikers and bikers, transit vans full of amps and refreshment vans full of ticketless stowaways were all making the same slow haul to a fenced-off wonderland of rolling hills and hollows.

In 1969, Dominion had performed at the very first Avalonia festival. It was sunset on the Sunday evening. The sky was streaked with Jacob's ladders, the site bathed in biblical light. Five thousand disciples raised their hands in ecstatic appreciation as the band dropped garlands from the godhead. Over the years, the Avalonian disciples had swelled to ten, twenty, twenty-five thousand. Come sun-baked meadow or mudslide the fields always filled. This year marked the festival's twentieth anniversary and the fields were filling again.

There were faces here that Keith Gear only ever saw once a year and here they were once more. Road crews and rig builders, stilt walkers and stewards, flamenco dancers and flautists, magicians and mime artists, buskers and beat poets, painted prophets and pamphleteers. And here again were the bit-part players, the casualties, the crazed old heads that wandered through the crowd all weekend, the characters who looked like they had just emerged from the hedgerows and copses, the odd-balls and out-theres and strange brains who made you wonder where they went for the other three hundred and sixty-two days of the year. They certainly weren't serving in the bank or standing behind you in the post-office queue or working at Kwik-Fit or Kwik Save. Or anywhere. They only seemed to manifest themselves at Avalonia.

Keith Gear flashed his performer's pass and followed the hand-carved wooden signs to the Artists and Crew area, a sizeable secluded paddock next to the perimeter fence. He parked his car in a triangle of space between an old bread van, a Second World War ambulance and a huge billowing bivouac, home to a mini-township of children's entertainers and their extended family of kids, the youngest of whom were excitedly playing chase, gleefully weaving in and out of their ready-made obstacle course, stepping and stumbling over guy ropes while their older siblings sat in a semi-circle, affecting boredom and flicking lit matches at one another.

Half an hour later, he was standing on a gentle slope at the edge of one of the camping fields. Gazing out over the festival site he marvelled at the spontaneously woven patchwork of canvas spread out before him, this temporary settlement of multi-coloured tents, tepees and marquees, their homespun banners and flags fluttering in the breeze. At the centre of it all stood a spectacular geodesic stage, the festival's pivotal landmark, but just one of seven designated performance areas among a multitude of undesignated ones. In the distance, a platoon of electricity pylons was stomping brutishly across the wheat fields and green hills, the only smear on the landscape. Still the Avalonia legions came streaming in like soldier ants.

Once he'd got his tent up Keith Gear sat and rolled a ceremonial spliff. Three tents to the left of him two teenage girls and a boy were struggling to construct a joint of their own. It was a strenuous collective effort, entailing much under-the-breath cursing as the Rizla papers fell apart, once, twice, then a third time.

'God, you have no saliva do you, Blin?' said the annoyed boy in the 'No Nuclear' T-shirt and the chain-store camouflage jacket to the anaemic girl in the 'No Animal Experiments' T-shirt and the baggy Ravechester jeans.

'Here. Let Kate do it.' The anaemic girl began sulkily chewing her split ends as a thickset girl in a studded dog collar and greasy hair bunches got to work on the taxing business of sticking three skins together. Time passed. The sun blessed the festival acres. Keith Gear buried his head in a book of Sufi wisdom.

'Oh, Chazzie! For fuck's sake.'

Keith Gear looked up from his page just in time to see an eighth of Nigerian bush scatter like dust as the boy belatedly cupped his hands against a sudden gust of wind. Several minutes of frantic and futile endeavour ensued as the teens got on all fours and finger-raked the ground for microscopic grains of windblown grass.

'Look, you hold the skins. I'll sprinkle what's left,' said the hard-faced Kate to the crestfallen Chazzie.

'That was meant to last us all weekend,' whined the anaemic one. 'Go and find us some roach, Blin,' barked Chazzie.

Spotting that Keith Gear was smoking a well-constructed cone of his own, the Blin thing got to her feet and approached him tentatively. 'I'm sorry to bother you,' she said in her best polite-teen-talking-to-adult voice. 'But do you have anything we can use for . . . any spare cardboard.'

Close up, he noticed that she had deliberately uglified

herself by shaving her eyebrows, making slits of her ice-blue eyes and emphasising the scowl line that ran across her forehead. Her black nail polish was chipped and her shoulder-length dry fair hair was splitting badly. But her smile, although distant and watery, sufficiently disarmed Keith Gear into reaching over to his bag and pulling out an empty Rothmans packet.

'Here, you can have this.'

'Oh, thanks,' said the Blin thing as she began to rip off the top of the packet.

'It's OK,' he said, going back to his book. 'Take it all.'

'Oh, thanks.'

'Have you got any cardboard?' mocked Kate loudly as the Blin thing returned with the roach.

'Only where her brains should be,' sneered Chazzie and they both laughed at the hapless Blin thing.

'Oh, shit, where's my earring,' shouted Blin, clutching her left lobe theatrically and initiating a whole new saga of angst as the three of them got down on their knees to search again for microscopic items in the afternoon sun.

'They're my nan's. She'll kill me,' said the tearful Blin thing, frantically pawing at the grass.

'Let's all search for Granny's earrings,' said Chazzie with practiced sarcasm.

Their voices gradually dwindled to a background buzz and Keith Gear was able to delve deep into his book once more. A few pages later his peace was broken again by an American accent. 'Keith? Keith Gear?'

He looked up to see a small straw-haired woman in an oversized lumberjack shirt and shapeless denim jeans shielding her eyes from the sun.

'Abby?' she said. 'Remember?'

'How could I forget?' He grinned 'It's only been three years.'

'86,' confirmed Abby. 'It rained all weekend.'

Keith Gear got to his feet and politely offered Abby a drag on his spliff.

'Uh-uh. I'm on a health kick nowadays. Strictly granola and purified water.'

Abby threw down her tent and wriggled out of her huge rucksack. 'Is this a good spot?'

'I think so.' He glanced at the three teens still dragnetting the grass for a lost earring. 'You still living on that commune in Oregon?'

'Yeah, still living the dream,' said Abby. 'But I'll always try to make it back to Avalonia. As long as the spirit's willing.'

'Yours or the festival's?'

'Whichever holds out. You still making music?'

'What else am I going to do?'

'Oh, I'm really pleased that we're going to be neighbours,' said Abby through a mouthful of tent pegs as she got busy with a rubber mallet. 'Are you performing?'

'Tomorrow,' he said. 'Between the gamelan and the ballet. That's the plan anyway.'

Keith Gear knew that with the best will in the world you could never truly plan Avalonia. The itinerary could be fluid at the best of times and with performers dropping in or out at a moment's notice billing was never more than a notional concept. Anyone who turned up unannounced could usually be accommodated into the scheme of things. Keith Gear knew this better than anybody did. That's what had happened in 1986. He'd shared a tent and body fluids with Abby that first night and they'd fallen asleep in each other's arms, only to be woken before dawn by the white noise of torrential rain drumming down on the taut canvas inches above their heads. When the downpour finally relented twelve hours later the whole site had been transformed into a bottomless bog. 'Only one way to survive this,' figured Abby, sticking her head out of the tent after a morning of relentless water torture. 'Psilocybin.' She diligently brewed up a pot of mushroom tea on her camping stove and the pair of them spent the next forty-eight hours tripping their squelchy heads off.

That's where the idea for *Tree Music from the Early Beech Period* had come from. At the height of his hallucinations, as he gazed out over the primordial swamplands of Avalonia, Keith Gear visualised the evolution of botany and geology as a sequence of distinct historical epochs, each with its own genetically coded characteristics and unique indivisible formulae for alchemical transmutation. There was some sort of intricate colour coding involved too, linked to refracted rainbow light and the harmonic properties of the electro-magnetic spectrum, but he'd forgotten the specifics of that by the time the mushroom trip had worn off. 'Out of his tree,' said the *Music Maker*. How little they knew.

Walking around the site that first evening a few familiar faces came up and said 'Hello' and 'When are you playing, Keith?' One old veteran of the first festival asked, 'When are Dominion going to get together again, Keith?' Someone asked him that every year.

He sampled the macrobiotic delights of the Crew food tent, supped a spiced hot toddy and talked about FreeFrom LPs with a knowledgeable couple of jazz-heads from Sweden.

'Drum's supposed to be here this weekend. I'm supposed to be meeting up with him,' said Keith Gear.

'I didn't know he was still alive,' said one of the jazz-heads.

Stumbling through a field full of kinetic sculpture and robot stilt-walkers at one in the morning, he noticed a bunch of young kids twitching and Dalek dancing around a makeshift totem pole that had a couple of speakers nailed to its wings. The music was all synthesiser bleeps and programmed pulses, the kids blissfully oblivious to their surroundings as they jerked and gesticulated like choreographed string-puppets, ecstatically ensnared in their own little private-public domain.

Back at the tent Abby from Oregon sat talking to a guy she'd met earlier. Keith Gear offered her a smile, but as she glanced up her eyes gave off subtle signals, so he left the lovebirds to it, softly speaking in semi-darkness, bodies close in the warm starless night. A few spots of rain were beginning to fall as he curled up in his sleeping bag with only his words of Sufi wisdom for company. The teens were inside their tent, arguing over another badly rolled joint.

'Oh, this is unsmokeable. It's disintegrating,' said the Kate voice.

'Yeah, well that's the last of it, thanks to him,' said the Blin voice.

He heard someone say, 'Go and ask that man if he's got any to sell.'

Then there was some hushed squabbling about sleeping bags and smelly feet. Then came a fanfare of breaking wind and a theatrical chorus of disgust.

'Oh, Chazzie. You're repellent,' said the Blin thing.

Keith Gear fell asleep and had that dream again. The one he often had.

When he stuck his head out of the tent late the next morning the sky was grey and the campsite was subdued. The teens were sitting outside their tent looking truly shit in a way that only teens truly can. The hard-faced Kate, now dressed in a fluffy jumper adorned with alphabet letters, fixed her dog collar and bunches, made a sour face at the weather, cupped her hands against the wind and lit a cigarette. Chazzie sat picking at the ground with a Swiss Army penknife. The Blin thing, still wearing the same animal rights T-shirt and Ravechester jeans, swept her hands rhythmically through the grass and continued to search for her earring. When Abby eventually emerged from her tent, Keith Gear was surprised to see she had slept alone. She too made a wrinkled face at the dull day. 'Only one way to survive this,' she said. 'Mint tea and granola.'

Keith Gear had made vague arrangements to meet up with Drum, so after sharing a mug of mint tea with Abby he made his way to the truck trailer that doubled as the comedy stage. Drum was sitting on the edge of the trailer when he got there.

They embraced with the briefest of touches and went off to find an isolated spot. You could always do that at Avalonia – walk to the perimeter where the fence was battered or broken and find an empty meadow. Even within the vast expanse of the site there were always little nooks and copses where no one ever explored. It was like tourism: get a couple of miles off the beaten track and stake out your own little piece of nirvana. As they strode through a gap in a hawthorn hedge and across a steeply banked ditch on the other side they almost stepped on a young couple enthusiastically shagging. They appeared to be completely oblivious to onlookers as they bumped gracelessly down the gradient together. 'Sorry,' said Drum, raising an invisible hat. The shaggers just smiled and carried on unabashed.

The two men huddled together on a windswept hillock, smoking joints in silence as they surveyed the blanket of grey and listened to the wind distorting the distant amplified sounds of the festival. As they sat there, Keith Gear contemplated how little they had to say to each other these days. When rain threatened they sought shelter in an empty crash tent, thoughtfully provided by the organisers for those Avalonians who hadn't anywhere to sleep. Drum brought out his hash pipe and they choked on grade-A gold seal for a while. Outside the crash tent a fine drizzle started to fall and time stood still, as it so often did at Avalonia.

Later, as they stumbled back to the main site, t'ai chiing ineptly through ground pegs and guy ropes, Drum remarked on the number of tents that had marked off their territory with roadblock tape or decorative ribbon.

'It's real my-pink-half-of-the-drainpipe stuff, isn't it?' he laughed, trailing several yards of yellow material in his wake. 'The gentrification of Avalonia.'

'It'll be white picket fencing next year,' ruminated Keith Gear.

'Electric fencing,' corrected Drum. 'Electric fencing and moats. Ah well.' He sighed, wrapping the accumulated ribbon into a tight ball and tossing it into someone's elaborate gazebo. 'Let us meet upon the morrow.'

'Where are you camped?'

'With the Outsider Crew,' said Drum. 'They seem to have adopted me as their court jester.'

'When are you performing?' asked Keith Gear.

'Whenever,' shouted Drum, disappearing back to his township.

As Keith Gear walked back to his perimeter field the clouds finally parted and a loud ironic cheer went up around the site. People began to emerge, as if from hibernation, out of their canvas cocoons. Layers of clothing were ceremoniously shed. Stoners began to stretch like lazy cats in the afternoon sun. Keith Gear started to feel good about plugging in and laying some tree music on the people. As he approached his tent he was surprised to see the anaemic girl, the Blin thing, sitting alone on the grass. As he got closer, he could see that her face was puffy and red, and her eyeliner had run to clown tears. When she saw him she hastily wiped her snotty nose on the back of her hand and smeared it on the grass. Keith Gear was hoping to have a quiet contemplative smoke before his performance and hadn't accounted for this awkward emotional intrusion, but as he sat there drawing on his spliff the sniffing and snivelling showed no sign of abating. 'Would you like some of this?' he asked eventually as he softened to her plight. The Blin thing looked up, smiled her watery smile, walked hesitantly towards him and took the spliff in her bony hand. Taking a polite drag, she spluttered slightly as she exhaled and handed it back. Keith Gear was loath to ask what was up, fearing that such an enquiry might suck him into the quicksand of teenage tribulations, but against his better judgement he did. She blurted it all out in one pent-up adrenalin rush.

'Kate and Chazzie – my so-called friends – have copped off with each other even though she promised me she wasn't going to get off with him. She didn't even fancy him, she said at

Jemma's party – and she could have copped off with him then.'

Having no solution to her domestic woes, Keith Gear offered her another drag.

'Sorry,' she replied, suddenly aware that she was laying her problems on a complete stranger. 'God, you roll strong joints don't you?' she added, apropos of her instant fuzzy-headedness.

As he still had to organise his stage requirements, Keith Gear tactfully made his excuses and got up to go.

'It's OK,' said the Blin thing. 'I'm thinking of going home anyway. I'll just leave those two to it.' She gestured at the tent as if Kate and Chazzie were all conjugated inside. 'But I think I'll see the ballet first. Might as well get something for my twenty-eight quid.'

'The ballet on the orchard stage? Seven thirty?'

'Yeah,' went the Blin thing.

'I'm on before them.'

'Oh.'

Keith Gear crawled into his tent to change his shirt, his one concession to stagecraft. When he emerged, the Blin thing was sitting on the grass studying her festival programme. She looked at the profile and the photo of the tall, bedraggled man on page nine, then looked up at her neighbour and said, 'You must be Keith Gear, then.'

'I suppose I must be,' said Keith Gear.

'Are you famous?' she asked. 'Sorry,' she added with unsubtle haste. 'Sorry. That was a really stupid thing to say. If you were famous you wouldn't be camping up here, would you?' She bit her bottom lip, realising that this was probably a bit insensitive too. 'God, you've made records and everything,' she said, holding the programme closer to her face to hide her embarrassment.

'I'll walk down with you if you like. But I have to go to the Crew area first to organise my gear.'

'I'll help you,' said the Blin thing, perking up for the first time.

'Well, they have a golf cart to ferry stuff up to the stage but you can carry a couple of things if you like. Nothing too heavy.'

'Nothing too heavy,' she mimicked in a baritone-deep parody of hippie-speak.

As they walked, they talked; the gangling avant-garde muso in his fortieth year and the skinny kid he couldn't put an age to, who gabbled on enthusiastically about whatever came into her stoned head. 'Do you know the Outsider Crew?' she asked.

'Yeah, a mate of mine is camping with them.'

'Yeah. They've got their own field. I think that's where Kate and him have gone. They think the Outsider Crew is really cool. It's all they talk about at school. What's *Tree Music*?' she asked, suddenly remembering what she'd read in her programme.

Keith Gear, explained, without concession or condescension, his hallucinogenetically inspired evocation of geo-botany and its subsequent rendering in musical form. He knew no other way of expressing it. He didn't do idiot-speak for pop teens.

'Wow.' She went all thoughtful. 'Like in the same way that sentient things have souls . . . like the soul in the rocks.'

'Yeah, like the soul in the rocks.' He laughed. 'The ancient wisdom in the ancient rocks.'

'Yeah, I believe in that,' she said, without expression. 'You could call your next LP *Rock Music from the Early Pebble Period*.'

Keith Gear looked at the Blin thing and laughed at her undemonstrative dry wit. 'Yeah, on the dust label. I don't know your name.'

'Belinda,' she said. 'Everyone calls me Blin.'

'I shall call you Belinda,' said Keith Gear, recoiling at the ugly abbreviation. Ugly eyebrows. Ugly nickname. He was warming to the person though.

He asked her about the animal rights T-shirt and got a

diatribe about factory farming and banned beauty products and weekends which involved walking into high-class furriers and setting off the sprinkler systems or grinding chewing gum or squirting superglue into the display racks. 'Or ink pellets. Ink is good too.' He was surprised at how militant she was. He readily assumed that ten years of exposure to Boadicea's government had given rise to a generation of apolitical unquestioning saps, but as she chatted knowledgeably about vivisection and Draize tests and the inalienable right of the ALF to put bombs under scientists' cars if they spent their days sticking needles into cats eyes for a living, he reasoned that two decades ago she might have supported the Angry Brigade.

'Did you know that when those chimps on the TV chatter their teeth it's because they are showing fear?' she asked.

'Yes, I did know that.'

'Did you know that to train circus animals to behave you have to crush their spirit and thrash them till they obey you?'

'No, I didn't know that,' he replied.

'Are you a vegetarian?'

'Sometimes.'

'You either are or you aren't.'

'I was for a while, in my late teens,' he said defensively.

'Yeah, but you gave up,' she said reproachfully. 'That's the trouble with your generation. Do I need a pass to get in here?' she asked as they reached the Crew area.

'No, it's OK. I'll say you're my dietary adviser.'

The Blin thing smiled at that.

He traded tokens for two portions of macrobiotic mush at the Crew food tent and they sat on the grass picking at their paper plates.

'Oh, wow,' said the Blin thing, taking in the backstage facilities. 'Showers. Can I use them?'

She was walking towards the nearest blue cubicle before he could reply.

'They don't provide towels,' he called out, suddenly sounding like a parent talking to an errant child.

She disappeared into the shower and emerged several minutes later in her damp clothes, having thrown them into a corner of the cubicle before putting them straight back on to her soaking skin. 'A proper wash,' she enthused, squeezing water from her hair, 'there was shampoo in there and everything.'

'You'll catch your death of cold,' said Keith Gear, his transformation into the father he had never been now complete. The Blin thing ignored him.

'Clean!' she exclaimed. 'At a festival. This feels decadent.'

'Ready to be my roadie now?' he asked. 'The car's over there.' The kids he had seen the previous afternoon were still sitting in the same semi-circle. They had graduated from flicking lighted matches to constructing a makeshift bong out of a toilet-roll holder, and were now enthusiastically hacking their young lungs up between industrial-strength drags.

As Keith Gear was unlocking his car a maternal vision in size-sixteen rainbow dungarees came bustling across the field, beads and bangles jangling. 'Oh, well done, Josh. A bong,' she shouted from some distance. 'How inventive. Can I have a hit?'

'Build your own bong, Mum,' said Josh.

Keith Gear clocked the look on Belinda's face. A mixture of contempt and disbelief. 'Are your parents like that?' he joked.

'My parents are dead,' she said sombrely, fingering a single silver fish earring through her still wet hair. 'I live with my nan.'

Keith Gear winced at his faux pas, opened the car door and leaned in.

'Do you have any copies of your *Tree Music* with you?' she asked. He handed her a CD and a small shoulder bag full of gadgetry. 'Are you OK carrying this?'

'Fine,' she said. He threw a larger bag over his shoulder, gave instructions to the golf-cart man he had entrusted with his guitars and sent him on his way, leaving the pair of them to scuffle along a short dusty backtrack to the Orchard stage.

'Are you going to perform this?' asked the Blin-thing as she studied the CD cover, a photo negative of bleached rocks and a solitary tree bent against the wind.

'Something adjacent,' said Keith Gear. 'I mostly improvise.'

'Oh, I'm really into that,' she enthused. 'We do it in drama class. I'm reading this book for theatre studies. Stanislavski. The Method. Have you heard of that? You could, like, be a beech tree from the old days.'

Christ, thought Keith Gear. *I'm being patronised by a school kid.*

'Is he singing to the rocks?' added the Blin thing, still engrossed in the CD cover. 'The tree. Is he . . .'

'Now you're taking the piss.' He smiled and she smiled back.

When they reached the Orchard stage, a twelve-piece Javanese gamelan orchestra was making stately sonorous music in the warm evening sun. Keith Gear explained the rudiments of the gamelan to his companion. How some ensembles were made up of royal court musicians, while others were village amateurs. How the Balinese gamelan was generally faster than the Javanese version they were listening to.

Belinda stood with her head cocked, transfixed by the chiming gongs and drums. 'It's beautiful,' she whispered, curling her bony hand around his arm. Keith Gear froze with the unexpectedness of the gesture. She detected the tension and hastily withdrew her hand. They both concentrated on the gamelan for some time after that.

Keith Gear stepped onto the stage to warm welcoming applause. He sat on the chair that had been provided for him, checked his array of effects, focused meditatively for a moment, and then in a voice that barely reached her mumbled, 'This is for Belinda.' She watched in amazement as he sat hunched over his guitar and began to conjure unearthly magic. She had never heard anyone play that fast or that slow.

At times she wondered how just one person could be making all that noise. At others, the music seemed to merge with the rustling trees and was barely there at all. The applause at the end was tumultuous and snapped her out of her reverie. There couldn't have been more than three or four hundred people in the Orchard field but every one of them was on their feet and cheering wildly.

Afterwards a queue formed at the side of the stage. So many people wanted to shake the hands that made those sounds, a few even exchanged cash for *Tree Music*. Belinda hung back hesitantly and waited for the fans to disperse. She now saw a different person to the one she had walked and talked with, and was nervous about what to say should he ask what she thought of the performance.

'What did you think?' he asked when everyone had drifted away.

'Very contemporary,' said Belinda, making an involuntary grimace the moment the words gushed out. Very contemporary! Of all the things she could have said. Of all the lame expressions. It reminded her of that time she told a boy she fancied at school that his new trainers were 'snazzy' and everyone took the piss out of her for weeks. She never had the right vernacular for the occasion. Confronted with the unearthly beauty of this music all she could come up with was 'contemporary'. She might as well have said 'snazzy'.

Suddenly Drum was there, blind drunk and oozing belligerence. He was accompanied by a couple of lunkheads with neck tattoos and mullet haircuts. 'Good show, old chap,' he slurred. 'Very wind chimey.'

Belinda found his arrogance unnerving and decided to make herself scarce. 'I'm going to watch the ballet,' she said, hastily reverting to formality and politeness in the company of slightly scary pissheads.

'Yeah, you go and watch the ballet, kid,' said the inebriated Drum.

'Will you be all right now?' asked Keith Gear paternally.

'Yeah, thanks,' said Belinda and went off hugging her *Tree Music*.

'Who's that?' sneered Drum.

'Oh, just some girl who's camped by me.'

'Nice bit of jailbait, that,' leered one of the lunkheads.

Drum offered to help load his friend's equipment and take it back to the Crew area. Before Keith Gear could say no, the lunkheads had commandeered a golf cart, and the four of them were soon roaring back along the dust track, scattering walkers and eliciting jeers and middle fingers as they cut a petrol-perfumed swathe through the good vibes of Avalonia.

Later in the evening as he stood by a burger stand talking to more friendly strangers, he saw Belinda again. She was reunited with her tent-mates and everything seemed OK once more.

'Nice to see you eating proper food,' she shouted mockingly and then was gone again, a busy blur in the night.

The following morning, over a camp-stove kettle and herbal tea, Abby announced that she was leaving that afternoon. 'Too many creeps here this year for my liking.'

'You heading back to Oregon?'

'No. I've got friends in Bath. I'm going to stay with them for a few days. Come down and see us. They're nice people. I'll leave you the address.'

They sat cradling their mugs and contemplating.

'Have you heard of the Outsider Crew?' asked Abby.

'Yeah.' He thought of Drum, thought of the Blin thing.

'Well, I'm hearing all kinds of crazy stuff,' continued Abby. 'I don't know what's truth and what's lies. People are telling me they send their young ones out stealing from tents and vans. Can you believe that?'

'Sounds like the kind of thing the press hacks would think up,' said Keith Gear, wary of festival rumours.

'Yeah, that's what I thought,' said Abby. 'Except that I was talking to my friends who run a jewellery stall and they told me about this little kid who just kind of adopted them on the first day. They let him sit in the van. Y'know, pretending to drive and stuff. Anyway, yesterday morning they found their day's takings missing from the glove compartment.'

'Maybe they left the van doors unlocked all night.'

'Yeah. Maybe.'

They stared at the ground some more.

'And I hear that they're having TV crews in next year,' said Abby.

'Yeah, I've heard that. And sponsored stages, apparently.'

'That's going to be the death of it then, isn't it?'

'Could be,' said Keith Gear, swigging the dregs from his cup.

'Ah, well. Thanks for the memories.'

'Thanks for the mushrooms.'

They laughed. Abby had been overjoyed when she read the personal dedication to her on the back of *Tree Music*.

When he came back to his tent later that morning all that was left of Abby was a rectangle of parched grass, all flattened out.

He went to the Comedy Truck in the afternoon to watch Drum 'performing' to about thirty people, mostly Outsiders. Drum was playing to the crowd. Lowest-common-denominator stuff. No bits. No skits. No sharpness. No jokes at all in fact. Just stoned patter and platitudes. The Outsider Crew had been holding a 'people's sculpture' competition and Drum was displaying the winning entries; a cigarette packet with burn indents in the shape of a Celtic cross and a plastic cup with a felt-tipped face drawn on. He attempted a few comedy riffs, as if to remind himself of why he was supposed to be there and who he used to be, but they were just remnants of former glories, bereft of timing and topicality. He riffed on the lovemakers they had stumbled over the day before, but it was embarrassing to listen to. The way Drum now told it, a field full of naked love children were all having wild orgiastic sex. 'You had to be there, man. The *News of the World* would have freaked at these fuckers!' The Outsider Crew whooped and cheered and lapped it up. Keith Gear crept away, hoping not to be spotted from the stage.

He walked back to his camping area depressed at what he'd seen, reflecting on what had become of Drum since his bubble burst. From a distance he spotted the boy called Chazzie hanging around the tents. As he drew closer, he could see that Chazzie was quite clearly tugging at the zip to his own tent. He was within five yards of him before Chazzie heard the muffled footsteps and swivelled round, panic in his demeanour.

'I was, uh . . . looking for Blin's earring.' He looked like someone had picked at a thread in his face and unravelled a line of stitching. Keith Gear stared at him in accusatory silence.

'She's been moaning about it all day. You know what girls are like.' He attempted a laugh but still looked bang-to-rights guilty.

'Where are your friends?' said Keith Gear, still fixing him with an accusatory stare.

'They're on their way. Just been watching bands,' said Chazzie, regaining his composure and walking nonchalantly back to his own patch of grass.

Keith Gear unfastened his tent zip, crawled inside and checked that nothing was missing. He sat there for some time, pondering, seething about this thieving little shit in his midst.

When he crawled out of his tent again, Chazzie was sitting on the grass, holding a broken slither of Kate's compact mirror in his left hand and hacking at his hair with a pair of nail scissors. 'How was your gig?' he asked, without averting his eyes from the mirror. 'Blin told us.'

'Told you what?' said Keith Gear, still trying to contain his anger at what he'd witnessed.

'About you and the trees,' said Chazzie. Keith Gear detected the faintest trace of sarcasm.

He'd watched this kid on that first afternoon flustered and

blushing and sheepishly go-fetching, flinching and recoiling when the girls teased or berated him. Awkward, ungainly, gauche, typically sixteen. Now he saw a different person. Steely and cocksure. Slyness in the set of his lips. Malice in his tone. Mockery in the eyes that met his accusatory gaze in the slither of mirror that he held to his face.

'She lives with her nan, you know,' he continued as he snipped away. 'Dunno why you gave her a CD. She hasn't even got a CD player. Always scrounging. She's never got any money.'

'That's nothing to gloat about,' said Keith Gear. *You sneering little shithead*, he wanted to add. 'She seems a bright intelligent person to me,' he said, suppressing an urge to kick this kid's head clean off his shoulders.

'She's all talk,' scoffed Chazzie, brushing snipped hair from his forehead. 'One week she's going to be a ballet dancer. Then she's going to be a singer. Then an actor. She's only doing drama cos me and Kate do it. She hates to be left out. I expect she'll want to be a musician when we get back to school.' Pause. 'Or a tree surgeon.'

Keith Gear stared at the horizon, eager to be somewhere else, anywhere but where he was. 'You're not really getting the spirit of the thing, are you?' he said quietly.

'I hate this place,' said Chazzie, admiring his unevenly cropped fringe. 'Everyone's walking around pretending to be having a good time and saving the planet. They're all fakes.' He glanced at his neighbour contemptuously, daring this sad old hippie, with his car full of unsold CDs, to disagree.

Keith Gear crawled into his tent and stared at his green-domed ceiling for some time. He heard the girls come back. He heard them all go out again. He read until it got dark then he went out himself for one last look at Avalonia. The lanterns that illuminated the walkways and thoroughfares seemed to give off a sickly yellow light, making festival faces look jaundiced and haunted as they drifted into their glow. In one narrow lane a cockney voice called out, 'Had anything stolen from your tent? Come and take a look.' Keith Gear noticed an eager queue forming around a makeshift canvas screen, which had been hastily strung up in the woods. Behind it he could hear the muffled sounds of retribution in full effect. 'Roll up, roll up,' repeated the cockney voice, like a sideshow barker. 'If you've had your tent nicked this weekend come and dish out some punishment to the scumbags responsible. Roll up.' He left the kangaroo court to its laws of natural justice and hurried on down the lane. Back on the main thoroughfare trucks and transits were whipping up the dust, shrouding a long line of backpackers as the Sunday-night exodus got underway. Some people had jobs to go to. A couple of beat-up old cars shot past, pulling open trailers. One had a car engine on the back, the other a 50 cc motorcycle.

'It's the Outsider Crew,' commented one early leaver to another as he adjusted his backpack. 'They do repairs. It's how they make a living.'

'Yeah, right,' said a sardonic second voice in the dark. 'Repairs.'

By the time Keith Gear reached the end of the thoroughfare he estimated that the trailers had gone down empty and come back loaded at least three times.

Later, as he lay in his tent listening to the faraway throb of an all-night rave party, he conceded that this wasn't the Avalonia of old, and that he would be glad to get away. On a previous occasion – 1975 was it? 1976? – he remembered sitting at his steering wheel with tears in his eyes as a long line of vehicles crawled slowly along the country lanes, leaving the hedgerows and the locals to their peace for another year. He'd looked back over his shoulder into the misty Vale and sensed that this truly was Albion's promised land. Now he just wanted to get back to his studio.

He'd been asleep for a couple of hours when a scuffling sound outside his tent made him sit up with a start. Someone was pulling at the zipped-up entrance to his tent again. He sat there in the darkness, silently sifting through three days of debris with his fingers, frantically trying to locate something with which to defend himself. Finding only a biro and a guitar capo he called out, with as much aggression as he could muster, 'Who is it?'

'It's me,' answered Belinda, as she comically wiggled her head through a six-inch gap. 'God, your zip's hard to open, isn't it?' She giggled.

'Obviously not that hard,' said Keith Gear wearily, as the Blin thing crawled in wearing a satin black party dress and red ballet shoes, the only change of clothing he'd seen her in all weekend. Obviously her last-night outfit.

'I thought I'd come and say ta-ta and have a goodnight spliff with you.'

'I thought you'd be partying,' said Keith Gear, listening to a distant pulsating bass line.

'Nah, they're off with the Outsniders again,' she said with breezy indifference as she crawled into a corner, sat cross-legged and smoothed her dress over her knees.

Someone from a nearby tent made a shushing sound.

'It's a bloody festival,' shouted Belinda indignantly. 'Oh well, better not annoy the grown ups, I suppose,' she added quietly. 'Are we going to have a goodbye spliff or what?'

'Just turn that torch on so I can see what I'm doing,' said Keith Gear, twisting round onto his side and reaching up behind him to a small net pocket in the tent lining where he kept his stash warm and dry. As he did so his body rode up out of his sleeping bag, exposing his nakedness down to the thighs. He heard his nocturnal visitor catch her breath. He eased himself back into his sleeping bag with as much decorum as he could muster and constructed a spliff in silence.

'What have you been doing tonight?' he said finally, roaching the spliff.

'Oh, hanging out with a load of morons,' sighed Belinda. 'Burning plastic cups on a big smelly bonfire and listening to the Outsniders banging on about which quarry they've been moved out of this week. Bor-ing. Do you think I talk too much?'

'Why do you ask?'

'Only when I was sitting with the Outsnider lot they were going on about Native Americans living close to the land and we had this lesson in school about that in World Cultures, so I said about how many Indians on reservations are alcoholics and all the diseases they suffer because of poverty and I was talking about all this and all the things I knew about their art and their beliefs and stuff and this bloke just goes, "You know a lot, don't you?" Really sarcastic. Made me look an idiot in front of my friends and Chazzie goes, "Yeah, she loves talking." And they all laughed. I don't think they like conversation much, not unless its about quarries and dogs and smelly vans.'

Keith Gear passed Belinda the spliff. 'Are you cold?' he asked quietly. 'There's a blanket there if you want it.'

'No, I'm fine,' she said softly. They passed the spliff back and forth in the failing flickering torchlight, their hushed voices giving a frisson of intimacy to this shared moment. When they heard Chazzie and Kate arriving back at their tent Belinda suddenly went 'shush' and threw herself down flat beside him. 'They'll start going at it now, you listen,' she whispered, her eyes glinting in the fading torchlight. They were lying inches apart now, their faces almost touching.

'Why did you shave your eyebrows?' he whispered.

'I didn't,' hissed Belinda. 'Kate did them for me. Then she chickened out of doing her own. Her mum would have killed her.' She looked into his eyes. 'They make me look ugly, don't they?'

'They don't quite succeed.'

Belinda thrust her fingers down her throat and made a gagging sound. Then she smiled. Then she leaned forward and kissed Keith Gear on the cheek. The torch battery flickered one last time and gave out. They lay there in the darkness together, their hearts thumping in unison.

Keith Gear's art-life dissolved into memory vapour. All existence boiled down to this moment, lying next to a slender shell of a girl, the Blin thing, breathing heavy beside him, sweetly tainted and nicotine stale.

It took him a while to realise that she had fallen asleep.

He reached over, draped the spare blanket across her huddled form, and drifted into dreams with her hair in his face.

He heard her slip away in the early light but pretended to be asleep. He heard snide recriminations from a nearby tent.

'Where have you been all night?' said Kate.

'I just wandered around,' said Belinda.

'Why?' insisted Kate.

'I just wanted to. For the experience.'

'For the experience,' drawled Chazzie sarcastically.

Keith Gear didn't get out of bed until his neighbours had packed away and gone. An hour later, as he was rolling up his tent, the back of his hand brushed against something sharp on the ground. A trickle of blood dripped from his middle finger and there in the grass sparkled a single silver fish earring.

His car sat waiting for him in the Artists and Crew area, deficient to the tune of one engine.

HAVE YOU GOT IT YET?

1995

Keith Gear stepped out to buy his morning paper. The air was good and the day was bright as he walked the short walk to the precinct. When he entered the newsagent's, however, the first thing he noticed was the mess. Instead of the neatly stacked piles of *Spectrum*s, *Herald*s, *Britannia*s, *Vulcan*s, *Victory*s and *Vanguard*s that normally greeted him, all the newspapers and magazines were strewn about the shop, carpeting every inch of floor space and heaping into small pyramids at irregular intervals along the aisles. At first glance, it looked as if the place had been ransacked – either that or a sudden whirlwind had swept the pages up in a swirling vortex and deposited them again in sculpted conical pyres.

Normally the gargantuan Mr Fazil sat wedged in his favourite corner cubbyhole. From this position, he could keep one eye on the TV screen permanently tuned to his favourite Asian movie channel and one eye on the merchandise. Today though there was no one at the counter. In fact, there was no one in the shop at all apart from a rather bemused Keith Gear. Bending to scoop up a handful of *Daily Vanguard*, he noticed that random pages from other newspapers had attached themselves to the crumpled segments of his favourite publication. On further inspection he noted that there was nothing random about the sequence at all. Miscellaneous pages seemed to have been carefully and deliberately inserted sequentially. *Vanguard* page. *Vulcan* page. *Vanguard* page.

Victory page. *Vanguard* page. *Spectrum* page. And so on. It all seemed too meticulous to have occurred by chance. Reasoning that if he gathered up a huge enough bundle he would still be able to compile a complete edition of the *Vanguard*, Keith Gear paused momentarily to contemplate the puzzling absence of Mr Fazil from his own premises, thrust a thick portfolio of newsprint under his arm, threw down his money and fled the shop.

He thought he heard the muffled sound of laughter as he left.

Keith Gear normally returned home and read the paper before setting off for work. A pot of lapsang souchong, two rounds of toast and a leisurely perusal of the arts pages would usually see him through to ten. But this morning he had to be somewhere. He'd received a letter from the bureau asking him if he might want to consider retraining for an occupation more suited to his skills. He wasn't happy about the letter. He was happy being a freeform musician and assumed that the meeting would be a formality. How many more times did he have to explain to the bureau that the soundscapes he created for his clients were a most satisfactory and lucrative way to earn a living?

Before he set off for the meeting Keith Gear had to go to the post office. He could have sent his music down the fibres like everybody else but he preferred the authenticity of the little mustard yellow bag and the real people he rubbed shoulders with at the post office. He liked masking tape and staplers and glue. It felt like you were communicating something of substance if you packaged things that way. All you did on a computer was press SEND. Then you waited for the client to contact you either to confirm that the music had arrived safely or to inform you that it had corrupted en route or been eaten by viruses. Sometimes, if he was in a malevolent mood, Keith Gear sent the music deliberately infected or incomplete. More often than not, the client failed to notice. Occasionally he even sent out review copies like that just to see if the more impressionable music journalists would notice. They never did.

Keith Gear arrived at the post office just as the shutters were opening. There was already a long queue of customers outside, blank and morose faces all staring silently ahead. It was the same every Monday. The same desperate people, pockets empty.

'Just one minute, sir.'

The young counter clerk looked quizzically at the package and disappeared behind a partition from where Keith Gear heard the unmistakable sound of tearing and cutting. The clerk re-emerged moments later with the package. It was covered in razor slashes.

'Thank you, sir,' said the counter clerk. 'Everything seemed to be in order.'

Keith Gear noted the past tense, looked at the lacerated package, then back at the counter clerk.

'You said, "Everything seemed to be in order"?'

'That's right, sir. In order. Everything. All stamped and ready to go. Good day.'

Keith Gear waited by the bus stop and flicked through his newspaper pages. Soon it clouded over and started to rain. He found his mood darkening with the sky. Eventually a bus appeared on the horizon. Even from a distance, he could see that the driver was steering erratically, crashing gears and veering dangerously across traffic lanes onto the wrong side of the road. From the constant stalling and restarting Keith Gear assumed that the bus was being driven by a trainee under supervision and wasn't in service. He went back to reading his newspaper. *Vanguard* page. *Vulcan* page.

When the bus eventually reached the stop, the trainee driver applied the brakes just in time to avoid mounting the pavement. 'Hop on aboard,' he shouted cheerfully as he leaned from his cab, dye-stained sweat running from the brim of his peaked black cap down each bright red cheek.

'Hop on aboard,' repeated the bearded instructor from the

back platform. Reluctant as he was to 'hop on aboard', Keith Gear was running the risk of missing his bureau appointment and there were no other buses in sight.

'Does this bus go to the bureau?' he asked.

'What do YOU want to know for?' the driver shouted above the growl of the engine.

'It's OK. He's training. He's a little nervous,' said the instructor. 'Hop on aboard.'

'Bureau last stop. End of the line,' barked the driver, sarcastically.

'Yes. Bureau last stop. End of the line,' confirmed the supervisor, ticking a box. 'Then back again.'

'Plenty room up top. Hop on aboard,' shouted the driver again, putting on some sort of ridiculous fake oriental accent. 'Plenty of seat upstairs.'

Keith Gear sat downstairs. Safer that way.

The bus lurched out into the centre of the road causing him to drop his newspaper. The supervisor quickly moved alongside him and helped him scoop up the pages.

'Twenty minutes,' he said, as if anticipating a question. 'Twenty minutes. No more. Put your money away. No charge.'

Keith Gear settled down in his seat to read his paper again but now the pages seemed to take on a life of their own, tangling and intertwining with every twist and turn of the driver's erratic steering. Some pages began to flake and feel sticky as if they were somehow de-evolving back to wood pulp. Others stuck fast and ripped when he attempted to part them. Others still had been torn into thin strips, then shuffled, rearranged, and put back together again, making a Brian Gysin cut-up or Dada-esque collage of every news story. When Keith Gear attempted to open the centre pages they unfolded as origami, and he found himself holding a chain of paper lanterns. Defeated by the futility of the exercise he laid down his newspaper and looked out of the window.

Endless rows of redbrick suburban houses gave way to

business-zone units of steel and smoked glass. He no longer recognised the route he was taking.

'I thought you said twenty minutes.'

No answer.

'Excuse me.'

The supervisor turned round, smiling.

'Soon be somewhere,' he said.

'So far, some morning,' added the driver, tsking away to himself in a parody of resignation. 'Tsk, some morning,' he kept repeating.

The bus wound slowly through the business zone, figure-eighting back on itself and passing the same office block three times. Finally, it came to a halt in a deserted lay-by opposite a large park.

'Careful when de-bussing, mister,' said the supervisor, giving Keith Gear a sudden sharp prod between the shoulder blades as he disembarked.

'Good luckee,' shouted the red-faced driver as he roared off again, zig-zagging and grinding gears.

The bus had dropped him next to a park called The Patchway. He didn't recognise the topography or the district he was in. All he knew for sure was that he was still some way from the bureau building. He knew that because he could see its distinctive mock-gothic facade looming above the fir trees that lined the far side of the park. Estimating that he was at least twenty minutes walk from his destination, he hurried through the entrance gate and headed in the direction of the distant bureau building. He found himself on a narrow pathway, walking towards a bandstand in the middle of the park, but as he neared the bandstand the path suddenly veered, steering him into an impenetrable maze of bushes. Undeterred, he backtracked on himself, negotiated a route out of the maze and strode on. Again, just when it appeared that he was within reach of the bandstand the path narrowed to nothing and once more he found himself wading through thick thorny undergrowth. When this happened a third time he paused to contemplate his predicament. His appointment grew ever nearer and here he was trapped in a labyrinth of unyielding shrubbery. Finally, in frustration, he clawed his way through a bramble thicket, tearing his overcoat and badly gashing the back of his right hand as he did so. Having hurled himself through a hedge backwards, he found himself in yet another interlocking maze of narrow lanes, each seemingly identical to the last.

It started to become dark. Now the situation was getting ridiculous. Keith Gear knew that he had been stumbling around for a while but not for eight whole hours. Someone must have tampered with the climatiser, he reasoned. There had been a lot of this lately. He'd seen it on the news. Saboteurs. The Meteorology Liberation Front probably. Sitting at home, channel surfing, Keith Gear approved of their tactics, applauded them even. If it stopped people from getting skin cancer on ozone-depleted days then he was all for it. Now he gritted his teeth and decided there was something altogether shallow and pointless about the MLF. For every person saved from a trip to the melanoma bank, another, caught off guard by the sudden enforced change in meteorological conditions, was raped or robbed or beaten senseless in a prematurely dark park.

The artificially induced dusk spread rapidly, shrouding the park in sinister pinks and flickering purples. Keith Gear now found himself drawn towards a grid of glimmering beacons. They looked some way off, but with the dusk light playing tricks with distance and perspective, it was hard to tell. Keith Gear hurried along a winding lane towards the beacons, but as he walked, the lane began to arc, turning a perfect three hundred and sixty degrees and depositing him back where he had started.

By now, he was utterly disorientated, and not a little nauseous. He lit a cigarette and pondered his next move. Applying reverse logic he decided to walk the thickest, most impassable route, a precarious unlit cobbled pathway made more hazardous by overhanging tree branches and a lattice of exposed roots.

It worked.

Within minutes, the pathway had delivered him to the source of the distant glimmering lights. These revealed themselves to be not the lights of a building at all but the lighted windows of the very bus that had dropped him off and left him lost some time earlier. Number 74. 'The Patchway', it said on the back. The instructor stepped off the bus to greet him. He began to back away, having endured enough disorientation for one day. 'Have you got it yet?' called the instructor, advancing towards him, right hand outstretched in greeting mode.

Keith Gear thought he heard the sound of muffled laughter again, as he had done in the paper shop. Now it came from the bushes, from hollowed-out tree barks, from everywhere in fact, beckoning, rustling, rising, a taunting tee-hee, swelling to a crescendo of raucous guffaws and invisible sniggers.

The instructor continued to stride purposefully towards him, arms outstretched as if welcoming home some prodigal son. As he got closer, he threw off his hat, unpinned his hair and theatrically shook his long black tresses until they reached down past his shoulders. Next, he carefully removed his false beard, exposing himself as herself. Then she slowly, teasingly, unbuttoned her jacket to reveal a hidden microphone, a black sports bra, and a familiar tattoo emblazoned across the top of her right breast, a setting-sun motif embossed with emerald-green rays. The universally recognised logo of the Game Fun Girls from Game Fun TV, a subsidiary of Game Fun Corps.

'Have YOU got it yet?' she shrieked in tones of friendly mockery. 'You soon gonna have, boy-son.' She placed a friendly hand on Keith Gear's slumped shoulder, positioned herself for the hidden lens, and subtly manoeuvred her dupe, her prey, to his marks. Even though the game was up, the punchline inevitable, he still couldn't tell which of the bushes hid the surveillance camera.

They all did. This was a big-budget number. The show got everyone it wanted to get. No exceptions.

'Especially for you, Mr FreeFrom music man. Today Game-Fun Girls ask you on behalf of everyone who requested us to mess with your mind and reverse role of art and life to "SEE HOW YOU LIKE IT".'

Out of the bushes stepped Mr Fazil the newsagent, Mr Fazil's beautiful daughters, Raissa and Naima, and the tell-tale bad driver who had wished him good luckee. He should have picked up on that at least. It was the *See How You Like It* show's most familiar catch phrase. Lastly, triumphantly, out stepped Mr Pi from the bureau, brandishing a copy of the fake appointment letter he had sent out, requesting Keith Gear's attendance at a non-existent meeting that very morning.

Keith Gear kept having dreams like that.

DUST MUSIC

1999

Keith Gear walked the short walk to the post office. The day was grey, the air was fumes and his melancholy was kicking in. He held in his hand two packages, each containing a letter and a cassette tape. One was addressed to *ArtFist* magazine, the other was going to Jonty Harris, producer of *The Inn Thing*, Radio Fun's new late-night live music show for 'mavericks, misfits, and madcaps'.

'Window number four, please.'

As he shuffled forward slowly in the queue he noticed a woman leaning against the counter at an unattended serving hatch, sniffling quiet tears. He wouldn't have noticed she was crying at all if she hadn't looked up suddenly, glancing nervously at the clock, then at the queue. That was when he spotted her black eye, puffy lip and shivering skin. He thought of asking her if she needed help but the moment for conspicuous chivalry passed and he shrivelled back into the anonymity of the line.

'Window number two, please.'

With only two customers still in front of him, she was still there, nervously trying to cram tokens into an envelope. She was tall, about nineteen or twenty, he guessed, but she had the bearing of a much older woman. The way she carried herself spoke of a hard life. Keith Gear looked on, puzzling over her circumstance, saddened by her demeanour. Nobody spoke to her. Everyone seemed oblivious to her existence, and one another's.

'Window number four, please.'

As Keith Gear walked to the counter the tall woman turned towards the exit, still sniffling. Just inside the doorway her partner, six inches shorter and light years less human, held out his hand in expectation. She passed him the envelope of tokens and trailed out behind him.

Keith Gear posted his packages, then wandered around the Christmas market in the cold December drizzle. A street trader stood in front of a boarded-up shop shouting, 'Last-minute shit presents for people you don't really care about! Last-minute shit presents for people you don't really care about!'

A Christmas office party clattered by, joking loudly.

'Come on, ladies!' shouted the trader. 'Step right up. Stolen goods! Counterfeit CDs! Dodgy perfume for nostrils that can't smell the difference anyway!'

The office posse shrieked as one and descended on his wares. 'Tell you what I'll do, ladies!' he shouted, putting on a compilation of party hits from the 60s and trying to sell them the scrapings from the aroma bucket. One of the women started to make 60s dance shapes with her hands. Wavy shapes. Fluttering shapes. Mystic Shiva shapes. Shapes that Keith Gear once saw from a Hyde Park stage, rippling like Technicolor wheat all the way from the Serpentine to Tyburn in the clear blue cloudless afternoon. Damask-clad dollies and chisel-jawed bikers from the Shoeburyness delta, all bowing down in the heat, all offering up garlands to the godhead in the presence of the Dominion.

Keith Gear wandered around the indoor shopping centre. Piped carols sucked the soul out of the yuletide. By the broken escalator, a promotions booth announced the live-in-person presence of Kevin Aaaargh, the madcap midday DJ on Radio Pus. And there sat the man himself, mirthlessly and mournfully chain smoking and ignored. The floor around the booth was littered with screwed-up request forms, all emblazoned with the Radio Pus logo, a screaming red-faced man. Most of the forms were blank, although a few had been partly filled in and then discarded like half-hearted tips on betting slips. It was as if the spelling or the task itself had defeated Kevin Aaaargh's silent legion of madcap fans.

Keith Gear waded over the paper scraps, through the exit doors and out into the car park, where a small crowd had gathered to watch a man chasing another man towards the distant perimeter fence. The man being chased was younger and fitter than the chasing man, who was carrying a little too much weight for the task, but the chaser kept good pace and stayed doggedly close to his prey. Despite the chaser's tantalising proximity, the other man would slow down occasionally in order to wriggle out of an item of clothing – first he peeled off a hooded top, then a sweater, then a shirt – before resuming his run. It was like some game they were playing to entertain the Christmas shoppers; indeed the onlookers were finding the spectacle hugely entertaining, far more entertaining than Keith Aaaargh and his seasonal dedications. Even the policeman on precinct duty found it amusing. As he sauntered across the car park to greet an arriving squad car he pushed his hat back on his head and rubbed his eyes as if he could scarcely believe what he was seeing. The chasing man was dressed as Santa Claus, while the younger man, a shoplifter disturbed in the act, was fleeing the scene of his crime while simultaneously shedding the evidence.

It was clear from his piss-take demeanour that the younger man was toying with the encumbered Mr Claus. As he wriggled free of each stolen garment he slowed down to let Father Christmas get that little bit closer, before sprinting off again, one layer lighter, one quick skip and hop nearer to freedom. The final disrobing left him naked from the waist up, revealing a skinny ribbed boy, flesh as white as snow, probably no older than fifteen or sixteen. He reached the ten-foot perimeter fence, clambered expertly up, swung with gymnast's agility over the spikes and ran across six lanes of busy traffic and an acre of waste ground, before disappearing into a labyrinth of alleyways and boarded-up houses.

The panting Santa paused to get his breath back, then busied himself picking up discarded clothing from the car park. The crowd quickly dispersed, drifting off in ones and twos to buy last-minute shit presents for people they didn't really care about.

ArtFist printed the first paragraph of Keith Gear's communiqué in its February issue. The rest of his rant received little more than a cursory glance from the recently installed editor, who knew nothing of his legacy and cared a portion less. Upon reading his truncated correspondence he made an angry phone call. The editor, a man of sensitive disposition, accused him of drunken belligerence and held the phone as far from his ear as possible. When Keith Gear asked him if he had played the enclosed cassette he said, 'There was no cassette.' Keith Gear accused *ArtFist* of conspiracy. *ArtFist* accused Keith Gear of paranoia. Keith Gear was airbrushed out of *ArtFist* history.

Both packages contained rough mixes of 'One Long Tension', 'Dusk Eerie' and 'Monastic Atmos', the three tracks on *Dusk Music* and his first new recordings in thirteen years. Both jiffy bags bore all the hallmarks of the artist's current financial plight. A multi-layered mosaic of labels, franking and stamps had been peeled or steamed off or crudely blacked out with a marker pen, betraying the number of times the cassette had already been sent, circulated, rejected and returned. Both cassettes were dubbed from an oxide-clogged VHS tape that contained what passed as a master recording. The tape had previously been used to record various wildlife documentaries, numerous nocturnal Open University transmissions, an old Peter Sellers movie, and an hour-long Channel Raw celebration of the life and music of May Grey, which he hadn't meant to tape over. The tape, wiped and wiped again, stretched and distressed with every generation of use, was full of drop out, grit and multiple sonic imperfections. As each rerecording added its own fresh layer of abrasion, these imperfections became part of the grain, part of the very fabric of the thing. By the time Keith Gear came to dub a final 'mix' of *Dusk Music* on the tape it sounded like no fidelity ever as leakage and spillage from other sources seeped through onto the tracks. A faint, almost imperceptible trace of May Grey's theremin fluttered hauntingly throughout sections of 'One Long Tension'. Due to a faulty pause button on his video a sudden burst of unerased dialogue from the Sellers movie filled the gap between 'Dusk Eerie' and 'Monastic Atmos'. 'Turn them into love junkies,' it said. The sentiment seemed appropriate, so he left it in.

One of Jonty Harris's minions at Radio Fun took one look at the jiffy bag, etched in loser font and brimming with low expectation, and tossed it unopened into his state-of-the-art Mondrian-print wastepaper basket which sat next to a matching Mondrian-print angle-poise lamp placed there to aid his inner illumination, as recommended by the office feng shui consultant for a fee of £2000. When Keith Gear made a follow-up call several weeks later, something he'd rarely had to do in the past, he spoke to another of Jonty Harris's minions, who denied all knowledge of the package.

'What's it called again?' she asked.

'*Dusk Music*.'

'Sorry, sir,' she said. 'We haven't received a CD called *Dust Music*.'

'*Dusk Music*. *Dusk Music*. It's on a cassette.'

'I'm sorry, sir,' she said, 'we don't normally consider cassette material.' When he started to explain who he was, she interrupted him. 'How old did you say you were?' she asked.

'I didn't.'

'It's just that *The Inn Thing* is a leading-edge show aimed at the sixteen to twenty-four demo–'

Click.

He'd tried to hand over the tape in person. That had gone badly too. He sat in the palatial foyer of the Boadicea

Broadcasting Company, watching people come and go, arrivals being greeted and schmoozed off to hospitality, departing guests being helped into taxis or chauffeured away in limos, switchboard enquiries being politely rerouted. He told the woman at the reception desk who he was. He watched her look up an extension number and, at her gestured request, sat himself down among the day's other visitors in a quadrant of comfortable armchairs, and waited to be called. The foyer was warmly lit by Christmas tree lights and extravagant decorations. Even the stentorian security guards were wearing tinsel round their peaked caps. Statesman-size portraits of celebrity presenters hung from the walls, studies in manicured blandness. Outside it began to rain, which made the foyer feel even cosier, the sense of seasonal goodwill even stronger. Colleagues greeted one another like long-lost friends as they stepped out of lifts or bustled in from the driving rain. Keith Gear waited as instructed. And waited.

Twenty minutes had passed when he looked up from his newspaper to see Becky Drake walking across the foyer towards him. He and Becky went way back. She had been Earl Raven's personal assistant from the mid 70s through to the late 80s and had been present at several of his sessions for the programme. They'd hit it off straight away. He recognised instantly that she possessed twice the intellect and, as it turned out, twice the qualifications of her male 'superiors'. Becky Drake discovered the first musician in her life who didn't patronise her or ask her to fetch coffee or alcohol like she was some glorified skivvy. They'd even had a brief relationship after Keith Gear had broken up with Helena Kirsch. The last time they'd spoken, in 1990, Becky had moved to the Overseas Drama department where she was producing first-rate plays with second-rate actors for third-world audiences. Now here she was again, looking fantastic in a two-piece suit and a geometric bob as she strode purposefully across the foyer. She held out a hand in greeting, her eyes creased as she smiled her familiar smile. Keith Gear stood up to reciprocate and tucked the tape under his left arm in anticipation of a warm handshake, a hug and a welcome return to the inner sanctum.

Becky paused and executed a lingering girly step. There was something almost coquettish in her posture. The smartly dressed man seated next to him got up from the sofa, and in a microscopic moment, Keith Gear realised that she was walking towards the smartly dressed man, and that he, the less than smartly dressed man, wasn't even in her eye line. He doubted if she'd even registered his existence. She greeted her appointment by name, Alan, and they walked off together, engrossed in animated chatter.

Keith Gear felt foolish beyond words. His face flushed. He hoped no one had noticed. The fact that no one had noticed made him feel even worse.

What hurt most was the memory flash. His girlfriend Anna, his first real love. Both of them sixteen. They used to do that on the school playing fields, at bus stops, across car parks and municipal recs, on the ramparts at the Tower of London, by the Flamingo pen at London Zoo. In the caravan park at Cromer. Across dunes and tide-battered beaches. Their running joke. Literally. They would bound slow motion towards each other, melodrama heaving in their hearts, celluloid clichés in every step, arms outstretched, pulses racing with the anticipation of touching. Then at the last moment they would both pull away, running blindly on past each other in opposite directions, eventually turning to face each other again, laughing, panting. Then they would embrace, conscious only of each other, oblivious to any audience, oblivious to the notion that this playful charade could have any other outcome, or that time would one day fashion such pathos out of their innocent adolescent mockery.

He walked over to the receptionist and asked if she could dial the *Inn Thing* office again. She regarded him frostily, as if the time that had elapsed since their previous dialogue had transformed him into an un-person. She reluctantly dialled the number, listened for a moment then replaced the receiver with prim fingers. Without looking up from her paperwork she informed Keith Gear, in flat nasal tones, that the voice-mail was on and that the *Inn Thing* team had gone for their annual Christmas lunch. Keith Gear asked if he could leave the tape anyway. The receptionist eyed the suspect package and mumbled something about the current climate.

'So it's OK if I go away and post this anonymously but it's not OK for me to hand it to you in person with that security camera trained on me so that I can be identified should there be an explosion.'

Silence. Forty-below-Fahrenheit silence.

'Well, is it?' bellowed Keith Gear, fixing the receptionist with a hostile stare.

'Everything all right, Sarah?' A security guard, alerted by the raised voice, flexed into border-patrol mode.

'It's OK, Clinton. Mr Greer was just leaving.'

Mr Greer, limbs like lead, slopped off into the Regent Street throng, clutching his dust music.

He hadn't intended to spend Christmas on his own. He'd hired a cottage in the Welsh mountains but everyone else had cried off. Drum hadn't returned his calls. Truelove was in prison, serving time for fraud. His increasingly sparse circle of musician friends all had 'commitments'. Keith Gear was surprised at the sheer weight of 'commitments' that his friends had accumulated down the years. Families. Children. Step children. Other scenes. Other circles. As he approached fifty he seemed to have fewer commitments than at any other time in his life. He had forsaken all that for his art. Music was supposed to get him through. Music was supposed to shore him up in preparation for the long dark afternoon of the soul, for whatever else was coming, for whatever else lay in wait. He went to the cottage anyway.

Everything that could go wrong did go wrong. The van

he'd hired was returned late. He was supposed to pick it up at nine thirty in the morning on Christmas Eve. Instead, he spent a frustrating morning kicking his heels in a windswept breaker's yard waiting for a Mr A. Inskip to return the vehicle. At a quarter to twelve a rotund little man with a bald pate the colour of spam drove the van into the yard, apologised profusely for its condition, for which he surrendered the return of his deposit, and sheepishly scuttled off into the December gloom. The hire-firm and breaker-yard boss disappeared into his Portacabin with some paperwork, came out again with a bucket full of disinfectant and hot water and invited Keith Gear to start scrubbing.

'Sorry about this, Mr Gears. The van's a bit of a mess. Turns out his son had it for a couple of days and someone's puked their guts up in the back. Tell you what I'll do though, as it's Christmas. You can have the van for an extra day. No extra charge. There's more disinfectant in that blue container there. Just help yourself.'

Keith Gear did the best he could on bended knees in cramped conditions. The stench was unbelievable. The vomit had the consistency of shit and the endurance of varnish. After a quarter of an hour the boss man came out again and asked if Mr Gears might like to drive the van outside the gates and finish off the job there on the industrial park arterial road, what with it being Christmas Eve and the lads all wanting to knock off at twelve for their piss up.

'Just sling the bucket and mop over the fence when yer dun.'

He watched the boss man padlock the gates. He said something to another man in a blue checked shirt, who shot Keith Gear a sneer. The pair of them drove off in a diesel haze.

He drove all the way to Wales in the rain with a dodgy fourth gear and the windows wide open. It was dark by four. He negotiated narrow country lanes, hopelessly lost, Welsh village syllables turning to road-sign Sanskrit in the relentless rain, momentary panic giving way to weary resignation as the windscreen wipers packed up.

The van finally gave out in the steep winding lane that led up to the cottage, leaving him to trudge the last few hundred yards of his journey in complete darkness. Once inside he stocked the kitchen fridge with his meagre provisions, made a log fire in the living-room fireplace, and hung his steaming wet clothes to dry on an old wooden clotheshorse. Then he smoked a joint or two and watched the kindling spark and the flames dance. The silence was only broken by the refrigerator hum.

On Christmas morning he awoke at first light, threw open the curtains, and gazed out over sheep-dotted hills and sunlit valleys. Smoke drifted from the chimney of a distant farmhouse. A clutch of stone cottages nestled in their nook and cloud shadows swept the land.

He washed and dressed, then finding that there was no light bulb in the bathroom, shaved himself at the kitchen sink. While he was waiting for the kettle to boil on the gas cooker he listened to Radio Parish Pump on a paint-spattered transistor radio that sat on the draining board. The station's Christmas-morning show was in full swing and a local Anglican minister, who had clearly partaken of sherry, was garrulously rolling his 'r's, exuding false bonhomie to everyone from his host to the Holy Ghost and heartily wishing early risers 'A merry krishmash and all the very besht for the whole of the new millennium.' Keith Gear slowly dunked his tea bag and pondered who among the Radio Parish Pump listenership was going to see out the next thousand years. Meanwhile the happy-clappy clergyman continued to chuckle avuncularly at his host's every asinine comment. When the road-report girl urged everyone to drive carefully this Christmas season he congratulated her on her 'pretty frock and lovely long legs'. When the weather girl broke the awkward silence that followed by confirming earlier reports of widespread power cuts throughout the region, the happy-clappy clergyman, his closely miked heavy breathing now clearly audible, said he hoped that 'Shanta Claus had enough light to shee to the end of all those children's beds'. He made Saint Nick sound like a pederast.

It was only when Keith Gear went to open his fridge door that he realised the motor hum from the night before had been replaced by silence. He tried all the lights. Nothing.

It could have been worse, he reasoned. At least he could boil water and cook with gas. At least he could re-string his Spanish guitar and strum the Christmas-without-electricity blues. At ten thirty he decided that he no longer needed the radio for company. The inebriated vicar, having long outstayed his welcome, was now braying inarticulately in the background of the next programme. Keith Gear turned off the radio and basked in the silence. No phone. No media. No banality. Bliss.

At lunchtime he sat and ate in solitude with all the trimmings. The bare cottage walls compounded his sense of isolation. A watery December sun illuminated the early afternoon. Wood smoke trailed in listless wisps from distant unlit houses. A scrawny ginger cat emerged from the cottage outbuildings, strode confidently up the shale path and glanced suspiciously at the kitchen window where he stood staring into deep unending space as he vacantly washed up a single cup, single spoon, single plate and single saucer.

At two thirty the cat invited itself in via a rusty window hinge, licked the fat from the turkey tray, curled up next to him on a fusty sofa and slept contentedly while the sitting tenant strummed his Spanish guitar and took stock of his life.

He thought of the strangest things that Christmas afternoon. He thought of the celebrity killer and couldn't shake off the feeling that somehow their paths had crossed, if not in this life then perhaps in some previous one. He often had feelings like that. He called it his proximity to the notorious. It had begun in childhood, fuelled by the comics he read and the cheap murder mysteries that sat around the house. His dad collected penny dreadfuls and devoured them enthusiastically. Maybe that's where it came from. All he knew was that from a very early age he imagined ghost footprints and phantom grid lines all over London. He sat on tube trains and imagined that the man opposite was a murderer, rapist or bank robber. He imagined such people brushing past him in the street. Many of his random infant musings were spent calculating the statistical possibilities of this happening. He drew pictures of these apparitions in his sketchbooks, glowing with what he later learned to call an aura.

He thought again now of his childhood and his fevered imaginings. He remembered that time his father took him, as an eight-year-old boy, to the spot by the Thames at Putney where they caught Christie, the mass murderer. 'It was right here, Keith, here on this very tow path,' his dad said. He remembered a time even earlier when he was taken in his pushchair from the terraced house he was born in, down to the embankment to watch the start of the Boat Race. The huge crowd cheered and waved the Oxford and Cambridge crews off to Mortlake. He remembered everyone by the riverside getting their feet soaked by the backwash that came with the flotilla of following crafts. He remembered the sensation of seeing it coming before everyone else. They were all watching the main event. He was looking into the space where the boats had been.

It was the same with ghost footprints and phantom grid lines. All trod by dark men with darker minds. Streets, back alleys and bus routes coated in evidence. Blood trails sniffed by hellhounds. Villains slipping through airports, murderers and sometimes the murdered taking their seats on trains, turning the pages of newspapers with their mugshots on the front. When he was ten he confessed this to a school friend. 'I see where murderers have walked. I see the places they go.' This was the moment he discovered that not every ten year old thought like he did. Not every ten year old smelt the death scent or sensed the presence of menace so keenly.

It lasted until his early teens. Then it stopped for a while. Or rather, he stopped it. He buried his macabre imaginings and put all his energies into his guitar instead. Other children flourished as opening batsmen or Latin scholars, grew confident or gauche at church socials and youth-club ping-pong. Keith Gear sat in his room experimenting with tunings, tensions and pedals. Strumming four E strings and two C strings, spending whole days high on drones. Resting a Cuban heel upon a brand new prototype wah-wah pedal, pushing its capacity to the very edge of disintegration. Or flexing a tremolo arm, feeling for the optimum angle, forever suspended between regular pitch and precipice. Currents whiplashing through guitar leads, forking like lightning between earth tones and ether-magic, surging through circuits and shattering into feedback.

There hadn't been a celebrity killing since – when was the last one, he pondered – Kenny Cash, wasn't it? 1995. Arrests had been made. False confessors had come forward, but no one had ever been charged. The killings had stopped as mysteriously as they had started, but still Keith Gear had that nagging feeling of proximity. He was also convinced that they'd find him – if it was a him – one day. He hoped he would live long enough to find out who was on the grassy knoll that day in 1963, transforming Lee Harvey Oswald into a patsy with one magic bullet, and he hoped that they would eventually unmask the celebrity killer. He might be in jail right now. Or dead. Who knew? It would only take a deathbed confession from some Mafia hit man sometime in 2013, or some undiscovered papers in an abandoned lot, and it would only take something similar with the celebrity killer. He suspected, though, that the denouement, if it came, would be sudden and shocking or commonplace and drab. Because that's how the world is. He thought of that teenage girl, Lucy May, who had gone missing in 1975. University undergraduate. Bright young thing. Bright future. Just disappeared off the street. One minute she was at a bus stop on the Fulham Palace Road. The next minute she was gone. Thin air. Ptoof. The story received lots of coverage on the TV news. The

Thames was dredged. Local loonies were hauled in and released. And nothing. On each anniversary of her death right up until 1980 the papers or the TV news would do a feature on her mystery disappearance. Then she slipped out of the public consciousness as easily as she had evaporated from that busy Fulham Street. All that was left was a grieving family and the memory of that faded newspaper photo of a bright bookish girl in bookish specs and 70s curls. Fast forward to the mid 90s and the capture of the notorious Palmers Green pathologist, Sidney East, responsible for an estimated seventeen murders. And there was Lucy May, all that time, under his floorboards, along with several other trusting young girls who had climbed into the car of a well-dressed stranger without ever suspecting he had a chloroform-soaked stocking in his pocket. And that's how it is, thought Keith Gear, as he gazed out over sunlit valleys and unlit cottages. We're presented with the outline of a life, a news item, and the incongruity of unexplained circumstances and then nothing more for ten, twenty, thirty years until one day someone is cleaning out an attic or investigating a blocked drain and we discover what really happened. That's how existence is. There's no convenient storyline. Life doesn't have a narrative arc, not one that's visible to the naked eye anyway. There are simply events, some sequential, some not, interspersed with fragments of realisation. Sometimes. If you're lucky. The rest is random and chaos and chance encounters and dark matter and groping and twilight and sin.

He thought of many things that afternoon. He thought of Sonya and Celia and Cindy and all the sex he'd had. And he thought about all the sex he'd never had and all the sex he'd never have now. At fifty, he figured that he had more life behind him than in front of him and assumed that the same went for sex. A warped sense of proportion enveloped him as the afternoon wore on and he began to muse wistfully about the ones that had got away. All that spontaneous joy in Swedish hotels and Midwest motels, at seedy Belgravia orgies, at May Grey's mad parties, and all he could think of was the unconsummated quests, the misunderstood signals, the diary blanks and love-empty numbness. By four he had distilled it all down to a tentative early morning knock from Guy Truelove in 1974.

'Can Nancy sleep on your floor? Only she can't get home tonight and there're no taxis.'

So Nancy steps politely, almost apologetically, into his bedroom. Keith Gear constructs a makeshift bed of spare blankets and cushions on the floor, curls up in his single bed and listens to her breathing, knowing she's not asleep and knowing the moment has passed when he should have said 'If you're uncomfortable down there . . . would you like to . . . I don't suppose . . .' and the reason he can't say any of this is so tragi-comic that it hurts him as he lies there listening to Nancy not sleeping.

And the reason is this. One of the legs on his bed has rotted away with woodworm and is propped up with phone directories and dictionaries. The absurdity of it. The unmasking of blatant intent should he offer to join her on the floor. He lies there in scrotal agony, erect, dry mouthed, estimating the leverage of his mattress and the optimum pressure that could be exerted on A–K, L–M, the *Yellow Pages*, and two volumes of the *Oxford English Dictionary*. The next morning Nancy creeps out early, leaving a thank-you note written in blue felt tip and concluded with kisses.

He gets up. Guy Truelove is walking around disconcertedly naked, swigging the dregs from bottles and tentatively tidying up. Scratching his ginger pubes, he says, 'Hey, mun, did ya giv her one?' and Keith Gear explains the imbalance of his bed. Guy takes an inappropriately pedantic interest in which bed leg has rotted, and then fills Keith Gear in on what he didn't know.

'We met her at that FreeFrom gig in Liverpool. Remember? She started following us around after that. Often gave her a lift in the van. And the rest. Nudge nudge. We were driving down country lanes in Cheshire one time and she's going, "I've doon it in that field there and that haybarn there and see those stables, well the owner . . ." all the way to Stoke,' says Guy. A catalogue of shag landmarks. 'Her dad's a country squire. Woorth millions. Jeezus, Gee-ah. She musta thought you were quee-ah.'

Why did that still rankle? Why did that one missed opportunity swell in perverse proportion to every effortless conquest, every fuckfest, every twice-nightly grind? And a hundred other cases laid end to end from Land's End to John o'Groats.

He thought of that time they watched a programme on John Betjeman. Betjeman was visibly and audibly dying when the interviewer asked him if he had any regrets.

'I haven't had enough sex,' said the poet.

'Have you got any regrets?' Gear had jokingly asked Drum.

'Yes. I haven't punched enough people.'

He thought of that afternoon he'd gone round to Drum's to return an unread Hermann Hesse novel. He didn't like Hermann Hesse anyway. All quest and no resolution. But Drum had insisted he borrow it. Drum wasn't in but his wife Kim was. So they'd sat in the back yard smoking grass and drinking wine and talking small talk, and Kim had leaned forward in that black strapless dress she often wore, the one that didn't quite contain her. With one effortless unthinking action Keith Gear pulled at the loose elasticated top and a bra-less breast flopped out. Kim stood up, led him by the hand into the bedroom, wriggled out of the dress and engaged him in exuberant sweaty headboard-rattling sex that lasted until the doorbell went. Drum, who had forgotten his keys, expressed surprise to see him there. Keith Gear wondered if Drum had noticed he was only wearing one sock.

It got messy with Kim. One day she drunkenly called him when Drum was at his place. *Drum doesn't understand me. Can we meet? Can we talk? Can we fuck?* Keith Gear shielded the receiver, held his nerve, said, *I think you've dialled the wrong number.* Kim sobbed softly, desperately. *No, I haven't.*

Yes, you have, he said tenderly, tentatively, deceivingly, giving little away in his tone. Drum turned up the volume on the afternoon film, rolled another joint and said nothing for some time.

And now dusk seeped into the hills and the mist-shrouded valleys. The radio said that the Christmas Eve storms and heavy rain had brought down power lines all over Wales and the West.

The ginger cat cleaned, preened, and sauntered back down the gravel path to his waiting rodent stash. There in that isolated unlit cottage Keith Gear conceded that this man-as-an-island stance had little to recommend it. He eyed the low exposed beams in the living room and wondered if it might be possible to sling a makeshift noose up there. He'd never seriously considered suicide; certainly he'd contemplated it, like any other adolescent who has encountered existentialism a little too early in life, or read Dostoevsky and Turgenev without fully thinking them through, but he'd never considered the ultimate blank out.

He imagined himself hanging there, silhouetted through the window, turning on an E string, moonlit and choreographed by *Le Gibet*, Ravel's macabre evocation of a suspended carcass. His shape mistaken for innocuous shadows by a passing farmer and left there for days.

He imagined the absence of obituary, the meagre gathering at his funeral, the excuses made and the flowers sent.

He was in the process of selecting a sturdy beam when he was distracted by something in his peripheral vision, a tiny spark on a faraway hill. It came from a cottage window he'd gazed at all afternoon, the previously darkened dot of a distant unlit living room. He was still intent on testing his relationship with mortality to breaking point, but when a second light went on, illuminating another previously darkened dot in another hilltop farmhouse, he stopped what he was doing, stepped down from his rickety chair and walked to the window.

A third light went on. Then a fourth. Then a multitude,

sparkling like diamonds, threading through the valleys like grounded stars. In his own living room a dusty lampshade silently cast its dim halo upon the ceiling. And from the kitchen came a quiet click, as currents surged and the refrigerator switched on again and life resumed its relentless dull hum.

THE REQUIEM BLUES

1969–70

'Jimi asked me to marry him, you know,' Kay said casually as she took a cigarette from the pack and fumbled around in her bag for a lighter.

'I said, "Jimi, have you thought this through? It would be great for two weeks then you'd be off on tour again and there would be all those girls . . ."'

She lit her cigarette and inhaled thoughtfully. 'I mean, look at me. I'm totally impractical. I can't even cook. I couldn't ever be the little wifey waiting at home. I don't even own a purse.'

Keith Gear laughed. 'Kay, ever since I met you I've never known you to carry money. You're like the Queen.'

Kay smiled and shrugged. 'I said, "Jimi. Stop thinking with your dick." It wasn't a wife he wanted, it was . . .' She searched for the words to explain whatever it was that Jimi wanted. 'Of course, he's asked lots of other girls to marry him. I wasn't the only one,' she said eventually. 'So what are you going to do now?'

'I'm going to see if anywhere is open and try to get some breakfast, then I think I'm going home,' said Keith Gear.

'No, silly, I meant what are you going to do now that the band has split up?'

It had all fallen into place so quickly for Dominion. Recording contract. Limitless studio time. Prestigious gigs at prestigious venues. The Albert Hall. The Royal Festival Hall. The

Roundhouse. Avalonia. A Hyde Park concert in front of half a million people where by common and critical consent they upstaged the headliners, Blind Faith.

Music Maker had coined the term 'supergroup' and applied it to Blind Faith on account of their pedigree, the band members coming from Cream, Traffic and Family. After the Hyde Park concert, it was applied to Dominion too. Somewhat spuriously, Keith Gear thought. Just because he'd once been the new hotshot guitar gunslinger about town, and drummer Richard Simmons had been a member of Expression and Spencer Charles had been this whiz-kid producer/arranger with a couple of quirky hit singles to his name. This didn't exactly elevate them to the pantheon in his eyes, but he kept his opinions hidden and rode the acclaim. Which was immediate. The moment they hit the boards at the Albert Hall and surveyed that dome full of people who had all come for Hendrix and ended up worshipping Dominion instead. The moment the audience at the Roundhouse rose from its stoned stupor and welcomed them as one. The moment the same thing happened at The Fillmore East and The LA Forum on that first mini-tour of the USA. There were many moments like that in the early days.

All this before they'd even had an album released.

When the LP, *Garlands For Godhead*, came out in the autumn of 1969, its critical reception was mixed. The music papers loved it. The quality Sundays, who had started to take rock seriously after Sgt Peppers, they loved it too. The Underground press reaction was more qualified. Dominion's lack of dues paying won them few favours with the Ladbroke Grove street hippies at *IT*. And although *Oz* liked it they spent more time talking about record-company hype than about the content of the record. The biggest level of dissent came from *Rolling Stone* magazine, who scooped up a little of the vitriol they'd reserved for *Led Zeppelin II* and hurled it at *Garlands For Godhead* instead. The album title they called 'ego-maniacal'. The sound they said was 'quaint and backdated, like soggy leftovers from the summer of love'. They also cast aspersions on the evident schism between the band's meticulously crafted studio work and the more explosive and exploratory nature of their live set, as if one or the other betrayed an insincere impulse.

The band incensed the rock snobs even further when they played the Roundhouse a second time shortly after the album was released. At the end of another spellbinding set, where they wiped the floor with the West Coast's finest, Keith Gear stepped forward to the lip of the stage and gently bowed. A girl ran on from the wings and placed a garland of flowers round his neck. That was the picture that made the front cover of *Music Maker* the following Thursday. When *Rolling Stone* reproduced the photo a fortnight later, it was accompanied by the caption: 'English Rock Group's Messiah Complex. See inside for the full shocking story.'

In time, Keith Gear came to see that garland as a wreath, but in that brief burst of wondrousness which lasted from the spring to the early autumn of 1969 that Roundhouse moment seemed like a crowning glory, a culmination of everything that had been good about being in a band.

It didn't last. Nothing does. Kenny was already showing signs of the chemical excesses that would drag him to an early grave. Richard had indicated on more than one occasion that if this all fell through tomorrow he'd be happy living in a tepee in the Welsh hills. And if Spencer needed further confirmation that it was his song-writing buddy and not he who was the brightest constellation in the sky, then that Roundhouse garland sealed it.

The first time they went to America they were cosseted and watertight. They didn't have to lift a finger for themselves. Lucas, their strait-laced and totally-together-at-all-times tour manager, handed them an itinerary each day, outlining checking-in times, checking-out times, travel itinerary, gig location, and radio interviews. But really, all it needed to say was 'Need shoelaces tying? See Lucas.' 'Need milk shake stirring. See Lucas.' With everything laid on and paid for, Dominion could concentrate on having a gas from coast to coast. They laughed at the plastic TV. They laughed at the plastic radio. They laughed at plastic America. Within a week of landing in the belly of the beast Keith Gear realised that those early Frank Zappa LPs weren't just music, they were documentaries. 'Bow-Tie Daddy', 'America Drinks And Goes Home', 'What's The Ugliest Part Of Your Body?', 'Hungry Freaks Daddy'. It was all here. On every sidewalk. In every bar. In every squeaky-clean scientifically planned suburban housing project.

Dear sweet Kenny was a joy on the tour bus, a natural joker, the life and soul. He drank in America. Dear sweet Kenny with a girl on each arm at the Fillmore West. Dear sweet Kenny getting the kind of chicks who thought Ringo was cute. Dear sweet Kenny only trying cocaine the once on that first visit and not really seeing what the kick was. 'It was boring. I couldn't get to sleep.' Dear sweet Kenny.

The radio ads had them in fits. Those hippie dollars were up for grabs. All the marketing men and merchandisers were trying to get some of that love and peace action by 1969. Their favourite was the burger ad they kept hearing on KYCY in San Francisco.

'Hey, man, wanna score a groovy cheeseburger from Hoagy's? A Hoagy's regular will only set you back twenty-six cents. A Hoagy's deluxe is only thirty-three cents. What else can you score for those kinda prices? Hoagy's cheeseburgers. They're outta sight.'

The band sought out a Hoagy's the moment they stepped off the tour bus, asking the sourpuss Suzie behind the counter which one had the acid in it, the twenty-six cent or the thirty-three cent? She handed them a Hoagy's decal and asked them if they were 'from out of town'.

'Yeah,' said Kenny.

'Canada?' said Suzie.

'Mars,' said Richard.

There was another one that really cracked them up on KGG Los Angeles, where they were doing a promotional appearance on the day of the Forum gig.

'*Sally's an artist. Scorpio. Moody. Intense. With a sting in her tail. She wears velvet tops and flared hipster pants. Jenny's into macrobiotics. She's Aries the Ram. Wears earth colours cos she's in touch with mother earth. Then there's Rona. Rona's an Aquarian. Rona looks good in anything. Did I tell you what they all have in common? They all shop at Patty's Pattern Shop. Patty's has far-out patterns and far-out fabrics at affordable prices. Patty's Pattern Shop.*'

The KGG DJ, Dean Tracy, lobbed them a polite question about how they were finding LA. Kenny went into his Patty's parody.

'Kenny is a bass player. Born under Taurus the Bull. Gets kinda messy down there. Needs the kind of clothes that can cope with that amount of Bull. He shops at Bona Drag on Tooting High Street.'

The bemused DJ responded with a slightly less polite question about what it was like to be an unknown bunch of limeys supporting Jimi Hendrix at the Forum. Dear sweet Kenny was on a roll.

'Spencer Charles is a Capricorn. He's into PVC. Kinda kinky, I know. There's only one outlet for his fetish but unfortunately we aren't allowed to advertise it on the radio.'

The band was in fits, riffing away. Lucas fretted. Dean Tracy cast a nervous eye on the clock and put a red pen through the rest of his pre-arranged questions.

These were the happy times. The band's wit and camaraderie protected them from all the phoniness and fakery. It was Dominion against the world. They knew how good they were. 1969 passed in a joyous blur and ended on a high. Earl Raven's Christmas show that year included a section where all the top English Underground bands performed versions of their favourite hymns. Dominion did a waltz-time version of 'Immortal, Invisible, God Only Wise' which was the highlight of the programme. Nobody noticed the underlying sadness in Keith Gear's voice as he sang 'We blossom and flourish as leaves on the tree / And wither and perish but naught changeth thee . . .'

Keith Gear spent an extended Christmas break with Celia in her Chelsea flat. All of that winter was Celia. Walking in Portobello Road in the snow this kid came up to them, couldn't have been more than thirteen, and said, 'Hey, man, do you know where I can score?'

They looked him up and down and laughed in disbelief. 'How much are you after?' said the much-amused Celia.

'Ten bobs' worth,' said the kid.

They spent the rest of the afternoon collapsing into each other's arms going, 'Ten bobs' worth.'

Celia trawling through a tray of old buttons.

'How many are you after?' said the stall holder.

'Ten bobs' worth,' said Celia.

The window of an antique shop where the perma-tanned smoothy proprietor stood languidly surveying the passing trade from the doorway.

'I'd like some antiques,' said Keith Gear. 'Precisely ten bobs' worth.'

The barrow boys at the top end of the market. Shouting, 'Spraarts, unyuns, parsnips.' Ten bobs' worth please.

Celia bought him a copy of *Live Peace in Toronto* and they lolled around all Boxing Day making lazy love and listening to it. He preferred the Yoko side. She preferred the rock and roll side. Celia played the rock and roll side so often that he grew to hate it as the twelve days of Christmas wore on.

'That's the trouble,' he slurred after one glass too many. 'With music I mean. They all want to be Teddy boys again. Fucking "Lady Madonna". "Blue Suede Shoes". All these groups who were saying they were into Ravi Shankar a couple of years ago. Now you ask them who their influences are and they say Carl Perkins. It's all so phoney.'

Celia was unsettled by the violence of the onslaught and began to cry. 'Don't you like my present?' she said.

Keith Gear wiped her eyes and consoled her. 'That's the trouble with music, I said. Not with you. I didn't mean to hurt you.' But he did. He did hurt her.

It didn't sour the seasonal cheer but instinctively they both knew that something had come between them. Neither of them could put a finger on it. She vaguely put his outburst down to artistic temperament. He vaguely put her tears down to too much brandy, but the conflict spoke of a deeper divide. In some ways life, certainly the creative life, is like that, he concluded. Ultimately you're on either the Yoko bus or the rock and roll bus.

At one, precisely an hour into the 70s, they were lying in bed, cosy and post-coital, when he heard the sound of someone sobbing in the upstairs flat. 'That will be Jennifer,' sighed Celia. 'She's seeing a married man, works in the city. He promised her he was going to get away to spend the night with her.' She paused to listen to the lonely sobbing. 'That will be me one day,' she said. And it was. It was her one day.

Early in the new year Dominion went out on a UK tour with Free as their support. Buoyed by an unexpected hit single when 'Greenwich Dream Time' was lifted from the LP, Dominion still acted like they had the world at their feet. But each night the support band blew them offstage. It was like the wind had changed overnight and everyone but Dominion had noticed. Only a year earlier Dominion had been doing the same to Hendrix or The Doors when they had an off night. Now the roles were reversed. Standing in the wings, watching Free do their stuff in front of a rapt Newcastle crowd, Keith Gear recognised something of Dominion's early spirit. The music was different, he didn't care much for the riffs and the swagger, but he recognised belief when he saw it. That was the difference. Free were on a mission. Dominion were coasting.

The next night in Leeds it was the same. And the night

after that in Birmingham. And the night after that. And the night after that. At Bristol Colston Hall Kenny came tottering unsteadily into the dressing room in his stack-heeled boots and said, 'Hey, I've just been talking to Free's bass player. He told me their record company wanted them to change their name when they signed and he told them to forget it. "We're Free, man."' Kenny laughed at his own parody. 'Kid's only nineteen and he's telling the record company where to get off. Far out.'

Dominion's own bass player was only twenty himself, although he was already starting to look older. Keith Gear watched in dismay as Kenny arranged a thick line of dirty speed on a magazine. He was still gabbling about these headstrong kids who were blowing them off stage every night and saving their partying for after the gig, blissfully unaware of the irony of his sentiments and the tragi-comedy he was becoming.

Free's big crowd pleaser, 'All Right Now', was released the week Dominion set off for a twenty-two-date US tour. America offered no respite. In fact, America the second time was where it all started to unravel completely. On their first visit, they'd sailed in on a tide of goodwill and careful planning. Showcase gigs on the East and West coasts with Hendrix had sheltered them from the harsher realities of the rock life. Now they toured the real America with Canned Heat, Taj Mahal and Johnny Winter. What had wowed audiences at the Fillmores cut little ice in Shitsville, Kentucky or Piss Ant, Minnesota. No one wanted to see this fey little English outfit with their pretty little pastoral songs and their itty-bitty improvisations. What was it *Rolling Stone* had called them? 'Backdated.' They wanted the high-octane full-tilt boogie of Canned Heat, Johnny Winter, Taj Mahal. And every night Canned Heat, Johnny Winter and Taj Mahal obliged. And after they had all boogied on stage they carried on boogieing in the dressing room and when they got on the bus to head on to the next town they still carried on boogieing. Every moment that wasn't spent sleeping was spent boogieing as the collective unit sat up back and jammed its way across America. The bus was re-christened the Boogie Bus. Keith Gear sat on his own listening to the interminable riffing and felt his ennui coming on like influenza. Each night seemed to be worse than the last as the Boogie Bus boogied on to its next destination. Ann Arbor, Michigan. Providence, Rhode Island. Greensboro, North Carolina. Tuscon, Arizona. Fort Worth, Texas. It was like Dominion were being offered up as sacrificial lambs at every gig. Feast on these tender morsels, my children. Then let the boogie begin. There were nights on that tour when Keith Gear wanted to die, and others when he thought he actually had died and gone to boogie hell. On a good night, the crowd was merely indifferent, too loaded on ludes to care about these limeys riding their luck. On a bad night they booed and jeered and threw things until the booing and jeering and throwing things became another instrument, a percussive counterpoint. The band began to miss it if it wasn't there.

'I think we're all atoning for something we did wrong in a previous life,' said Richard one night as they watched the twinkling lights of a distant town from the Boogie Bus windows. And he wasn't joking. Semi-detached at the best of times, Richard started to act really strange on that tour. Most nights he threw the I Ching to determine how he should play the drums. One night the hexagrams told him to exercise apprehensive caution in order to achieve an outcome of good fortune. This he interpreted as an instruction to forego drumsticks and to only tap the skins softly with the palms of his hands, so that's what he did. The crowd didn't give a shit one way or the other. Kenny meanwhile pranced around the stage like a prick, too high to notice that he was fast becoming the chief catalyst for the crowd's derision. Whenever he heard feedback from the auditorium, any whoop, any hiss, any holler, Kenny would be there at the edge of the stage, throwing the rock-star poses, oblivious to the fact that he had transmogrified into a fully fledged object of ridicule. But no matter how fucked up he was on stage every night there would still be a steady stream of teen groupies waiting for the cutie little bass player so the cutie little bass player was content to play the fool. Pretty soon it was all he could play.

Spencer was becoming a wreck for different reasons. Unlike Keith Gear, who just got his head down and battled on through the boos and bottles – some nights he even thrived on the adversity – Spencer was terrified. Keith Gear would glance over at him as he struggled to get through the set and could feel only pity. This nice cultivated boy who was reasonably talented and well connected and had got lucky in 1968 with a couple of minor hits called 'Kinda Quirky' and 'Harum Scarum' which he had arranged himself, and who had scored himself a nice little publishing deal and found himself a supergroup, he wasn't cut out for all this, hadn't asked for any of it. But on it went regardless. Amphitheatre after amphitheatre. Night after nightmare night. The crowd was there for the booze and the ludes and bloooze and the boogie. They weren't there for Dominion.

Each night Keith Gear sat alone on the bus, watching the distant lights of distant towns and wondering how he'd ever let himself get dragged into all this. He wasn't just compromising his artistic purity now. He was compromising his sanity. Those distant lights became a motif, not merely for his art but for life itself. A far off town would loom up on the horizon, drawing slowly closer. Eventually they'd reach the town and speed through in a flash. And every town would look the same. Deserted main street. Motel. Diner. Gunsmith. Hosiery. Bowling alley. Gas station. A lone traffic light suspended and swaying above the emptiness of it all. Then on into the darkness until the next beckoning lights loomed up in the distance.

By 1970, the phoniness had spread everywhere. Even the underground radio stations had caught the phoniness bug. The band did an interview at KPPX San Bernardino which was preceded by a competition to design a record sleeve or concert poster for a forthcoming gig. 'Manifest your groovy talents in art and send us your visions,' drawled the DJ, Rick Dorn. 'All entries automatically become the copyrighted property of KPPX,' he concluded, without apparent irony. He turned to his visitors. 'Well, the time is, hey who cares what the time is? A big San Bernardino welcome to my guests, The Dominion.'

Keith Gear glanced at the script lying on the studio consol. It read: 'Well, the time is, hey who cares what the time is? A big San Bernardino welcome to my guests. Band name here.'

It was the same everywhere they went. There was a whole identikit network of these supposedly groovy radio stations with their hip-to-the-trip sponsors and their far-out DJs and their psychedelically phased weather jingles. They would play The Doors, the Stones, Jimi and Janis and the occasional fey little English band like Dominion. Then they'd go to the news, which would be beamed in live and direct from the Pentagon in association with the military-industrial complex, and they'd talk about how US forces had put down another Vietcong insurgency and taken out another guerrilla supply line. There would be some senator talking about how 'communist agitators are responsible for campus disorder.' Then they'd play a song about four dead in Ohio. Then there would be a public service announcement urging listeners to register for the draft. Then there would be an ad for some forthcoming avant-garde film festival. Then they'd play 'Fortunate Son' by Creedence. Then they'd read out a bunch of requests for soldiers on active duty in Vietnam. Then they'd play 'Make Me Smile' by Chicago Transit Authority. Then there would be ads for fake eyelashes for three dollars – 'Extra long, extra bewitching and easy to apply with special formula adhesive' – and fake tans – 'a darker richer tan in three to five hours or your money back'. There would be ads for fake everything. It was all one crazy psycho mosaic of merchandise, propaganda and love buttons and brain police and it was slowly,

slowly chewing up Dominion and spiting them out like pips.
They were glad to get back to Britain.

The band's flagging spirits revived a little with an appearance at the second Avalonia festival on Midsummer's Eve. Kenny lay off the powders. Richard lay off the hexagrams. Spencer and Keith Gear lay off the mutual animosity. There was even talk of a second album but when Earl Raven asked them to do a new session for his show there was no fresh material, just tired rehashes.

By August they knew the game was up. A short tour of Europe supporting Hendrix was announced. This would be followed by an appearance at the second of that summer's Hyde Park free concerts alongside John Sebastian, Eric Burdon and War and Canned Heat. After that, Lucas expected Dominion to fulfil their contractual obligation to record a second album and follow up with a UK tour. The band secretly convened and agreed there would be no second album and no tour. They agreed instead to announce that they were splitting up live on stage at Hyde Park.

Keith Gear hadn't seen Jimi in over a year. When he did, he was shocked at how tired and puffy he looked. He'd hustled a pass for the Isle of Wight festival and had spent the weekend watching the counter culture fracture and fragment before his eyes. Anarchists tore down the fences or watched for free from the hill. A bloated Jim Morrison sleepwalked around the stage, barking the dipso blues. In the short space of time since they had supported Dominion, Free had become one of the biggest bands in the land, and a short space of time is sometimes as long as it takes, reflected Keith Gear as Free blew the crowd away.

Jimi went on at two in the morning with the crowd sounding as if they were baying for blood. As he neared the stage, a French reporter shoved a microphone into his face and shouted inane questions at him. Jimi answered her with polite weariness. He seemed to be on autopilot. He was on autopilot for most of his performance too. Midway through the set, as radio interference broke through the PA and Jimi retuned his guitar for the nth time, underground-press music journalist Jaz Beaker came and sat next to Keith Gear on the stage-side scaffolding. He was in tears.

'It's funereal man,' he sobbed. 'We're watching the last rites here.' Jaz was a Hendrix disciple from his Afro hair to his buckskin shoes. He was inconsolable. 'Whatever was going on, man, it sure ain't going on any more. Face it. It's over.'

As Jimi churned out a lame version of 'Foxy Lady', Keith Gear found it hard to disagree.

'If you kept playing the same old songs you'd be ready to stop,' Jimi announced prophetically at the end of the song.

It was like that on the European tour too. Jimi churned out 'Stone Free' and 'Foxy Lady' and 'Fire' and looked like he couldn't wait to get off stage most nights. Keith Gear wondered what had happened to the space music. He wondered what had become of the *Rays of the New Rising Sun* album Jimi had supposedly been working on for the past year. When he came off stage Jimi was routinely greeted by a dressing room full of hangers-on and reporters ready to fire more inane questions at him. *Why are you into black power, Jimi? Why aren't you more into black power, Jimi? Why do you play so many old numbers, Jimi? Why do you play so many new numbers, Jimi? Are you an integrationist, Jimi? Are you the magic voodoo superspade witchdoctor, Jimi?* Everyone wanted a piece of Jimi. Everyone wanted to project whatever he or she goddamn wanted onto the increasingly blank canvas that was Jimi.

Most nights he didn't even go on stage in his showman clothes. He dressed down to suit his downbeat mood and wore what he wore offstage. Usually a plain brown suede jacket, a white cotton shirt and black pants. 'What DID happen to the *Rising Sun* album, Jimi?' Keith Gear dared to ask one night back at the hotel in downtown Copenhagen.

'Oh, man,' Jimi sighed. 'I'm still working on it, but the trouble is whenever I play any of that stuff live the audience don't want to hear it. You heard them tonight, man! They still shout for the old stuff.'

Jimi picked up his acoustic guitar and sat down on his hotel bed. The moment he began gently strumming a burden seemed to lift from his body.

'That's a pretty tune,' said Keith Gear. 'What's it called?'

'Its called "The Requiem Blues",' said Jimi.

Jimi's requiem blues took Keith Gear's mind off his own. It no longer mattered that Dominion were splitting. He was looking forward to getting away from it all. Everyone in the band felt the same. Even though Kenny was acting like a train wreck once again, relations between the four members were fairly convivial. There was a mutual feeling of 'let's just get through this charade one more time and get it over with. Let's do a good show at Hyde Park on Saturday and go out on a high.'

The day before the Hyde Park finale Keith Gear met up with Jimi again. Jimi was staying at the Cumberland Hotel at the Marble Arch end of Oxford Street. He called in the morning and said, 'Come on over. Let's play some tunes.' He sounded jaded and hungover. He said that his new bass player had returned to America feeling ill, but seemed optimistic about the future. He asked Keith Gear if he played bass and if he fancied coming to Morocco some time to get away from it all.

'Remember that caravan of music we dreamed up?' He laughed. 'Lets go and join it.'

He also mentioned that he was due to do an interview that afternoon with Harry Cole from *Discbeat*. Harry was an old-school music hack plying his trade for an old-school music publication. Keith Gear suspected that Jimi just wanted someone else there for protection, as a buffer against the inanity of it all.

When he got there, Jimi was already on autopilot,

answering every one of Harry the hack's questions with stoned politeness, agreeing with everything, revealing nothing. Jimi told his interviewer that he was thinking of working in future with a bigger group and that he was thinking of working in future with a smaller group. He wanted to play more live gigs and less live gigs. He wanted to play his space orchestra music. He wanted to play the blues. He thought he should be more of a showman on stage than he had been of late. He thought he should lay off the showmanship a little and concentrate on his chops. And so on and so off. None of this was conveyed with a wink or a twinkle. This wasn't Dylan playing mind games, conducting the interview like a piece of prime-time theatre of the absurd. This was a man who wasn't sure he knew what he wanted to do anymore. 'You should interview this guy,' said Jimi at one point. 'His band is splitting up tomorrow.' Harry Cole smiled his Fleet Street smile and moved on to his next question. He didn't even know who Keith Gear was. He assumed he was Jimi's tour manager.

After he'd gone, they had a smoke. Jimi said that maybe he'd come down and check out Eric Burdon and War tomorrow. Keith Gear said that maybe the pair of them should sit in with War when they played the MQ Club the following night. 'Yeah, then I think I'm going to split the scene for a while,' said Jimi. 'Get my mental shit together.'

On the Saturday morning of the Hyde Park concert it was raining hard. Lucas phoned, his voice full of foreboding. He thought that the concert would be cancelled if the rain persisted, but by lunchtime, when Keith Gear set off for Hyde Park, the sun was trying to break through.

There were nothing like the numbers that had attended previous gatherings but fifty thousand hardy souls had braved the overcast skies and the early September chill, eager to be there. Shortly after Keith Gear arrived it started to rain again. He stood and watched from the front of the stage as Michael

Chapman switched from electric to acoustic guitar and battled on gamely against the elements. His bitter-sweet songs about naked ladies and Scarborough postcards, all rendered in a grim and gruff accent, seemed to be in keeping with the ambience, but as the wind got up and the rain got heavier even he had to concede defeat. And that was pretty much that for the rest of the afternoon. Keith Gear retired to the back of an Avis rental van and smoked joints with Richard and Roy Harper. The crowd dwindled from fifty thousand to five thousand who sat under makeshift shelters of polythene and tarpaulin or retreated to the nearby trees and peered miserably into the unrelenting gloom.

Spencer arrived and immediately threw a fit about the billing. The original running order had been:

12.00 Roy Harper
1.00 Michael Chapman
2.00 Eric Burdon and War
3.30 John Sebastian
4.30 Dominion
5.30 Canned Heat

The weather had thrown all this into chaos and now Lucas was talking of everyone playing shorter sets.

Kenny arrived. He hadn't been to bed since Thursday and looked incapable of playing a note. Keith Gear gazed at the miserable weather and dreamed of Morocco.

Eventually the downpour eased just enough for Eric Burdon and War to risk electrocution. On the stroke of four, the leaping Geordie gnome with rain-matted hair and water dripping from his nose stepped up to the mike and addressed the bedraggled gathering.

'You must all be crazy,' he said, peering at the thousand or so saturated hippies huddled in front of the stage. 'But that's OK. Cos we're all crazy too.'

War then launched into ninety minutes of non-stop

percussion-heavy funk that had the crowd dancing itself dry. They exited to thunderous applause.

When John Sebastian walked on stage the sun peeped through the clouds for the first time since midday.

'How fucking corny,' said the increasingly agitated Spencer, as if John Sebastian had somehow choreographed the whole thing.

By now it was past five. There was a six-thirty curfew on the event and Lucas was fretting about how they were going to squeeze two more bands into little more that an hour's playing time. By now Keith Gear was past caring. Kenny was nodding out in the corner. Richard's hexagrams had told him that to encounter water would put him in a position of great peril.

Spencer continued to rant and rage. 'We spent an entire US tour being upstaged by Canned Heat. They're in our country now. It's not going to happen again,' he spat.

Canned Heat were stoned and sombre and no more happy with the situation than anyone else.

'Give it a break, Spencer. Their singer died last week,' said Keith Gear, referring to the passing of Al 'Blind Owl' Wilson.

'Why don't you go and form a band with Jimi Hendrix,' Spencer replied, petulantly.

As the sound of John Sebastian's sunshine music wafted backstage and Lucas continued to schmooze everybody with love vibes, all of Spencer's pent-up resentment continued to pour out until finally he could take no more. 'OK, let me make things easier for you,' he said. 'I quit.'

With that, he flounced to the back of the Avis truck, jumped down into the backstage mud, skidded, and landed flat on his velvet-clad arse. And that was the end of Dominion.

Keith Gear went and watched Canned Heat for a while, then he said goodbye to Richard, patted comatose Kenny on the head and made his way out of the backstage compound. As he trudged across the park he glanced back at the ever-dwindling gathering in front of the stage. Canned Heat were launching into 'Refried Boogie'. Keith Gear had heard more

'Refried Boogie' than he cared to remember. He'd heard 'Refried Boogie' in every city from Pittsburgh to Pasadena. Some nights that song went on for half an hour or more. He could still hear it when he reached Marble Arch. It went on for the rest of the show. It seemed to go on for the rest of his teens.

'So what are you going to do now?' asked Kay.

'I'm going to see if anywhere is open and try and get some breakfast, then I think I'm going home.'

'No, silly. I meant what are you going to do now that the band has split up?'

They were sitting in the waiting area of the St Mary Abbot's Hospital in Kensington where Jimi was taken to have his stomach pumped. The doctors had said they were going to keep him in overnight for observation.

On the Tuesday following the Hyde Park concert Keith Gear sat in with Eric Burdon and War at the MQ Club. It was the first time in three years he'd performed with another group and it was nice not to be in the spotlight. He just sat quietly at the back scratching out rhythm, playing lock and go with the conga player. No one asked him about Dominion. No one bothered him at all. It was a gas. A couple of nights later he went down to the MQ again to watch Jimi jamming with War. Jimi wasn't on it. He was barely there at all. He sat in on Tobacco Road and Mother Earth, unplugged, with the minimum of fuss, and went back to his hotel saying he was tired.

Keith Gear was surprised therefore to see Jimi at an impromptu after-gig party at the function suite of The Damask Hotel in the Grove. Most of the musicians had gone on to the Speakeasy. Keith Gear hated the Speak. He'd never quite forgiven them for barring him the one time he'd optimistically tagged along with Jimi and Kay back in 1966. He loathed the whole elitist attitude of the place. This gentleman's club for the rock aristocracy. *Fuck that*, he thought, *where are those Isle of Wight anarchists when you need them most?*

The Damask couldn't have been more different. The Damask was where the dregs had washed up. Local junkies, local winos, loser musicians from loser bands, pimp landlords who rented out rooms by the hour, and the girls they rented them to. Every girl there claimed to be Jimi's girlfriend. Jimi had already nodded out in a corner and there were all these people ripping him off even as he slept. Someone went through his pockets and helped himself to his stash. Someone else made off with his acoustic guitar. Some Afghan-clad parasite even prized his boots off, claiming to be 'helping the cat get more comfortable'. The last thing Keith Gear noticed before he too nodded out after one toke too many was the Afghan-clad parasite slipping out of the back door with Jimi's boots.

When he came round, this German girl, Helga, was leaning over him, slapping his face, speaking in a panic-stricken whisper. 'Wake up,' she said. 'Wake up, mister. I can't wake Jimi.' Keith Gear focused and looked around the function suite. Everyone had gone. Jimi was lying slumped upright in the same corner, head titled slightly back. Thick saliva was dribbling from the side of his mouth. Keith Gear had the presence of a very stoned mind to gently ease Jimi onto his side and put his fingers down his throat in an attempt to clear his airways. When that appeared to have failed and Hendrix started to turn blue he placed his own lips gently onto those of the overdoser and gave him the kiss of life.

'No one recognised him,' he said to Kay, as they sat in the empty waiting area, watching the clock tick slowly. 'The ambulance men. The police officer. The hospital receptionist. The doctor. No one.'

'I didn't recognise him,' said Kay, brushing cigarette ash from her knee. 'He came up to me in the Kings Road. Last week I think it was. He looked so tired. Withdrawal symptoms probably.'

'The weird thing was when I went to call for the ambulance the hotel was deserted. I mean entirely deserted apart from that Helga girl. There wasn't even a receptionist or a porter and the front door was locked. I couldn't work out how to get an outside line on the phone. I was in a blind panic. I found a way out through the fire exit and found a phone box. When I got back, this Helga, or whoever she is, she'd fucked off too. I sat there in the darkness, cradling Jimi's head till I saw the ambulance light outside.'

'Something like this was always going to happen sooner or later,' said Kay. 'That's why I got out. It was a case of get out or go mad.'

'I know the feeling.'

'This is unreal, isn't it?' Kay lit another cigarette with the one she was finishing.

Keith Gear nodded in agreement and blinked at the unreality of it all. The harsh hospital lights were beginning to hurt his eyes. A tramp wandered in from the street and asked them if they had any money so that he could buy seed for his budgerigar. The receptionist got up from her desk and ushered him out. All that the situation needed to compound the surrealism was for a small boy to come in with a saucepan stuck to his head.

'I'm glad you phoned me,' said Kay.

'I didn't know who else to phone. When the copper arrived, he said, "What have we got here then, another dead junkie?" He actually said that. "What have we got here then?"'

The receptionist looked up from her paperwork and regarded them like they were shit.

Daylight filtered in with a sickly yellow tinge. A swing door opened and a shoeless Jimi stood there looking fragile and frail. 'Just call me Lazarus,' he said, grinning goofily.

'Christ, what does that make me then?' said Keith Gear.

APOLLONIA

2001

On a bright clear Monday in September, Keith Gear went to the precinct to buy food. A semi-circle of punters had formed round the window of One-Eyed Joe's and from a distance he assumed that Joe, or more likely one of his pretty assistants, was giving a shop-window demonstration of the latest piece of digi-vid gimmickry to hit the mass market. When he reached the shop Keith Gear was surprised to see that everyone was staring at the regular window display, a bank of wide-screen TVs all showing the same Hollywood blockbuster images of a war-torn cityscape reduced to smoke and rubble. A blue information strip ran along the bottom of the screens, giving the apocalyptic scene a sheen of newscast authenticity.

Keith Gear went into the greengrocer four doors down. He noticed that the assistant seemed distracted as he weighed his customers' provisions and kept glancing out of the shop towards the swelling throng outside Joe's.

'Spect Joe's got one of his girls in the window,' he mused.

'No. It's just some war film,' said Keith Gear.

'Porn film?' replied the grocer man. 'Might go and take a look myself then.'

'No. War film,' repeated Keith Gear. 'War film.'

He counted his change, noticed that the shopkeeper had given him a pound too much, then took the lift to the eighth floor of the multi-storey, got in his car and drove home.

As he walked in the door the phone was ringing, but it

stopped the moment he put his shopping bags down. There were three messages. All from Drum.

'Keith, pick up the phone if you're there. Pick up the phone.' Click.

'Keith! Are you there? For fuck's sake put down your music and pick up the phone.'

Keith Gear heard the sound of a receiver being clumsily replaced.

'Keith. It's Drum again. Turn on the TV. I expect you're already watching. Give us a call. Chickens are coming home to roost, man. Chickens are – oh for fuck's sake! Oh, God!'

The 'oh for fuck's sake! Oh, God!' didn't sound like it was aimed at the telephone receiver. Drum sounded like he was reacting to some external source. He played the messages again, straining to hear the background ambience, suspecting for a moment that Drum had an unwelcome intruder. Then he turned on the TV and saw the pictures of a plane crashing into a tall building, then another plane crashing into another tall building. He watched the endless numbing loop of TV images until the buildings took on the consistency of potter's clay, absorbing the aeroplanes into their softness.

At home Drum was watching the same endless loop. He'd been watching for some time. He was watching when they showed that footage of a man in a hardhat who stopped what he was doing to gaze up at the sky. It looked like some sort of training film. Regular am-cam stuff. Then came the sequence the man in the hardhat would never forget. An overhead distraction. A roaring noise. A flicker of annoyance on his face as he realises that they've got to stop filming for a moment to let this extraneous object pass. But if you look closer, as Drum did many times, there's another flicker in that face. A flicker of confusion as he wonders why a plane is flying so low on this clear blue New York morning.

Drum often thought about that moment in the months that followed. That moment before the dawning of a new dark reality. That moment when inconvenience reigned for not quite long enough. That moment where a camera resented the intrusion and waited for interruption to pass. That frozen moment where these regular maintenance Joes were counting down the minutes to coffee and bagels, and history was somebody else's job. That moment where normality still existed and the sky was where it should be and the ground was way below.

The frieze unfroze. The scene resumed.

'Holy shit,' shouted somebody off camera.

'Holy shit!'

And that's exactly what it was.

Drum watched the endless numbing loop for four sleepless days and nights, then he packed his bags and took a cut-price flight to a cut-price life in Apollonia.

Keith Gear received a postcard from his comrade in exile two and a half years later.

> Keith,
> get yor gear out here. Get away from all that
> music industry shit before it kills you. I'm running
> a beach bar. There's room in my hut for two.

Drum was there to meet him at the airport. Keith Gear slung his bags and his beat-up old Spanish guitar in the back of Drum's beat-up old jeep and they drove through dusty heat and pinewood forest to the northwest edge of the island.

'I started off running a café in town,' shouted Drum above the rasp of the engine and the grinding of gears. 'But I didn't know that you're supposed to clear it with the boss man who lives in the house on the hill.' He pointed to a gap in a grove, high on a distant ridge, where a whitewashed villa stood gleaming in the hot midday sun. 'He bankrolled the airport you landed at. Everyone has to go to him if they want to set up here. Doctors. Dentists. Builders. Everybody. I didn't know that.'

Drum slowed down to show his passenger a brand-new hotel complex that stood empty and abandoned by the side of the road. 'They didn't speak to the boss man either.' Weeds were reclaiming the courtyard. Cracks ran like forked lightning across the car park.

'Is it my imagination,' said Keith Gear, 'or is the whole thing listing?'

'Yep,' said Drum. 'It's sinking. The basement's already under water. They built on swamp ground. I mean, they couldn't even grow bananas there before. The land's unmanageable. Another reason to listen to the boss man. It's not all menace and threats. Some of it's fucking common sense. There's my old place, there.'

Drum slowed down to wave to an elderly man sitting out front of a taverna sipping a leisurely espresso. 'I had a couple of warnings. A beer barrel through the plate glass late one night. Stock continually arriving all damaged. I got the message eventually. Heard they were going to torch me. Slept down the beach one night and thought, Hey, this is the place.'

Drum's bit of beach was only accessible via a dirt road that wound through olive groves to a headland ridge, which shelved steeply down to the sea. Parking the jeep in a clearing, the two men scrambled down an inhospitable incline to the water's edge, then clambered over a small rocky outcrop to a sheltered sandy bay.

'Paradise, eh? You wouldn't even know this place was here. You don't get any package tourists or coach parties. The boss man don't bother you. His henchmen can't be bothered to traipse all the way down here.'

Keith Gear walked in Drum's footprints to the furthest corner of the bay where a beach bar had been constructed between a curve in the cliffs.

'There was nobody but me and a few German naturists when I first got here. I built all this.'

Drum's bar was a work of art. It looked like it had sprung up organically as part of the landscape. Driftwood had been fashioned into furniture. Scrap metal into wind chimes. There were sturdy rushwork partitions and awnings weaved from tropical leaves. Conch shells dangled from forest twine, like mermaid's earrings. Every bit of washed-up beach debris had been incorporated into the grand design.

On that first afternoon Keith Gear took a siesta in the shade while Drum filled pitta for the beach gatherers. And at sunset, over grilled fish and a bottle of the local palm rum, Drum told him how he had come to hate England now that commerce and commodification had permeated every walk of life.

'Even the beggars are on a fixed rate these days, aren't they? Who would have thought that the homeless would end up selling magazines on commission?' He laughed scornfully. 'I had to get out, Keith. It wasn't the Jihad. It was the barbarity of everyday life. It was driving me insane.' He took another swig of rum and grimaced at his recollections. 'God, that ugly, ugly language everyone started speaking with its must-have acquisitions and its must-see shows and its best-buy gadgets and its wow factor and its factoring in. Everyone from the fucking weather girl on the telly to the politicians talking like they're auditioning or trying to sell you something. And everyone's got the irony tic instead of beliefs. Irony's the last refuge of the intellectually bankrupt, I'm telling you. I hate all that, man. Fucking hate it.' He stared into the crimson haze as the big sun sank slowly into the sea.

'So you really miss England then, Drum?' Keith Gear laughed.

'I'll tell you something, man,' said Drum. 'Here's how much I miss England. Someone left an English magazine down here one day and I was flicking through it. On the first page I opened it said: "In the 60s you either bought into The Beatles or the Stones." And I thought, no we didn't! We didn't buy into things. It wasn't a fucking down payment on a carpet or a washing machine. It was music. It was fucking art, man. It meant something. Fucking meant something to me anyway.'

'I'll drink to that.' And they drank to that. 'Everyone talks like that now,' said Keith Gear. 'It's wall-to-wall clichés.'

'Wall-to-wall clichés. Love it, man,' said Drum, falling off a rock.

Keith Gear spent the summer of 2004 living the simple life with Drum. During the day they sold food and drink to the beach bums who walked the woodland path and clambered over the rocky ridge to Drum's little piece of paradise. And in the evenings Keith Gear played his acoustic guitar for free on the beach, or for euros and cents in the old partisan bar in the hilltop village of Placida that they sometimes drove to. There, in the tranquillity of Placida, entire families had been slaughtered by the Nazis and memories died hard. Unsuspecting German hippies were still charged quadruple the going rate for everything. And while children ran unattended and free, or slept soundly in the arms of their softly conversing mothers, hashish of the finest quality was smoked through a hubbly-bubbly pipe by wizened old men with copper-coloured teeth. And late at night, those same old men sang the old Apollonian songs with their haunting choruses and wistful refrains. Keith Gear memorised what he could of these ancient melodies and would perform them on his Spanish guitar to the coastal trees and the soul in the rocks and the ceaseless ocean, skimming notes across the waves and out into the mysterious stillness beyond.

And on Sundays at sunset, there were beach parties where Gear and Drum enjoyed more sex than the British Board of Film Censors.

'I love the democracy of the nudist beach,' said Drum one day as he stood chopping garlic and watching a septuagenarian Russian couple going about their early morning constitution. 'I think it's the most unpretentious place on earth. Everyone's the same with their clothes off.'

Keith Gear begged to differ as he watched two bronzed

Brazilian women emerging from the ocean like Amazonian sea-priestesses, but he dug the sentiment all the same. 'The English are so hung up about nudity, aren't they?'

'Yeah,' said Drum, 'and that's why you hardly get any shit-for-brains Brits here. Those bottle-blond lasses flashing their Teflon tits on the telly, and those lardy lager lads showing their arses, they don't venture down here. Thank God.'

Every day they came. Clambering over the rocks. A parade of old ones, young ones, ebony ones, translucent ones, mottle skins, smooth skins, grey pubes, shaved pubes, oiled pecs, flabby no pecs, everyone under the sun equal in their nakedness.

'Change the tape will you, Keith?'

And everyday Drum dug deep into his box of cassettes. Customers lingered languidly, bathers lay drowsily, inching within earshot so they could listen to Drum's impeccable taste. Miles' *Sketches*. Fauré's *Pavane*. Ravel's *Enfant*. Arabic oud. Moorish choirs. Mediterranean alchemy. Filling the pine-scented air and azure skies.

Only rarely did a bather make the mistake of asking Drum to change the tape. 'Don't you have any boogie rock?' asked a polite German one day as he counted his change.

'Fuck off,' said Drum. The benign beach dweller looked wounded and confused. 'I mean it,' said Drum. 'Fuck off to the town and the boogie bars if that's what you want.'

He turned back to Keith Gear. 'And you notice the other great thing? What's missing? What is there a complete absence of?'

'Mobile phones,' guessed Keith Gear correctly.

'Precisely. The cliffs act as a barrier. No fucking signal. Magic. No fucking business cunts bringing their office to my beach.'

One Sunday night, in the midst of a mellow beach gathering, with the firewood crackling and a party of Berlin girls dancing to Mambo tapes, the two men found themselves in reflective mood. Neither had been much given to sentimentality in the past but the legacy of middle age, the accumulation of almost a hundred shared years, began to weigh heavily, and as the drink took hold regret rolled in quicker than hill fog. At first, they exchanged drunken generalities about not having enough money, about wasted opportunities and ones that got away. They even began to question their current beach Bohemian existence, knowing that it was no kind of no-rent compensation for an unfulfilled artistic quest.

'I wasted years with the Outsider Crew,' bemoaned Drum. 'People I was sussed enough to avoid when I was seventeen. And then suddenly twenty years later . . . What was it that Churchill said about eternal vigilance?'

Keith Gear, nursing a bottle and now singularly incapable of re-stringing or even tuning his guitar, made to respond, but Drum ploughed on.

'We were stuck in a field one day, having a standoff with the police. They were there, banging on their shields, ready for confrontation. And this toothless old hippie turned to me and said, "Look what they're doing. Why isn't anyone helping us?" and I just thought, man, you should have considered that before. Before you got into this mess. No strategy, you see. No understanding of how power works and how the state can crush you like an ant.'

The bottle passed back and forth and with every swig Drum got more caustic. 'No fucking strategy,' he kept repeating. 'They talked about the right to travel. The right to roam England's green and pleasant land. What fucking right? Go and ask the gypsies living under motorway flyovers and breathing in leaded petrol. Go and ask them about the freedom to travel. That's the trouble with England, it's all smugness and self-interest and single issues. No solidarity. You ask people what they believe in and they start twatting on about "the fweedom of the individ-wall". None of that means shit without the collective consciousness.'

'That's because there's no such thing as society,' slurred Keith Gear, parodying the words of the wise one.

'As Boadicea rightly claimed,' agreed Drum, waving an empty bottle at the moon. 'And, man, are we reaping the rewards. Do you know how watertight they were, Keith? My Outsider chums? I'll tell you how fucking kosher they were. As soon as they tightened up the regulations for claiming the dole all the fellow travellers went scurrying back to Mummy and Daddy. Of course, they'll all be writing their *Vanguard* articles and novelettes in ten years: "My life with the convoy". Meanwhile, the Outsider Crew was left with the real fuck-ups, the homebrew dregs, the smackies. I met some real damaged souls, unhinged kids, I tell you what, Keith . . .'

But Drum didn't tell Keith what. Instead he staggered to the waters edge and pissed in the ocean. Rum-soaked and bellicose he stood there braying into the night, the roar of the tide drowning out his words.

But after one slug of rum too many, Drum's antagonism began to seek out targets closer to home. Out of the blue, he brought up the letter that Keith Gear had sent to *ArtFist* magazine in 1999 and began castigating his colleague for biting the hand that fed him. 'They constantly praised you to high heaven in that magazine, you pompous twat. I remember once they compared you to – what was that line they used? – Charlie Parker playing Bach. They put you up there with the gods, and all you did was send them snidey letters. You really pissed on your chips there.'

'I could say the same about you, Drum,' said Keith Gear, and he did. He brought up 'Nice Shame: Legs About The Face'. He brought up the Cinderella's Ball debacle. He brought up the poignant spectacle of having to watch his old friend perform crowd-pleasing crap to a tiny gathering of Outsider Crew deadbeats at the Avalonia festival.

'Aw fuck 'em,' said Drum, squirting lighter fluid into the dying flames of the log fire. 'Fuck 'em all. Fuck all those show-biz charity slags. D'ya really wanna know why I sabotaged the Cinderella thing? It was because fucking Kenny Cash was standing there in the wings with his smug grinning face and his "I'm so fucking right on" red ribbon and his fucking fake bandwagon-jumping radical material and his f–f–f–'

'Fucking rich dad?' said Keith Gear trying to introduce a little levity.

'Nobody knows you exist,' snapped Drum. 'You've just retreated. There's a whole generation who . . . your trouble is you've always been too fucking purist for your own good.'

'Your trouble is, you never see anything through. You think discipline is some sort of sinister bourgeois plot.' There was no anger in his voice. Only regret.

'It is,' slurred Drum. 'Discipline is an illness. It makes you sick enough, Gear.'

The spite, the recriminations and all the pent-up resentment rumbled on, spoiling the tranquillity of a moonlit Mediterranean night for everyone who witnessed it. Finally, a kindly German tourist, the same one who had asked politely for boogie rock, had to step in to separate the two adversaries at the moment when, although barely capable of standing, they looked like they were about to come to blows.

Both men were contrite in the morning, with hangovers that registered on the Richter scale, but it was never quite the same after that. After months of easy living and busking for his supper, Keith Gear booked a cheap flight back to England, and returned to rheumatic rain, tax demands and music-industry bullshit.

Drum sent him the occasional conciliatory postcard. These continued for a couple of years. Gradually though the communiqués tailed off. When they did arrive, each one was progressively more resigned in tone and spirit. In one Drum mentioned 'a bunch of animal rights campaigners' who had come over from England to try to save the colonies of wild cats that swelled in number during the summer months, prospering on fishermen's scraps and tourist kindness, but were promptly poisoned or shot the moment the season ended and the tourists went home. 'Boss man and his henchmen ran them off the island. (The libbers, not the cats),' Drum's postcard read. A letter Keith Gear received that Christmas told of the growing English ex-pat community that was arriving on the island and buying up cheap property, setting up scuba schools and windsurfing classes just along the coast and whose trust funds and bottomless pockets were keeping the local bars going during the quiet winter months.

> They make peace with boss man and they've got euros to burn. Which is the quickest way to make peace with boss man. They are the most jaded bunch of gentrified arsewipes you can imagine, Keith. They cultivate beetroot tans and sit around the bars listening to shit colonial rock music and yah-yah-ing. Meanwhile they're pricing the locals out of their own housing while scamming every penny they can because they've sussed out how to qualify for regeneration grants. (Most popular scam at the moment is to say you've lost all your computer equipment in a thunderstorm. Get new computer. Get two new computers. Even if you didn't have one computer in first place. No one ever checks.) And even though they're ripping everybody off they think the local peasants are so exotic. They can't stand their own peasantry back home but they think the sweet little coolie agriculturals here are just so divine, darling.

And then one day the boss man in the hills finally came down to Drum's level.

The coastal woodlands were cut down. The winding dirt road was straightened and tarmaced, thousands of tons of sand were transported from the other side of the island to create a big artificial beach, complete with purpose-built bar and leisure complex. And finally the rocky outcrop that separated the commercial beach from Drum's now less than secluded bay was dynamited away.

Drum's penultimate postcard read:

The fat fuck son of Mr boss man turned up today. Lording it in front of everyone. Tells me I have to rent out sunbeds. It could have been worse.

And then it was.

The last letter read:

The tourists are driving the nudist crowd off the beach. They turn up in pleasure boats and coaches. Hundreds of them. The fat fuck son of boss man came down today and demanded a sunbed for free. I told him he could fuck off. All he does is sit and stare at the naked girls with a big obvious throb on.

The last postcard read:

I'm at the airport. Heading back. They trashed everything. They burned my clothes and emptied my tape box in the sea. Nothing left. Sighed (*sic*) Drum. Gloria In Transit.

THE CRESCENTS

2015

Keith Gear had started walking closer to walls. He'd noticed that. It's what he did when he felt the city arch over and fold in on itself. He thought that walking closer to walls might afford him more chance of survival should the streets fracture and crack and the blood start running in rivers.

He left his towering concrete monolith in the Crescents and walked the short walk to the post office to collect his sickness tokens. The air was petrol fumes, the day was ozone depleted and every white van that passed him was carrying screaming prisoners to the specially constructed penal colony on the Isle of Wight. Only he knew this, but he didn't know who else to confide in.

He sat by the water feature in the shopping centre and waited for his friends. The first day he'd gone there it was a Sunday. He'd woken frozen and early with no heating in his room. His toothpaste was solid in the tube. The water was ice in the pipes and his taps wouldn't turn. He walked across the park and stood shivering outside the centre until it opened at ten. He remembered the day well. The water on the ornamental lake had turned to ice in the night and there was a white swan, head and half a neck submerged, dead in the middle. He wondered how it had come to die like that. Had it been searching for food? Had the water solidified so rapidly that it hadn't enough time to withdraw that elegant neck? Or had it merely bowed to the inevitable, hungry, exhausted, unable to go on? He'd asked a man walking his dog but the man jerked the lead and hurried away.

He thought the centre would be empty at that time of day and was surprised to see so many people drifting in through the automatic doors as soon as they were opened. The Flotsam Parade. The Withouts. The Crescent Heads. All glad of the warmth and the dry and the respite from whatever their four lonely walls told them. All making for the benches and the alcoves and the water feature. It became his familiar Sunday ritual. Then weekdays too. He and his sector friends, backs to the fountain, baptised by its jets, blessed by its holy flow, illuminated by the gaudy glow of the hordings and showered in multi-coloured droplets.

Here comes Mad John in his 'Flux Of Pink Indians' T-shirt. It's all washed out and so is John. He says, 'They 'aven't got to say that to me, 'ave they? They 'aven't got to say that.' Over and over again. It's all he says till he slumps into silence. The correct response to 'They 'aven't got to say that to me, 'ave they?' is always a re-assuring, 'No they haven't, John,' and never a careless, 'Haven't got to say what, John?' And certainly never an ill-tempered, 'I haven't got a fucking clue what you're on about, mate,' as the bus driver replied one day. Which led to breakages, blood, security guards and some sort of neutralising spray and a muzzle, which John has to wear on community order days. John is six foot four but it's only at times like that, when an unsuspecting bus driver makes inadvertent eye contact and lets out an exasperated, 'I haven't got a fucking clue what you're on about, mate,' that you realise just how tall John can stand and how many men it takes to muzzle him.

There goes Rosemary. Headphones on. Lost in music. Caught in a trap. Listening to her coded messages. Lazy right eye. Wary of every passer-by. Warding off all but the briefest conversation. Danger averted in a cock-eyed glance. Thick red lipstick plastered on. Hair bleached blonde then black then back again with brown roots sometimes showing. Rosemary is dressed in a hooded blue sports top, charity issue, and a short tartan skirt that puffballs out and rides up slightly at the back, revealing the curve of her arse cheeks if she bends forward three inches. She's a little less than five foot tall. She's twenty-one or she's thirty-four. It's hard to say. She has three skirts, the tartan one, a pleated blue one, and a plain black one. They all puffball like that. She never wears anything on her short stocky legs. Sometimes she goes and stands with the security guards for some security. Sometimes she lets them listen to her tapes, which she picks from a skip on the market. And sometimes, later in the afternoon, around four say, she might disappear with one of the guards for a while because Rosemary needs food and fuel like everyone else and tokens only go so far.

There stands Baxter. He's outside the pound shop. It's been Eurosaver for years but everyone still calls it the pound shop. The handwritten sign in the window still says 'everytheng one pound'. Baxter is Scottish and bespectacled. He has thinning fair hair and a left-side limp from an old Gulf War wound. He has pale white skin and a fixed expression. He is watching the schoolboys come and go, looking for tender meat and a friendly eye. Here comes that beautiful black one. He sees him every day. The boy is usually with his little sister, talking, laughing, but he sometimes lingers by the pound shop and mimes an excuse and his sister walks on to the bus stop. The boy then goes into the centre toilets, lets his locks down and stands at the cubicles taking matters in hand to left and right. Baxter limps in and stiffens.

There sits Constantine waiting for the sun. He can usually be found sitting on a box outside the centre, strumming an old steel guitar. Its strings are slack as is his grip and his fingers barely make contact some days. Just a faint scritch scritch scritch that gets buried in the shuffle and the drift of passers-by. Today he has only four strings to play with but if he gets his tokens tomorrow he'll go searching for the whole tune. He's left some of his brain to science, pickled in a hostelry bottle. He's left his sane self back down that past road somewhere. He's left his sign outside rotting in the rain. Constantine always has a cardboard sign with him. It's part of his performance. It's a chronicle of wrongdoings and misdemeanours, slights and slurs, imagined and real, crayoned on the bottom of an old brown box. He calls it his bulletin. Today's reads:

> The man ON the 77 or 78 bus HE IS that badman who tells John and everyone that they should NOT Be on his bus if they behave that way or this. I was on his bus and knows he is not fit to be the bus driver. He should BE reporting to a high authority and will not receive forgivement on the judgeing day. These are the words of truth written by Constantine Theobald Hunt. I have stood and see these things as I am reporting them to you now. Read the truth. The harf nevre been told.

Sometimes he sings the card like it's a blues.

Keith Gear had watched the 21st century wither and perish. He had been beaten down daily by the sounds of surveillance, pulverised by property alarms, screaming through daylight and darkness. Even when they stop he can still hear them. He grimaces at the cacophony. He grinds his teeth at night. He thinks, *If I stood in the street in the night and played my music like that someone would come out and punch me or call the police, and I would be arrested and locked up for public-order offences.* He still could be, if he had any instruments to make music on. But property is sacrosanct and the alarms play on, unattended, unabridged, uninterrupted. Looted shops and trembling tenements call out to each other across the deserted curfew night.

He walks back to the Crescents, his home since he reached retirement age without a rainy-day income. The Crescents are monstrous concrete settlements. They stand twenty storeys high and a hundred apartments long and curve in a C shape, hence the name. All the trouble people are put there. The anti-social order people. The drowners from sunken sink estates. The uncaring and the uncared for in the community. Side by side by side. All the immigrants are put there too. They come seeking asylum and then they find one. They want an apartment and then they find out what apart meant.

When the blackouts aren't on, the Crescents light up the night sky for miles. The rooms are stifling hot in summer, ice cold in winter. The windows barely open and the walls are thin but they are insulated with some sort of aerated petrochemical jelly which turns toxic if the walls weep. The insulation deadens the acoustics in every room to the consistency of a mediaeval tomb. No one can hear you scream in the Crescents but everyone can see you. Many of the windows have no curtains. Constant surveillance has stripped people of their pride, their privacy, their dignity. No one seems to care anymore. Every night Keith Gear can sit and watch the unspeakable played out in flickering cameos from a multiplex of two thousand windows.

Three down, twelve across. By day he sits at a mouse, eyes trained on the unseen screen two feet above his head. She washes, tidies, washes, tidies. Keeping up appearances. They look respectable.

Two up, two and three across. He sits hunched in a chair, watching TV, like a spring ready to be sprung. He is young, pockmarked complexion, pencil moustache, jet-black hair slicked back. He is not watching the screen. He is looking right though it. Next door a small child is holding a smaller child, cradling it close, singing in soothing tones, her lips softly mouthing, *Don't cry, don't cry.* But the smaller child continues to cry. The young man springs from his chair, tears into the next room and beats the living crap out of his step-daughter, but first he closes the curtains not quite all the way.

Ten down, seventy across. A dark room will stay dark until

two or three in the morning. Then a dimmer switch is activated, the subtle light slowly rises until it illuminates a teasing silhouette, and there on a chair, Sacha begins her show. She sits with legs slightly parted and touches herself. She jiggles and licks her breasts in a parody of the censorship days when actors played softcore. She used to work for satellite subscriptions but since she's been in the Crescents she gives good window for free.

Three down, twelve across. Mouseman gets a crick in his neck and tidy wife massages it better.

Fifteen down, twelve across. A man and his daughter live there. The wife left to go and live with the woman at fourteen down, five across and now she only sees her daughter every other weekend. The daughter is ten. She has her mum's broad backside and is bulking out into not-quite-woman shapes. The daughter doesn't look like she wants to be with her daddy. That's what Keith Gear thinks. He sees her in the street sometimes. She speaks to strangers when she's with her mum, but never when she's with her dad.

She puts on her blue dress, then her red one, then changes her mind again or has it changed for her. It's very late, gone three, and she should be asleep, not trying on dresses. Once she's passed her dress test her daddy will lead her up twelve flights of piss-stained stairs to three down, twelve across where mouseman and tidy wife are greeting guests. Their curtains will remain closed for several hours.

Keith Gear walks to the centre. On a patch of grass by the burnt-out cars some kids are playing football with a dead puppy. It wasn't dead when they found it. It wasn't even dead when they took the first free kick. Outside the post office a young man gets out of a car, points a keyfob at his elderly passenger and zaps him trapped. The passenger is his granddad. The car radio plays titanium metal pulverisingly loud, but the old man doesn't appear to notice. He just sits there in black hat and black suit like he's all funeraled up and stares straight ahead. The car rattles with bass lines, fills up with noise fumes. He's still there when Keith Gear goes by an hour later. Emotionless eyes the colour of egg yolk.

Keith Gear's hair grew rat-tailed and ragged. His nails grew long. His eyebrows turned grey, his sight grew weary but no dimmer. If only.

He grew disconnected. He knew he was cracking up. He recognised it well. One dark December night he saw his reflection in the kitchen window. It moved a moment before he did. He walked around the kitchen for a bit, his ghostly doppelganger slightly ahead of him.

Keith Gear came home from a meal at May Grey's house. Everyone had said how pale Keith looked, how thin he was getting, and how he needed feeding up. He was glad of the meal and of the company and the conversation that flowed and halted, flowed and halted. He put his key in the lock but the front door wouldn't open. So he went round to the back of the house and looked in through the window. He saw his TV lying smashed on the floor and mess all around.

A six-foot-five police officer put his shoulder to the door and tutted at the familiar scene. Keith Gear stood in a darkened studio room and wondered why he was shivering and why his reflection wasn't seconds ahead of him, wasn't visible at all.

'That's where they broke in,' said the officer, stating the obvious, although it only became obvious to Keith Gear when the cop turned on the light to reveal a windowless room.

'Have they taken much?'

'Everything,' said Keith Gear.

'Oh well, make sure you put in a creative claim,' joked the policeman, taking another call on his radio and making towards the splintered door.

He didn't care to explain that the mess was normal and that he wasn't insured and hadn't been for years. He used to pay his yearly policy to a damp man in a damp office under the railway arches but on the one occasion he tried to make a claim the damp man got very annoyed. He said that he would call some of his dry friends and that they would go to the address on this form and hurt Keith Gear and his pets if he had any, so Keith Gear didn't go there again.

The scum patrol had taken his video, stereo, DVD player, PC, Portastudio, practice amp, guitars, CDs, fuzz pedals, wah-wah pedals, blank tapes, live tapes, rehearsal tapes, master tapes, *Wilderness Tapes*, *Tree Music*, *Dusk Music*. He had just spent six months negotiating back the rights to *The Wilderness Tapes* from the Boadicea Broadcasting Company and the daughter of the late Mr Schmidt of Bremen with a view to getting it reissued with all those unreleased Idiot Bastard Son tracks.

Guy Truelove had returned the master tape of *Tree Music from the Early Beech Period* when he got out of prison. Guy was promising to do a digital remastering job. Said kids were file sharing this stuff. Guy was talking about reactivating the Import Ant label. Said he would issue *Dusk Music*. Said a lot of stuff.

Keith Gear phoned Guy to tell him what had happened. Asked him what the opposite of zeitgeist was.

Mobile phones rang and their owners genuflected. It made him sick to see how slavish they were, scrabbling, groping, beholden to a ring tone. Lots of things started to make him sick. Eventually the sickness consumed him. He couldn't even travel on trains anymore because he'd attacked that man who wouldn't stop talking into his mobile. Just wouldn't shut up.

He started walking everywhere. One winter's night he walked ten miles in the pouring rain to one of May Grey's concerts. Arrived bedraggled and drenched two hours after the concert had ended. Walked another five miles to May Grey's house. That's when everyone noticed that things weren't right.

Then Keith Gear vanished. Ptoof.

* * *

And now Keith Gear sat by the water feature in the shopping centre. The day smelled like bleach. The air rained down desert dust. He listened to Constantine singing the cardboard blues. In all the time he had been listening, he had never figured out if Constantine could play that damn thing, but then Constantine would probably have said the same about him.

Music became an unfamiliar thing. The incessant bombardment began to baffle him. He turned on the radio one day and a boy and girl – Chinese, possibly Japanese – were jabbering in monkey language. He turned on the cable TV one night and a young couple were lying in bed, brick-patterned quilt covering everything but their talking heads, like drugged-up little Chads. Their eyes glowed and their pupils were large. They were discussing a club they'd been to and all the things they'd seen. All drawled out in dry exhausted exuberance. All night long.

He started to hear his *Dusk Music* through the ether. Just a fragment. Just enough to flip his instability up a notch. One day he heard it piping out of a bar. Another day he heard it coming out of a room in the Crescents. One up, four across. One night he was sure he could hear it in the background on the cable channel. They were reporting from a club called Ticket to Waterfall. The music was preceded by a clear strong voice saying, 'Turn them into love junkies.' A Californian voice. He was sure of that. He recognised the accent, but he couldn't recall the source. 'Turn them into love junkies,' it kept saying. He had no idea how he should act upon those instructions. One morning it all got too much for him so he pulled the system out of the wall and left wires and leads trailing from the bare plaster. In the afternoon, a man came round and fixed it. The heating could be off for weeks in the winter but the cable guys and the radio engineers were always round within hours.

He began to dream fragments of poetry. Chinese or possibly Japanese. He couldn't tell. Borne on the wing down century breezes, delivered through the medium of sleep. One night after another. Each night a different set of images spilled out.

the sun on bare winter branches
a moment's hesitation
a bird settles

the still water
the sky without stars
no light reflected on the frozen lake

as fleeting as the shadow from a falling leaf
is the distant peel of bells
my lover's footfall recedes
I cannot return to the temple

when night comes again
will the moon be gone from the mountains?
what bright star illuminates my solitude?
I cannot follow the birds to where they fly

two travellers are approaching
I have drunk the last of my wine in silence

Wordplay was the gift he had squandered long ago. And now it returned. A lifeline tossed into the abyss. Sanity gifted from the depths. Sedentary silted layers disturbed by what psychic undertow? Winched up in a rusty bucket from the dank waters of the dreamwell.

He saw the bird hesitate then settle. He saw the still waters and heard the distant bells. He shivered in the mountain cold. He saw the travellers approaching and recoiled in drunken dishevelled guilt. The dream poetry began to manifest itself in daylight apparition. One morning walking to the precinct, he hallucinated the approaching travellers. One looked like Guy Truelove, a Guy Truelove sent from the Anglo-Saxon days, fashioned in sackcloth. The other looked like May Grey, in silken threads and rickshaw drag. He wondered if anyone else could see them too. He asked a man walking his dog but the man jerked the lead and hurried away.

Then, just as suddenly as the poetry had begun, it ceased. No more illumination. Only darkness. A recurring nightmare. Marsh mud, a pale flickering dawn, more immutable darkness. A feeling of being mummified, entombed. A sensation of carrying something unfamiliar inside him, like a womb. Some nights he could almost piece it together. Unravel the layers. He inhabited a woman's skin. That was one of the layers. He was encased in sheness. Inside the sheness was a womb. And inside the womb grew a death seed, a stillborn child. On some of these dream-nights the sheness felt rain on its skin. Arriving at the same place night after night, flailing desperately in the relentless dreamdark. And cold. So cold. Rain falling in the never-ending blackness. Pouring for all eternity. Washing a brief unaccounted life away in its torrent. Then the sheness was in mud again, and numb again, the weight of some force crushing her.

He asked Rosemary what it all meant. Rosemary removed her headphones and her mouth made the shape a smile makes. She said, 'See Marie.' Marie lived in Crescent Six. She threw coins, called cards, traced the prophecy route through gnarled hands and wizened fingers. Held readings for the quiet believers and the discreetly desperate. 'Don't let the warden see you,' warned Rosemary. 'If he does, say you are buying lottery tokens.'

Marie was a burned-out relic from the hippie days. She resided at seven down, seven across. Long grey tresses with wisps of silvery blonde, remnants of her golden years. Gap toothed, gin skinned and rouge cheeked, she padded barefoot across her floor to answer the door. She made honey tea, which they both sipped slowly.

Her hands shook as she outlined her rudimentary numerology. 'This explains your energy flow and your number lines.'

K E I T H G E A R
2 5 9 2 8 = 26 2 + 6 = 8 7 5 1 9 = 22 2 + 2 = 4

8 + 4 = 12 1 + 2 = 3

'Now. Ah. I see. Ta-ta-ta-ta.' She sing-songed softly to herself. 'Your first name adds to eight. Eight is the unconscious mind, transmutation, your vessel through timelessness and endless space. This will explain your visions. Your surname is rooted in logical thought, in practice, materiality, empirical reality. The here and now. This will provide the context for your visions. If we add the first to the last we reach twelve. We split twelve into its numerical parts. We get one and two which adds to three. See? Ta-ta-ta-ta. Ego plus duality equals action. Being squares imbalance equals service to mankind. Tell me more about the dreams. And come here tomorrow. Don't let the warden see you. If he does, say you are buying lottery tokens.'

When he returned the next day Marie was still in her nightdress and seemed excited to see him. She pulled him into her room, hung a pentagram-adorned purple curtain over her window, lit a scented candle and asked him to be seated.

'I've made a graph of your energy lines. This is very special but it took me some time to work out. The eight. The four. The one plus two equals three. So many possibilities. Ta-ta-ta-ta. But only one outcome. The eight of your forename, the unconscious, the transmutable. These are your incarnations. You are reborn every eight hundred years. You were a Chinese poet during the T'ang dynasty. I think you died young or the gift within you died young. In your next incarnation in the 1600s, you were a young woman. You were accused of practising dark magic and you carried a child, which didn't survive. You were raped and left to die. You died a slow lingering death.'

Marie paused and wiped her brow. Her breathing was heavy and her tone portentous.

'The number total puzzled me for some time. The eight plus four equals twelve. The one plus two equals three. First, I thought about the logic line. It tells me you have had three incarnations, of which this is the third, and possibly last, but look at this transverse line, interrupting your material life. This means that your third incarnation comes early. The sequence is interrupted. Eight becomes four. See? This is your third incarnation. Now. This is what the numbers reveal.'

She twisted her tresses nervously, looked towards the door and lowered her voice.

'Then I went back to the four again. See the straight line here. Practice. Rooted reality. See this dominant line. This means you have four incarnations not three and the sequence should go year nought. Year eight hundred. Year sixteen hundred. Year twenty-four hundred. So, what has interrupted the sequence and brought you forward to now? Why are you so out of synch with yourself, Keith? Are you ready to receive what I am going to tell you?'

She gripped his wrists and looked deep into his eyes.

'Listen to me. The root number is nought. Your dividing line between endless receding incarnations. Eight hundred BC. Sixteen hundred BC. Twenty-four hundred BC. The male/female duality. See? The stillborn child. See? Did you have children of your own in this life? No. I thought not. Now let us look at your name again. G-E-A-R. 7-5-1-9. Seven is the limits of time. The limits of the material. Five is your spiritual aspiration. Your learning. One is ego. It is also leadership. And nine? Nine is completion. The divine. You are Jesus Christ come again, Keith Gear. You are Jesus Christ. You have been brought back by divine intervention four hundred years early in order to lead your flock. You are Jesus Christ, the saviour.'

Marie paced the room, gripping her nightdress tightly in her fists. 'You have been sent to the Crescents for a purpose. We are the unwanted here. The meek and the poor. You will lead us to the Promised Land. How old are you now?'

'I'm sixty-six.'

'Twice the age Jesus was when he died. Oh, God. You must go to your flock. There is work to be done.' Marie knelt and kissed her messiah's feet.

He backed away, groped for the door and hurried back to the sanctuary of his room.

Even in the midst of his madness, he knew she was wrong. He had dreamed himself into sheness. He had carved out beautiful fragments of poetry. He still didn't know where they came from but he knew the readings were wrong.

How he hated his name. Keith Gear. Keith Gear. Keith Gear. Keith Gear. Keith Gear. Keith Gear. Keith Gear. Keith Gear. Keith Gear. Keith Gear.

When he was thirteen he began to practise it as a signature. He carved it into school desks, onto the toboggan he made in woodwork class, onto folders and maths books. The Merseybeat was to blame. The moment he first heard it. This noun that became an adjective. This naming word that became a describing word. A phlegmy guttural utterance that poured from thick gobby lips. And the word was flesh. And the word was gear. And music would never be the same again. Before was 'Listen With Mother', 'Dashin' Along With A Smoothing Iron', 'Foxy Went A Courting And He Did Ride' and 'The White Heather Club'. After was winkle-pickers and Cuban heels and purple corduroy ties and backstreet Italian tailors and 'Love, love me do' and his mates going, 'Gear, Gear, that's Gear that Gear is' until the word was flesh and the flesh was Keith Gear.

His real name, the name on his birth certificate and passport was Lyons. Keith Lyons. He had an Aunt Elsie, who had a husband called Walter, stage name Lenny.

* * *

Keith Gear walked the short walk to the post office to collect his sickness tokens. The air was ammonia, the day was asthmatic, wheezing out short bursts of breeze and sucking all the colour from the sky. There sat Constantine waiting for the sun. His sign said:

> The air here is not good. The bread is no good eithre. They putting something in it and the water. I don't know what it is in the bread. If you heat it up toast it makes your lip dry and your brain hotter. All the cakes are bad too. DON'T touch them. It is the word of gospel truth. These are the words written by Constantine Theobald Hunt. I have stood and see these things as I am reporting them to you. Read the truth. The harf nevre been told.

Constantine was playing in waltz time, strumming a regular 3/4. For the first time Keith Gear realised that Constantine could really play that thing. 'Nobody in the centre,' he shouted. 'They move everybody away now. Everybody is gone.'

Keith Gear ignored him and headed habitually for the water feature but when he got there he discovered that Constantine was right, everybody had gone. The fountain was still there, shooting spray jets through a rainbow of light but around its perimeter the benches had been replaced by infomercial screens. A young man's face appeared on all of them. Pakistani? Turkish? Armenian? He couldn't tell. The voiceover – mid-Atlantic, Disney-bland – explained that at six years old he had passed his general certificate in Computer Studies and when he was ten he had passed his advanced certificate in Information Technology. Only last year this young man had sold the rights to his music machine and was now a millionaire.

Keith Gear began to see his face everywhere. In newspapers. On magazine covers. On infomercial screens. This young man with beautiful almond eyes confidently explaining in a soft, educated accent how his Omega Mk 11 would revolutionise the process of music making.

A few weeks later Marie approached Keith Gear in the precinct and began to explain that she had got her readings wrong. She had not worked through the full implications of his number lines. There must have been a kink in the energy flow. When Keith Gear ignored her she began to loudly accuse him of trying to take advantage of her. 'Me, a vulnerable women living alone in the Crescents. And you still haven't paid me. You still haven't paid me!' she screamed as the female security guards led her away. 'And that's the saviour,' she said, jabbing a finger at the infomercial screens. 'That's the saviour. His name is Saladin. Birthed in the year of the new millennium. S-1 A-1 L-3 A-1 . . .' She was still screaming when they dragged her through the exit doors and threw her roughly into the back of a white van, which drove her away to the specially constructed penal colony on the Isle of Wight. Keith Gear told all this to a man who was walking his dog but the man jerked the lead and hurried away.

STILL

1971

'The next-ext-ext artist-ist-ist has travelled-ed-ed all-all-all the way-ay-ay back-ack-ack from Paris-is-is just-ust-ust to do this-is-is one gig-ig-ig. Some of-of-of you-you-you may-ay-ay remember-ber-ber him from-om-om a band-and-and who played-ayed-ayed here two years-ears-ears ago-go-go called Dominion-yun-yun. Avalonia-ya-ya would you please-ease-ease put your hands-ands-ands together-ther-ther and welcome-come-come Keith Gear-Gear-Gear-Gear.'

The distortion on the PA sent the announcer's voice echoing across the Vale of Avalon. The audience waved like poppies, rippled like the sea.

Keith Gear had drunk a pot of mushroom tea shortly before going on stage. He figured that if he gripped the neck of his guitar really tight everything would stay still. He positioned the tuning keys so that they aligned with the serving hatch of the ice-cream van at the perimeter of the field. As long as he kept the guitar pointing at forty-five degrees towards that ice-cream van, everything would stay centred and eventually settle down.

It didn't help that the audience rose the moment they heard his name. First those at the front then those further back because they couldn't see and so on all the way to the perimeter, waving like poppies, rippling like the sea.

He'd joked before with Cindy about how mushrooms always made him paranoid and gave him the Charlie Manson eyes.

'All that hippie shit about a natural organic high,' he screamed, recoiling from the mirror. 'Give me chemicals on blotting paper every time.'

'Yes, but you're only supposed to take a handful,' said Cindy.

'How many is a handful?'

'About fifteen, twenty, I guess,' rationalised Cindy. 'How many have you taken?'

'The lot,' said Keith Gear.

'How many is the lot?' asked Cindy, astonished.

'I dunno, about four hundred.'

'Helter Skelter!'

Cindy was Lucas's girlfriend. Twenty-six years old with a ball of black hair like Nancy in the funny papers. Lucas had met her on that ill-fated day in Hyde Park when it rained on Dominion's farewell parade and Spencer plunged ignominiously into a mud puddle. Cindy was in charge of backstage catering. Pretty soon she was catering solely for Lucas and his ever-increasing fiefdom of bands.

After a winter of indolence and prevarication, Keith Gear had spent some time hanging out with Jimi in Morocco and had then made a tentative low-key return to live performing. Just him and his guitars and his box of tricks. In France and Italy he was considered a god and greeted like an underground hero. At Farx, Potters Bar and Friars, Aylesbury, he was a tousle-haired curio, an uncategorisable oddity adrift from the dominant tide. Neither prog nor pop, fish nor fowl. Lucas arranged most of the dates. Living in Stevenage, he found it convenient to organise gigs within a thirty-mile sweep of the mock-Tudor pile that his twenty per cent of Dominion had paid for. Secretly he still harboured hopes that Keith Gear would kiss and make up with Spencer and fulfil his contractual obligation for a second Dominion album. Realistically he knew that wasn't going to happen. Keith Gear wouldn't even do press or TV. But he would do Farx or Friars for £250 and a sofa to crash on.

Sometimes Cindy was there and sometimes she was away catering. One day Lucas had to go off on urgent business and she and Keith Gear were alone in the house together, so she catered for Keith Gear instead. They had room-wrecking sex and afterwards Cindy poured it all out. *Lucas doesn't understand me. Lucas has no sense of humour. Lucas is so straight.* Keith Gear already knew this. On the tour bus they used to call him 'The Good Mr Square', after the Pretty Things song. Lucas was thirty going on middle-aged. He had probably always been middle-aged. He was probably middle-aged when he was eight. 'It's a lovely day isn't it?' Cindy had said. 'Help me tidy this room and we'll do some mushrooms.'

Keith Gear watched a lizard as it sat spreadeagled against a sandstone wall. When he and Jimi first arrived in Morocco he only noticed the wildlife when it moved, a sudden darting from rock to rock, a sensuous slithering across wind-combed desert rivulets. Gradually, though, he acclimatised to the dimensions of the landscape, to the chameleon hides and grainy shapes that zigzagged from crack to crevice. He grew familiar with the subtle stillness of it all. The way it all curved and snaked and merged in the shimmering heat haze that was everywhere, that was vision itself.

They wandered the medina in traditional robes. They bought herbs and mats from the market. They sat and drank sweetened mint tea with their hosts. They smoked kif from water pipes. They were careful to observe local etiquette. Both left-handed, they learned instinctively to eat with their right hands, warned that to do otherwise was an insult to all Muslims.

They were invited to attend the sacred music festival and sat in a palatial marble palace as the Orchestral Ensemble of Fès performed Cantigas from the Castilian Court of King Alfonso. Afterwards their host explained how the Moors were driven out of Spain and that Morocco was a welcoming host for political and cultural exiles of many persuasions.

Jimi was more at home with this concept than his companion, who felt a certain Englishness strike home at times. Keith Gear could never get used to the way the women wouldn't look him in the eye, or even speak unless spoken to first. And even though he knew he carried more money in his pocket than some of the local people saw in a year, or maybe even a lifetime, he could never get used to the constant throng of begging children and the ever-present bustle of the market. Something in his constitution rebelled against the food too. The first day he went to the market he wondered why the meat was black. It was only when the butcher brought his knife down suddenly on the slab and the black coating lifted that he registered the flies. And later, as he lay in a foetal crouch on his bed, bathed in hallucinary sweat, the hum of the ceiling fan torturing him, he concluded that his physical self was less attuned to this world than his musical self. This was confirmed for him the moment he stretched his legs slightly to ease out a fart only to feel a hot jet of faecal liquid splash against his ankles with a ferocity he would barely have thought possible.

Keith Gear scuttled from Stevenage precinct to Stevenage precinct one warm July evening looking for Lucas and Cindy. *Meet you at the venue. Seven o'clock soundcheck*, Lucas had said. *Be punctual.* But when Keith Gear arrived at the venue it was all locked up. Maybe he'd got the time wrong. Maybe he'd got the date wrong. Maybe he was in the wrong place altogether. Now he was scuttling from precinct to precinct, guitar case in hand, conspicuous in the evening sun. Darting from alcove to alley avoiding the skinhead gangs who owned everything. It reminded him of that summer with Sonya. Except then it was Battersea bikers, leathers and Enfields. Now it was bovver boots and cropheads, Ben Shermans and braces. Same difference. You can usually hear them before they see you. Everywhere he went their scent and their sound seemed to follow. Phlegm rattling off concrete. John Player on the breeze. One step ahead of his shadow. Five minutes away from getting the next train back to London. Where the fuck are they? Forget it. It's only a gig.

'Keith.'

Cindy called out across an empty square.

'Thank God we found you,' she said. 'There are skinheads everywhere.'

Lucas didn't look like he was about to throw out a protecting arm. He was sullen and twitchy, his eyes swivelling to every arcade echo. 'Problem with the licence,' he muttered. 'Had to find a phone box. Ever tried finding a phone box that hasn't been vandalised?'

Keith Gear was sandwiched between a couple of groups. He and Cindy watched from the wings. First on was some corny combo called Abbey Rogue, dressed in monk habits and squawking saxophonically. A prog group for people who like gooseberry-in-a-lift jokes. Cindy liked. Keith Gear pretended to like because he liked Cindy. Then Keith Gear hurled his incendiary noise bombs into the semi-darkness. The crowd liked also. They even asked for an encore. Then the headliners, Brain Box, played. Twiddly muso music for proper music types. Lucas fussed around making sure everything ran smoothly. Monitors. Check. Lights. Check. Door receipts. Double check. 'Let's go for a walk,' said Cindy as Brain Box twiddled and Lucas fussed. In sweaty darkness she took his hand and slipped out of a fire exit door.

'Let's go to Blind Park.'

'What's that?'

'It's a park especially designed for the blind with handrails and scented flowers and everything. It's this way.'

Keith Gear thought she might be joking but five minutes later they were writhing in the midnight dew, surrendering themselves to the rich heady aroma of jasmine, honeysuckle and each other. 'Let's get back before he notices,' said Cindy, snagging a zip in the perfumed moonlight.

It went on like that all summer. Snatched moments. Surreptitious liaisons. Acid tabs. Mushroom tea. Hash cakes. Sky pie.

They listened to the *Oz* trial verdicts on the radio one drizzly morning and then they went and sat on the mossy seat in Cindy's garden, rain dripping from the trees. Cindy said, 'The older generation really despise us, don't they?'

He didn't know if this was true or not. He'd always had a hard time embracing the idea of us and them. From what he'd seen, a lot of those who should have been us were them. Record companies were them. Lucas was definitely them. And didn't the underground press say rude things about Dominion? But when the Free *Oz* campaign came calling he let bygones be gone and said, 'Yes, I'd love to play on your benefit record.'

It was so quiet and peaceful that morning in the garden with Cindy, the rain dripping from the trees and the *Oz* men sat in stocks on the village green.

'Why do you stay with Lucas?'

'I could ask you the same question?' said Cindy.

'I'm contractually obliged.'

'I'm not. I can walk out any time I want.'

'So why don't you?'

'Because he's useful to me,' said Cindy, cradling his head in her lap. 'He's good for business contacts. He opens doors for me.'

'So you're using him then?'

'Basically, yes,' said Cindy, brazen and unrepentant.

'How do I know you're not just using me?'

Cindy looked down at her man, amused at the insecurity. 'Ah, there there,' she said, stroking his hair. 'Poor little superstar.'

Keith Gear watched a scorpion as it scuttled from rock to rock. He thought of the conversation he'd had with Jimi the previous evening as they watched dancers sway in a Tangier courtyard. Jimi's new album, *The First Rays Of The New Rising Sun*, had just been released and had received mixed reviews from the music press. He'd sent Keith Gear a test pressing some months earlier. Attached was a note crayoned in Jimi's looping childlike script. 'Some of my peoples all the time,' it said. When the album eventually came out the tracks had been rearranged and remixed. A couple of the more spacey instrumentals had been left off. Keith Gear liked some tracks more than others. 'Drifting' he liked. And 'Angel'. And the ones where Jimi sounded like he'd been listening to Dylan. But he didn't care much for the bluesy stuff and too much of it sounded like he was trying to please everybody. Once he'd listened to the finished album a couple of times he understood that crayoned note.

'It's a muddle,' conceded Jimi. 'I have all this music in my head and there's infinite possibilities and sometimes infinite is too many.'

Keith Gear said, 'Uh-hu,' and took a ferocious toke on a passing pipe. The bowl glowed fiery red.

'It's like those mosaic tiles,' said Jimi, pointing to the wall. 'Because of the way those patterns . . . those interlocking shapes, y'know, you could arrange them in any order and they would still look beautiful. That's the problem I had with *Rising Sun*. No matter how many ways I re-arranged the pieces it all . . .' His voice trailed off. The dancers continued to sway. The musicians struck up a curious arhythmic clapping which corresponded with no known beat.

'I don't know which way to go next,' said Jimi. 'Gil Evans wants to work with me. He wants to orchestrate some of my music. We've been talking about it for a year. Can you imagine it, man? Knowing what he did with *Sketches of Spain*. Miles too man. He even phoned me one day. In New York when I was up-country getting healed. I didn't know it was him at first. There was this weird silence and kind of breathing noises. I could hear music in the background. Sounded like a rehearsal. And suddenly there's this voice and it's Miles and he goes, "Hear that, man? Not as good as you?"' Jimi laughed.

An evening breeze blew across the courtyard.

The dance ended and everyone applauded. Their host came over and asked them whether they were enjoying the entertainment. 'Tomorrow we shall head for the mountains and you will visit the Master Musicians of Joujouka,' he said.

Jimi had visited the Master Musicians on his previous visit to Morocco in the summer of 1969 and told his fellow traveller how much he would enjoy them. Their host asked them what other concerts they had attended during their visit and they told him about the Orchestral Ensemble of Fès.

'That was a magical time,' said their host. 'During the time of the Moors in Medieval Spain the music was Muslim, Christian, Judaic, all mixed up. You can still hear that when it is performed. Just look around you. The musicians dress in Occidental, Islamic and Jewish styles. They play instruments from Europe, North Africa, the Middle East. All togetherness.'

Jimi and Keith Gear had another blast on the pipe and babbled excitedly about the pan-global music in their heads.

'This is one of the only places I've ever been where I don't feel like a nigger,' said Jimi.

'Will you play the Hyde Park concert'? asked the Good Mr Square. It was the last one of the summer and the first anniversary of Dominion's passing. Two years previously the band had reigned triumphant. A year ago their world had ended in a mud splash.

'Who else is playing?' asked Keith Gear.

'Roy Harper. King Crimson. A few TBAs. I'm working on one solo, one band alternating all afternoon. It'll be a groove.'

Hyde Park wasn't a groove. It was hell with choc-ices. The flotsam of a washed-up underground scene stumbled around backstage. A shit PA system crackled out shit records all afternoon. Somebody spiked Keith Gear with STP and when his turn came to play he sat cowering in a portable toilet studying flecs of freshly jettisoned junkie blood on the walls. He could hear the PA playing Frank Zappa's *Live at the Fillmore East* album.

An acid casualty was stomping around outside. 'Yeah, sock it to 'em, Frank,' he was shouting. 'Minge and Muff. Minge and Muff. Plenty of minge for me to stuff.'

It was all too much. Keith Gear had really liked the Mothers of Invention. He'd even liked Flo and Eddie when they were the Turtles, and who cares if 'Eleanor' was a piss-take of a pop song. Etcetera. It was still a great pop song. Etcetera. Now they were just Frank's dirty old henchmen with an acid casualty as a cheerleader.

Keith Gear sat in the portable toilet until his STP hell trip subsided a little. When he opened the door the backstage area was full of road-crew hippies formation idiot-dancing to ELP's 'Tarkus'. A limo was pulling into the backstage area with another of the groovy underground groups that Lucas had booked. 'Hype Park,' said a passing cynic and if Keith Gear could have got his paralysed hands to move in unison at that moment he would have clapped the sentiment.

'Look after him,' said Lucas. So Cindy looked after him for the rest of the afternoon.

Later, in a Soho bar, everything Keith Gear said went numb on his tongue. 'When are you going to record again?' everyone asked.

'1949,' said Keith Gear, still gamma-rayed to fuck.

'You're a fucking mess, boy,' said one old jazzbo, ready for a fight.

Yes he is, isn't he, said Cindy's startled eyes.

Lucas and Cindy were both too pissed to drive so they left the car in Berwick Street and took a train from King's Cross back to Stevenage. Cindy led the STP-fried Gear like he was on a lead. On the train everything stayed stupid on Keith Gear's lips. Every utterance came out wrong. Things that would have made Cindy smile in July made her wince in

September. She looked at him with pity. That's when she looked at all. Mostly she talked franchise talk with the Good Mr Square.

They got off the train at Stevenage but there were no taxis so they wandered into town in search of fish and chips. Lucas and Cindy walked several paces in front, wrapped up in business propositions and percentage points and venue licences. They got further and further ahead of the dazed and drifting guitarist. A narrow cinder track ran off the road, dwarfed by overgrown bushes on both sides, winding down to an industrial estate. Keith Gear turned off at the track, bursting for a pee. He thought of shouting to them to wait a minute but just as quickly thought why bother. He stumbled down the track, round a bend, and was soon some way from the road. Eventually, in the distance, he heard muffled shouts as the preoccupied couple stopped and retraced their steps.

'Keith,' shouted Lucas.

'Keith,' shouted Cindy.

'Keith,' they shouted together.

It's that easy to walk away. Keith Gear never forgot that moment. Just head off the straight and narrow and down the winding track. He waited till they'd gone – the shouting didn't last – then staggered back to the station. When he walked onto the platform the train they'd got off earlier was still there. Engine failure obviously. Just waiting for a tow. Keith Gear walked the length of the platform towards the footbridge to cross to the London-bound side, but when he reached the last coaches of the broken-down train a policeman barred his way. Men in British Rail uniforms were inspecting the end carriage. He noticed that someone had splashed red paint on it. Vandals obviously. Early season football hooligans. The paint ran from the open window above a carriage door, ballooning in thick splatters, then ebbing to specks and drips, and it wasn't paint.

'Sorry, mate, you can't get on this train,' said a British Rail man.

'I don't want to get on this train,' he said. 'I want to go back to London.'

'Well, you'll have to walk down to the other end of the platform and cross there,' said the British Rail man. 'There's been an accident.'

'What's happened?'

'Some kids were fooling around. They held their mate out of the window and that's what's left of his head.'

Yeah, thought Keith Gear. *That's about the size of it.*

Weirder still, because things always can get weirder still, he bumped into Spencer and his girlfriend Hilary on the concourse at King's Cross. They'd been to Hype Park as well. Keith Gear told them about the brain train and asked them what they'd thought of the concert. Spencer talked like he'd just stepped out of one of those CBS Rock Machine adverts. Jack Bruce, he said, was 'jazz-rock with opera leanings'. King Crimson were 'intense techno-rock'. Formerly Fat Harry were 'country flavoured folk'. He asked Keith Gear why he hadn't played.

'I was death-ray head blues with a dash of stab-me razor girl,' said Keith Gear, and headed for the underground.

'This music is wonderful,' said Keith Gear.

They were on the last leg of their Moroccan visit and staying with Collette, an old girlfriend of Jimi's, in the harbour town of Essaouira. 'It's like one note is every note,' said Jimi.

'There's a purity in this music which might never come again,' lamented Keith Gear.

'Oh, such sadness in one so young,' said Japhy, the old Californian beat poet who had accompanied them to a simple oud recital given by an octogenarian Berber who sat and played cross-legged in the shade of a spreading fig tree.

'Are you going to form another group?' asked Jimi.

'No, the group thing has been and gone. I'd like to get back to some sort of simplicity. It's like, y'know, when I first started playing I mastered some Bach and I mastered some blues and after a while I –' the oud player finished the piece he was playing and everyone applauded '– realised that all I really wanted to do was play "Taxman".'

They all laughed. Jimi laughed loudest of all. 'Oh, I know, man. I know exactly where you're at. Sometimes I don't know if I want to play outer-space music or inner-space music. So I just play "Red House" or "Hear My Train" and I feel better.'

They all laughed again. Summit meeting of the big boss alchemists. 'Too many options you see,' said Japhy. 'It's not a blessing. It's a curse. It's the same with words. Sometimes you need to pare it all down. Down to the essence.'

'The truth is,' said Keith Gear, 'even if I worked at it for a hundred years, a thousand years, I still couldn't do anything as perfect as that.' He nodded towards the old oud player. 'The purity of that. I can hear it in my head often enough but when I try and translate, it only comes through in fragments.'

'That's all we have my friend,' said the wise old beat poet. 'Fragments is all we have.'

'Even my fragments have fragments,' said Keith Gear.

'Words are just sculpted ruins,' said Japhy. 'The remains of some ancient memory.'

'Vapour trails,' said Jimi. 'That's all my notes are. That's as near as I can ever get to what I hear.'

'Perhaps it's too near,' said the wise old beat poet. 'Maybe you're flying too close to the sun.'

'Is anyone hungry?' asked Collette.

'Yeah, let's go and eat,' said Jimi, rising slowly.

'I'm all right here for a bit,' said Keith Gear. The oud player continued to pick out notes of unfeasible beauty with gnarled and wizened fingers.

'Where are you going to be?' asked Keith Gear. 'The Riad?'

'No, let's go to the French café,' said Jimi.

He watched the three of them walk off together, Jimi, Japhy and Collette, shimmering in the late afternoon sun, robes billowing in the breeze. A lizard sat spread against a sandstone wall.

His music sounded to him like a scrapyard full of dustbin lids, even though he was playing with great delicacy to an awestruck audience. At one point, he looked down and saw stigmata blood pouring from his open palms. Never again, he said, never again will I go on stage after consuming mushrooms.

He continued to aim his guitar at the ice-cream van, but now the ice-cream van seemed to be sliding down the valley. Perhaps someone was working the field like a huge fairground ride and everything was pivoting on some central axis; maybe the stage was that axis, maybe Keith Gear was that axis. He tried not to think about it.

Blue sparks gushed from his fingernails. A jet stream of blood was pouring from his hand and dripping into his pick-ups. Blood music from the early Rhesus period! Yeah! Eventually he realised that the blood was real. He'd scrubbed his plectrum to shards and was down to flesh and bone. He took this as his cue to stop and stepped away from the microphone, holding his guitar aloft and accidentally unplugging it as he did so. The field seemed to sway again. It was merely the audience doing its poppy-waving, sea-rippling thing but it caused Keith Gear to stagger slightly and hold on to the microphone stand to steady himself. He gripped it for dear life.

A photographer snapped away. The photo would look epic.

Eventually everything settled again. The applause died down, his dizziness subsided and he managed to walk off stage even though the boards had the consistency of unset concrete beneath his feet.

Faces loomed. A long-haired man with a wild expression said, 'You're the man who saved Jimi Hendrix aren't you?'

'No,' said Keith Gear. 'I'm just the man who delayed the inevitable.'

'Wally!'

Rod Stewart bellowed at the crowd at the Weeley Festival. Everyone was requested to look for a lost dog called Wally. Thousands of sun-baked hippies roused themselves onto their elbows and shouted, 'Wally.'

'Wally!'

Keith Gear lost everything except the clothes he was wearing. That was the highlight of the Weeley Pop Festival for Keith Gear. That and playing to the sun-baked hippies on Saturday lunchtime. It was a blazing hot August Bank Holiday.

'Let's do it,' said Lucas. Prestige gig. Mucho dinero. Scorched eyelids. Heat haze. Cindy was in charge of backstage catering. Her presence cast a bad spell. To avoid her, and to show how defiantly underground he was, Keith Gear decided to forsake the cosy backstage facilities and hang out with the people. The people in this case being two Glaswegian Dominion fans called Nil and Neil who wore excrement breath and sewage socks.

Keith Gear played a majestic set, plucking at velvet strings in the breezeless early afternoon, but at night it was cloudless and cold and the three of them, Nil, Neil and Gear, compensated by getting blasted round their campfire. And when Glasgow Neil, or was it Nil, came staggering through the crowd on Sunday and said, 'The tent's on fire,' Keith Gear thought, *you Scottish jokers*. No. Here's the joke. Get the festival organisers to put down lots of straw so the hippies can keep warm. Now light some camp fires and stoves. Now add sunshine and tinder dry nights.

Keith Gear's weekend was oblivion after that. There was Cindy dishing out healthfood to the hungry. There was the PA playing that Carole King song, 'It's Too Late'. And there was Keith Gear pouring it all out to Nil, or was it Neil? And

Nil or was it Neil or was it neither said, 'Plenty more fish in the sea, Keith. Plenty more fish in the sea.'

Help, I'm a cliché! he thought.

'Come on. Let's go and look for that lost dog,' said Nil.

'Wally!'

A rumour began to spread around Avalonia that Jimi was dead. There was always some sort of rumour doing the rounds. In 1969, the big story was that Nixon had been assassinated. In 1970, someone said that Manson had escaped and was on a Californian killing spree. Someone also said that Dennis Wilson had replaced Neil Young in Crosby, Stills, Nash and Young and that Crosby, Stills, Nash and Wilson were going to be headlining Avalonia on the last night. By the end of the weekend Dennis Wilson and Charlie Manson were helter-skeltering their way towards the White House with the intention of rubbing out Richard Nixon.

That sort of thing was always happening at Avalonia. It had something to do with the landlocked valley and the way all radio contact with the outside world ceased the moment those hills surrounded you. Some said it was the ley lines and the mystical properties of the terrain that cut out radio signals. Either way, the geo-physical properties of the electro-magnetic spectrum counted for nothing the minute you checked in your senses and your sanity at the gates of Avalonia.

Once you'd made your pact, Copernicus was up on trial, moon men walked the earth and Avalonia was a primordial vortex of unreality where rationality feared to tread and Nixon lay gasping his last.

But this one refused to go away. It arrived on site like a dirty virus late on Saturday afternoon, mutated round the midnight campfires and spread across the fields throughout the hazy hallucinatory night. The fact that the source of the rumour was a Hawkwind roadie didn't give it much credence initially, particularly as this was a Hawkwind roadie who had been up for three days and nights, feasting on every pharmaceutical compound known to man and some that didn't even have names or numbers yet. He gabbled out his truth-lies all afternoon to anyone who was prepared to listen or couldn't get out of the way fast enough. 'I tell yer, man,' he said, braying his prophecy like some demented sermon from the mount. But when the sun started to go down and he was still 'telling yer, man', people began to listen.

He'd had a phone call from New York. It was Battalion's manager, the X-Ray Kid. He was in tears. 'You better be putting me on,' said the roadie.

Instinctively Keith Gear knew it was true. He'd often thought about that night he saved Jimi from choking on his own vomit, breathing life through sick-stained lips, clogged airways and wheezing lungs, his action taking on metaphorical life of its own as he kneeled over Jimi's slumped and wasted body. It was as if Keith Gear was breathing life into the culture itself, giving it renewed energy and sustenance. But when he saw how quickly Jimi lapsed back into his old ways, how tired and beat up he and his music seemed, he knew that the muse had exhausted itself and that some dim and distant star had imploded thousands of light years away. Subconsciously, at least, he always knew this day would come. A day, a month, a year, a decade hence. The timescale hardly mattered. In fact it was almost exactly nine months to the day since that panic-stricken kiss. Some gestation.

In September, he played the Grantchester Free Festival. Nothing to do with Lucas. Lucas was of the breadhead persuasion and didn't embrace the concept of playing for free. Richard from the Dominion days drove him down there. That's what he did now. A bit of roadie work. And house removals. Still throwing the I Ching to determine removal fees. The cosmic Pickfords.

The meadow was sunny green and the day was autumn

perfect. Richard was still a strange fish and hardly said a word all the way there but when they got to Grantchester they drove past pretty white cottages with ivy growing, and down a dusty track to where the meadows spread and Cambridge hippies went merrily stepping to a stage by a winding river. There was no acrid smell of burnt burgers, no one selling stale donuts or STP or aspirin acid. There was just Donovan's Open Road without Donovan, Carol Grimes' Uncle Dog, Keith Gear and an assortment of raggle-taggle harlequins and jugglers and underpass buskers. The joints passed freely among friendly strangers and when the bands weren't playing there was little to hear but birdsong and the river's gurgling. The only time the tranquillity was broken was when a girl on a bad trip got up and ran around screaming. First she did it with clothes on. Then she did it with clothes off. Then she ran to the river's edge and tried to drown herself in two feet of water. After a while, everyone sussed that attention was the name of her game and they left her to her paddling and her shallow madness. She was as safe here as anywhere with Donovan's Open Road without Donovan, Carol Grimes' Uncle Dog and Keith Gear, who peeled off notes that rippled like the water and merged with the distant bells of evensong. After his set, Richard rolled a huge joint, then passed it to Keith Gear who passed it to an Open Roader (without Donovan) who passed it to a Dog Uncle who passed it back to Richard. They warmed their brain cells on this thick dynamite stick of a reefer and watched the sunset set fire to the sky. No one spoke. No one needed to.

With the sun nesting in the lowest branches and the twilight crackling with neon sparks, Richard and Keith Gear climbed into the van and headed for the dusty track. Civilisation this way. Four hundred yards. Early leavers were scurrying back along the track towards them, cramming polythene bags and balls of foil into hedgerows and hollowed tree trunks. 'Hide your stash,' they said. 'The fuzz are pulling people out at random.' At the end of the track, where the meadow met the pretty white cottages, there they stood, a thin blue line blocking the road. 'Don't meet their eyes,' said one frazzled longhair whose own were helter-skeltering for Albion. 'Smoked it all,' said Richard, winding the window up. The longest sentence he'd spoken all day. He eased down into second gear, showing due care and attention to the roadside stragglers and the Cambridgeshire Constabulary. The thin blue line parted and waved them through. The moment they reached the top of the road, Richard accelerated and they blew smoke rings out of their arses all the way back to London.

That night Keith Gear went to bed with a head full of autumnal haze and meadow bird song.

It was Christmas Eve 1971. Keith Gear was in the West End looking for last-minute presents. Perfume for Mum. Check. Perfume for Aunt Moira. Check. Perfume for everyone. Let scent rain down from a thousand display stands. Keith Gear had sprayed so many testers on his wrists he was attracting the attention of elegant men with decadent appetites. He would probably have been attracting their attention anyway, drifting down Oxford Street bathed in a halo of curls. Just how he would look on the cover of his first solo album in a few months time.

He headed for the Boadicea Broadcasting Corporation to drop off a card for Earl Raven, whose patronage and friendship he respected. Earl Raven was a sincere spirit among charlatans and sharks.

Regent Street was framed by an arc of unlit Christmas lights. Everyone scurried in and out of shops, all wrapped up in the pandemonium of it all. A coffee roast aroma wafted from a side street. The alki-tramps fed pigeons on the steps of Langham Church. Dads stood vacant and forlorn in department-store doorways, arms limp and laden with bags. One woman turned to another and said, 'Leave him there, the soft sod, we'll go and have a cuppa.' Outside Chelsea Girl two twelve-year-old girls were learning how to smoke, while two twelve-year-old boys were learning how to smoke and gob while chatting up two twelve-year-old girls.

His bag rattling with Essence of Whores Handbag and Lily of the Forbidden Swamp, Keith Gear decided to buy his dad some driving gloves. Sensible practical present for sensible practical Dad. He checked John Lewis's Store Plan and plotted his course from the 'You are here' arrow to gentleman's outfitters. He headed up the stairs to the first floor. He paused halfway and gazed down at the seething heaving throng of bodies, all urgent and shoving and bustling and queuing and clicking purses. Then he walked through leather goods and millinery and on through the shoe department, barging and dodging and weaving his way towards his sensible practical present for sensible practical Dad. He edged his way through a narrow gap between two racks of ladies shoes. The crush subsided, the crowd parted momentarily and there in front of him, on her knees and carefully easing an old lady's stockinged foot into a slipper, was Sonya, frizzy locks all shorn and tightly permed, her face a portrait of boredom. She looked up and smiled a surprised smile.

'Hello, Keith. How's it going?'

They exchanged pleasantries while the old lady fiddled with the slipper, wriggling her toes and pulling at the heel.

Sonya babbled away like she always did. 'Do you go to the MQ these days? Haven't been down meself for ages. No time what with one thing.'

The one thing being Pete the Gas Fitter it seemed.

'Hope you're behaving yourself. Don't do anything I wouldn't.'

Keith Gear told her he was about to start recording a solo LP after Christmas. Sonya didn't even know he'd been in a group. No time what with one thing.

She picked up a shoehorn and eased the old lady's other foot into the other slipper. Her knee cracked as she stood up but she kept on smiling her 'keep on smiling' smile.

Keith Gear said, 'Do you fancy going for a coffee during your lunch break?'

'Can't really. I'm meeting up with Pete and his mum to do a bit of shopping.'

'How about after work then?'

'Can't really. Got too much to do. Gotta get my Pete's tea on, then there's presents to wrap and turkey to stuff and . . .'

And all the time she kept on smiling. Smiling and smiling until her smile was a grimace and she looked like she had lockjaw.

'Some other time maybe,' said Keith Gear.

'Yeah, some other time,' answered Sonya.

PAGES FROM THE UNBOOK

2019

Keith Gear had last seen Drum in 2006. He spotted him from an upstairs window as his bus crawled through rush-hour traffic. Drum seemed hunched, cowed, like he had some sort of spinal condition. He was jabbering to himself as he hurried along the road.

'Look at that old dribblist down there,' shouted a school kid.

'Yeah, real loonaliscious,' taunted his friend, banging on the window.

Keith Gear jumped off the bus at the next stop and they went and had a cup of subsidised tea at the Mission House. Drum told him he was playing trumpet again.

'With some young Tamil lads. And I'm doing an evening class in animation.'

'That's good,' said Keith Gear.

'You make it sound like physiotherapy,' said Drum, morosely. 'That's good. Keep taking the medicine.'

'Sorry,' said Keith Gear. And he was. For everything. They sat dunking biscuits in silence, with little to say to each other.

The two men parted outside the Mission House with a half-hearted embrace and an equally half-hearted promise to keep in touch. Keith Gear watched as Drum walked unflinchingly into the full force of the north wind and away off up the high street. That image of Drum hunched against the elements burned itself into his brain. He thought of it often in the months that followed, always believing that Drum would turn up again, always half expecting to bump into him round the next corner.

But months turned to years and Drum never was round that next corner. He was never far from Keith Gear's thoughts, though, memories resurfacing at the most unlikely moments. Sometimes these were fond evocations, at other times they were deeply unsavoury recollections that made him wince. More often than not, as Keith Gear understood only too well, he was recoiling as he recognised his own worst aspects reflected in his colleague. The circumstances may have differed but the bull-headed trajectory, the emotional cost and the impoverished outcome were remarkably similar.

Like many autodidacts who had worked it all out for themselves, Drum frequently wore his learning a little too loudly. He could spot mediocrity at a thousand paces and had the kind of untutored intellect that got people's backs up. He also possessed a self-destruct button of awesome capabilities. Nobody could fuck up quite like Drum. Keith Gear was there the day Drum was thrown out of Boadicea House after recording a session for the Earl Raven show. Everything was going fine for the first half hour and Drum's band had laid down a couple of tracks. Then a portly twentysomething producer from another show barged into the studio when the red light was on to consult one of the tape operatives about a forthcoming charity programme. As the insensitive young producer loudly explained the following evening's live telethon schedule to the technician, Drum slowly emptied the spit from his mouthpiece onto the carpet, then fixed his sights on the producer's T-shirt. Emblazoned across a huge pink teddy bear were the words 'Hugs Not Drugs'.

'Would you mind not coming in here while we're performing?' said Drum, quietly.

'I'm terribly sorry,' began the producer, swelling with indignation, 'but . . .'

'And would you mind removing that offensive T-shirt?'

'I . . . I . . .' stuttered the producer, blood rushing to his cheeks.

'I mean, would it be OK if I got a T-shirt made up saying "Hugs And Drugs" or "Drugs Instead of Hugs"?' continued Drum. 'And then swanned around thrusting my moral values in other people's faces from my great big sweaty corporation chest.'

Drum finished the session, but as far as Boadicea Broadcasting policy went, the session finished him.

When Keith Gear thought of Drum now he thought of a creative life that had promised so much, yet delivered so little. A few years of jazz improv. and a short-lived period of infamy as an alternative comedian hadn't left much of a legacy. He remembered Drum once telling him that he'd had to stop taking acid because every time he tripped he kept hallucinating visions of some greater indeterminate darkness that he suspected was lying in wait for him further on down the road. Keith Gear blamed the drugs at the time, conceding that there are certain people, even one's closest friends sometimes, who should never be allowed anywhere near chemical weaponry without full protective armour for the body, soul and psyche. Now that Keith Gear was peering into that great indeterminate darkness himself, now, as he wrestled with his own demons in the tomb-like confines of the Crescents, he thought of Drum constantly. Always buzzing with some new idea. Always working on four projects at once. Which was always three too many.

Keith Gear down on his knees in the studio, juggling with jack-plugs, frantically trying to find a way to channel the police messages that were crackling ethereally through his amp. Trying to trap them in a tape loop before the moment passed. Drum behind him, loudly rehearsing future schemes to sceptical band members who wished he would shut up and take less speed.

'I've got this great idea for a film based on Lord Haw-Haw,' said Drum. 'Opening shot, Joyce and long-suffering wife arriving in Berlin in 1939. Everyone else is frantic to get away. Refugees, Jews, communists – everyone's having papers stamped, heading in the other direction. Bird's-eye camera pan above everybody's heads: at the station hundreds of people crowding onto last trains out of Berlin. Just this one man and his put-upon wife going through passport control into Germany. That's the opening shot, here's the ending: 1945, Joyce and his wife flee to Denmark. Holed up in this cottage. Snow scene: he's chopping wood in the backyard. Two English soldiers from the expeditionary force are walking through the snow, patrolling the woods. Freezing cold day. Steam, breath blowing on their hands, cupping fags. Joyce calls out to his wife from the backyard. The sound travels across the snow to these soldiers. One says, "Wait a minute, I know that voice," and it's like a flashback to all those wartime broadcasts he's heard. The film ends with a long shot of them walking towards the cottage, these two little stick figures about to make history. The credits are going up. That's not how they caught him in real life – they found him in the woods. He could have just walked on by, they would have thought he was a refugee, but he couldn't resist speaking to them, couldn't resist shouting his big fucking mouth off.'

'You sound just the man for the job,' said Guy, dryly.

'All you have to do now is write the bit in the middle,' said Tony Maggs.

'I will,' said Drum. 'Do you think anyone will want to make a film about an unpatriotic loser?'

All that ambition, all that potential, all those projects pending.

The three of them, Gear, Truelove, Drummond, down New Mexico way. Vulturous sunlight bleaching through to the bone on the Sante Fe trail. Deep in trouble. Quicksand deep. Gear playing De Falla for gangsters and not-so-hot-shot guitar slingers. Drum licking sulphate off his fingers. Infused with that border bodega outlaw vibe. Writing eighty-eight page poems without punctuation because that's how many keys on the piano, he babbled, and babbled on, and oh how his babble towered above everyone. Wrote a leaning tower of words eighty-eight storeys high and kept all his speed notes in little red ready reckoners. That day in the desert heat he wrote the same line over and over and over and over. 'Old Dueloz, he tossed the Spanish coins.' Scribbling himself into mantra madness.

A thousand layered indentations later, Truelove wrenched the pen from his grip and said, 'Relax, Drum. I'm sure they won't be long now.'

The Drumhead all mashed up with I Ching and Spaghetti Westerns and Bob Dylan and Bill Burroughs. All invited to his pill party.

Drum sometime later. All cleaned up, teeth capped and bridged and two stone healthier, pacing Truelove's carpet, displacing ornaments with one enthused gesticulation. 'That novel your uncle wrote. Someone should film it.'

He was talking to Gear. He'd found the bleak little fiction book that Lenny Lyons wrote in the 70s. Light years removed from the barefaced act he'd been known for ever since he took the showbiz shilling.

'They wiped most of his 60s shows, you know,' said the nephew.

'That's fucking scandalous that is,' said Drum. 'One day his reputation is going to rest solely on what survives on tape. Memories don't endure. They oxidize like celluloid.' He tapped the book for emphasis. 'Someone should definitely make a film of this.'

They sat and reminisced, the three of them, Truelove, Drummond, Gear. Laughing at half-remembered skits and bits.

'Do you remember when he parodied *Ready Steady Go*? Every character! Cathy McGowan? Sonny and Cher?'

'Do you remember his Fellini? Six and seven eighths?'

The three shrieked and howled, pounding dust from armchairs. A tray of drinks went flying. Someone banged on the wall next door. A retaliatory TV was turned up. Canned laughter filtered in like Zyklon B.

'And some day,' said Drum, 'all people will remember him for is buxom wenches and a saucy grin.'

Keith Gear could see them still, sprawling left to right on Guy Truelove's cig-burned, beer-stained sofa all those years ago. Now as he stood in his kitchen pouring hot water into a cup containing a sachet of tannin dust, he could scarcely believe what he was reading. Scanning a torn strip of news page in a busy blur because he didn't want the words to be true.

'The body washed up on Blossom Sands . . .'

He was down on his knees, placing newspaper pages on the kitchen floor. The sink unit had been leaking for weeks and every day he replaced damp strips with dry ones.

'The body washed up on Blossom Sands three days ago has been formally . . .'

He was picking away with his fingernails at the pulped pages, all mashed up and trodden in.

'. . . identified as that of the missing musician and conceptual artist Malcolm . . .'

His hands were blackened. Ink was imprinted on the soles of his shoes.

'. . . Drummond. It is believed that Drummond, sixty-six . . .'

Two years younger. Always younger. Always would be now.

Industrious Drum pitching another screenplay. Another neatly typed and thwarted scheme. There was one on the life of the chess player, Bobby Fischer. Drum believed that chess was maths and maths was truth. There was another on the battle between Art Arfons and Craig Breedlove in the 60s to break the world land-speed record: to be the fastest man alive. Drum was interested in speed long before his addiction slowed him to a crawl.

'It's an all-American story,' said Drum. 'Craig Breedlove is the all-American hero with the patriot's gleam and the rosy red cheeks, as wholesome as mom's apple pie. He's LA born and destiny bound and his corporate-financed craft is called Spirit of America. Art Arfons is the renegade with the lawless grin and the faraway stare. He's an Akron man, born 1926, twelve years Breedlove's senior. Makes his rocket car from spare NASA parts out back in his shed. Picks up a big ol' Starfighter jet engine in a job lot and, when the military come asking for their engine back, Art tells them it's part o' ma car and I have a receipt. Calls it Green Monster and in three years between 1963 and 1966 he chases Breedlove through the 400, 500, 600 miles an hour barrier, topping and tailing the all-American boy and being the only man in the world to survive a crash at 672 mph.' Guess who Drum favours? Drum favours Art. Every time.

Drum's itinerary. Drum's art-life inventory.

Drum's instruction for the inaugural performance of Alexander Scriabin's unfinished composition *Mysterium* to be performed at Antonio Gaudí's Sagrada Familia in Barcelona upon that building's completion with precise directions regarding duration, colour-coded lighting and the suspension of bells from clouds, according to the composer's wishes.

Scripts and story boards for *The Vulva-nauts*, an X-rated cartoon that Drum managed to sell to a satellite station, holding out for syndication rights that would set him up for three full years of eating properly and scheming compulsively and art-life communiqués.

Complete transcripts of Drum's unreleased duets with May Grey, scored for trumpet and piano, trumpet and synth, trumpet and jenny ondeline, trumpet and theremin, trumpet and koto, trumpet and ondes martinot.

One copy of Drum's 1986 comedy album *Secret Handshake*

Lot, withdrawn due to multitudinous libels made against showbiz slags and alt.com con artists.

One copy of Drum's privately distributed comedy cassette, *Sic Drum: Gloria in Transit*.

An undelivered conference paper entitled "Where's the euphemism? Yes it does, doesn't it?" A treatise on the purgative properties and pleasures of punning and associated forms of worm play.'

Copies of all polemical rants, prankster prose, drunken declamations, sober reflections penned and sent to newspapers, magazines, radio stations, TV producers, Members of Parliament, captains of industry, friends, foes, and strangers.

Plus.

Reams of speed writing, diaries, expired passports, adoptive mother's death certificate, step-brother's death certificate, birth mother's birth certificate, his own birth certificate, evening-class certificates in composition, script-writing, screen-writing, animation, the accumulated residue of unswept attic corners and long-forgotten miscellany, all bundled into a box and driven to a late-night destination, and burned on a midnight beach.

Plus.

Drum's last will and testament. All spoken quietly onto a C-46 cassette entitled *Last Crap Tape* and hastily strapped to his skin but inefficiently adhered and insufficiently sealed and soon wrenched away by waves and now waterlogged and lost and never to be heard. Instructions for his meagre earthly funds to be shared equally among the only four people he ever really cared for: Keith Gear, Guy Truelove, Tony Maggs and Kimberley Clark, in sickness and in health.

Drum's last work. Fire cleansed and ocean bound. Purification. Obliteration. Pages from the unbook.

Keith Gear in his kitchen, thinking of what Drum said that day at his flat, the day after Kim left him. 'None of us really know shit about each other or anyone or anything.'

He turned on the TV. They had caught the celebrity killer and a distant relative was being interviewed by a news crew. She leaned on her gate, peered anxiously up the road as if he might still be coming back and said, in a blank emotionless voice, 'He was a lovely child, always polite and well behaved. Never thought he was capable of anything like this.'

'He always seemed a happy-go-lucky sort of boy,' agreed a neighbour, staring directly into the camera as if seeking confirmation. The neighbour's neighbour then said how shocked everyone was. And stunned.

DUSK MUSIC

2019

Keith Gear, a retired and impoverished musician, left his living space in the Crescents and walked to the shops to exchange tokens for a morning paper. The air was rationed, the wind wafted noxious currents, legionnaires' disease oozed from ventilation grills and outflow pipes as he made his way along the walkway from his residence at six up, six across. He hurried past the wilting bouquets on the third-floor stairwell, left in remembrance of an eight-year-old boy who had been stabbed to death with a school compass on that very spot. Keith Gear thought it very poor that people should commemorate a young child's life by leaving flowers on a piss-stained stairwell.

He walked the short walk along potholed pavements and disinfected streets to the newsagent, where Mr Jimahl sat reading the racing pages, his radio hissing with off-channel sibilance.

'Pick me a winner,' said Mr Jimahl brightly. 'I feel lucky today.'

Keith Gear handed over his tokens and smiled uncertainly. In the small room behind him Mr Jimahl's daughter Raisa chopped coriander and ginger, filling the shop with the sweet scent of leaf and root.

He normally went back to his room and spent all morning reading *The Vanguard*. Two pots of Net-Let leaf dust and a couple of slices of norjen starch loaf would usually see him through to midday, but today he had to be somewhere. He'd received a letter from the warden's office asking him to attend a meeting at eleven. No explanation. No hint as to the nature or purpose of this summons. Just three lines on a stark white page. You are requested to report. The last time he had received a summons of this kind, somebody had been duplicating his food-stamp card and obtaining free provisions from the Net-Let. On that occasion, a young Estonian girl had been led into the room, bewildered, shivering, all of fourteen, and Keith Gear had been asked if he recognised 'this wretch'. That was two years ago and he'd seen the girl again, weeks later, attempting to shoplift tampons from the same Net-Let. She was walking up the aisle ahead of him. He saw her trying to conceal something inside her Salvation Store overcoat. An overhead camera swivelled silently, a red light glowed, then shrank to a pinprick. Four female security guards rushed in and with choreographed efficiency bludgeoned the young girl to the ground with their karate blows and drop kicks. Keith Gear told all this to a man who was walking his dog but the man jerked the lead and hurried away.

Now Keith Gear was in his kitchen, whipping up eggs in a measuring jug, approximating the indigenous tribal rhythms of an African country he couldn't put a name to. He mused on the possibility of hiring a basic drum machine from the Pawn Mart and laying down some egg music. In his living room the TV droned on. He never listened to the radio anymore. There was a time when he couldn't turn it on without hearing fragments of his dusk music. He was stabilizing of late and didn't want his sickness delivered again at the flick of a switch. So the TV droned instead.

A movie preview show was playing. A middle-aged presenter, sporting a red velvet smoking jacket and hangdog jowls, mugged convulsively in front of a digital projection of a Broadway night scene. 'Coming up . . .' he said.

Keith Gear added some milk from a carton to his eggs and continued to beat out time in rapid rhythmic bursts.

'*The Resting Place* takes us back to 70s Baltimore and a

re-union of seven guys who used to meet up in a 50s diner. Effectively, it's an unofficial sequel to *Burger Boys*, the story of . . .'

He poured his egg mix into a chipped enamel pan and put two slices of starch loaf under the grill.

'. . . Director Billy Morton talks about her new film, *The People Lab*, and the darker side of her personal life.'

He scanned the letter from the warden's office again, all twenty-seven words of it, then placed it in a drawer.

'Where did the idea for *The People Lab* come from?' asked the TV host.

'I've had the idea since I was nine,' replied Billy Morton, a slender-boned woman of forty-five with a black curly perm and pinafore dress. The camera cut back to the host, who looked obsequiously over-attentive.

'I saw an item on the news about a nightclub in Las Vegas,' continued Billy Morton. 'Somebody had smuggled a camera into this club where they had circus acts between the singers and the showgirls; performing monkeys and dancing bears, that kind of thing. And they showed the animals on stage responding to the compère's commands. "How many hands am I holding up?" to a blindfold monkey. "Which card is the ace of clubs? Clever monkey." That kind of thing. Then they showed a clip, which had been secretly filmed backstage on a hidden camera. And there was this man, this brute with a whip in his hand, with a monkey on a stool. And he was–'

The woman's voice faltered. The camera exploited her face, which showed she was nervy, intense and close to tears.

'And I realised straight away, even though I was only nine, that that's how they train the animals, that's how they command obedience and respect. By instilling total fear into them. By beating them and punching them. I'd always wanted to make a movie about that and I thought, wouldn't it be cool to do a movie where a clandestine group of animal rights' supporters from England go to Las Vegas to take on these . . . Sicilian businessmen, you know. I originally wanted to call it

Animals, but there's already a film called that apparently. Then I thought *The People Lab* would be cool. Because that's what we are in a way. Lab rats and circus monkeys. We're all performing under laboratory conditions to other people's expectations. Aren't we?'

The host nodded vigorously.

Keith Gear mused on the myriad ways in which human beings perform under laboratory conditions to other people's expectations. His starch loaf slowly turned to charcoal under the gas flame. The smell of pan rust and scorched milk began to fill the kitchen.

The host gushed on in his platitudinous way. 'Sounds like *The Godfather* meets *Free Willy*,' he said. The camera closed in on his irony tic. His reference points dated him and his guest betrayed a flicker of an uncomprehending frown.

Then they showed a clip from the opening of the film. A lab raid late at night. The click of wirecutters. The sound of wind in the moonlit trees. Torchlight illuminating laboratory rows of rats, rabbits, kittens and minks. Silhouetted figures, open cages and clasp-cold frightened animals to their warm beating hearts. An alarm bell rings.

In his fume-filled kitchen Keith Gear surveyed his blackened eggs, scraped at the stuck-fast residue around the rim, sighed, soaked the pan in soapy water and looked around for edible alternatives. He imagined those monkeys taking those beatings and couldn't get it out of his head. Now it was in there, it was in there forever.

On the TV screen a montage fast-forwarded through Billy Morton's career. Her early life was rendered in garden-gate snapshots and Kodak close-ups. Here's Billy at seven, a slip of a thing squinting in sunlight, dressed in hand-me-downs, dragging a rag doll through the dirt. Here's Billy at fifteen, pouting and preening in a bus-station photo booth. Billy has painted eyebrows, a watery smile and ghost-white skin. Billy with her friend Kate. Kate has a greasy complexion and thick curtains of hair, hennaed black. There's a whole sequence of these, the impromptu sparkle of adolescence documented in every frame. Billy going boss-eyed. Billy's friend giving an assertive middle finger to the camera. Billy distracted by something to her right. Billy's friend inserting her left index finger up her left nostril. Both girls laughing. Both girls making pig noses. Then another face looms, a boy's face, thrust into the cramped kiosk, disproportionately bulbous in profile; he's making with the buck-teeth and the pug face and the girls are laughing hard. Then he's turning to camera, blowing imperfect smoke rings and clouding up the booth. Then he's gobbing at the lens, white spray and phlegm flecks dripping down the images, like seagull shit on a windscreen.

The background music shifted to ominous. A shaky am-cam zoomed and panned at random, spilling its gaze on autumnal moors, drawn to a frowning woman in her early twenties and a sky full of thunder clouds. The host, wearing his best cliché-concerned face, was asking Billy about her troubled youth. Billy shifted uneasily in her seat, curled her bare feet under her, began picking at the hard skin on her heels, her posture regressing to a mime of girl life. 'I had a very checkered . . . youth.' There was precision in her vagueness, understated deliberation in her tone, a bemused pause before the word youth. 'I was . . . I suppose because of my home life, or lack of it, I was always searching for security. I was . . . easily led. I had a series of relationships with older men.' You could hear the quotation marks when she said 'relationships'.

Something in those distant tones made the man in the kitchen twitch. It was as if some parallel tableau of his troubled life was arranging itself simultaneously. He plucked a tin of petrified soup from a dusty shelf, made two crude indents in the lid with a rusty and blunted tin opener, then swung round in one smooth clockwise motion towards the cooker, where in the periphery of his vision he had mistaken a full soaking saucepan for an empty one. That one ninety-degree swivel from shelf to saucepan took half a second.

During the second half of that eventful second Keith Gear remembered that he had just filled the egg-burned pan with water and stopped himself before he jettisoned a tin of soup into a pan full of scummy residue. And somehow, that *déjà-vu* flash unlocked everything. In that one domestic sweep, in that one preventative action, a chain reaction was unleashed and a fog began to lift.

They ran the footage of the celebrity killer's capture again. He had seen it so many times before. The same shots of helicopters hovering, the same heat-seeking surveillance, the bodies detected and ringed, the caravans on the moss, circled up like Custer's last stand, the surrendering suspects being led in a line, handcuffed and ankle chained; a middle-aged man with grey thinning hair and six inches of ponytail, clad in brown fisherman's jumper and black tracksuit bottoms. His accomplices trail out behind him, one woman, a second much younger woman, a third, a fourth, a fifth, a harem, a shaven-headed coven. The first woman is thickset and forty-something – bull neck, baggy dress and swollen arms. The others look no more than fourteen, fifteen. They are dressed in army-surplus commando chic, their piercings catching the gleam of the early morning sun.

There's the police chief explaining yet again how a vanload of officers had gone to the moss to investigate another case altogether. An impromptu motorbike race had taken place. Scrambling bikes built from scrap metal and skip-junk circling the travellers' camp, their riders fuelled on bath-tub wizz and industrial-strength home-brew. Five laps, ten laps, fifteen laps completed when a small boy wriggles free from his watchers and wanders into their path. When the ambulance arrives, the boy's family refuse to allow him to go to hospital. There is a stand off. Social services are called. The police take the opportunity to have an exploratory poke and probe. They make a note of untaxed vans, unroadworthy trailers, piecemeal stuff, routine harassment. An officer kicks a tyre to test the pressure and a hubcap comes loose. In the two-inch gap between wheel and hub sits an indiscreetly secreted gun silencer and a stash of bullets. The officer keeps his nerve, crouches and places the hubcap back in position. Back at the station, he says, 'Sarg, I think we should take another look at . . .'

And now the arresting officer is talking again. His TV voiceover documents the last days of the celebrity killer crew, from surveillance footage to defiant prison mugshots. 'There was no reason as far as I can see. People always look for an explanation but I'm not sure there is one. Who knows what set him off?'

Keith Gear had been starring at the punctured soup tin for some time now, his arms heavy by his side. His proximity to the notorious kicked in. His chest tightened. He wondered if he was having a heart attack.

Billy Morton was talking again.

'We all went for auditions to do this photo-story in one of the teenage comics. For a laugh. It was my friend Kate's idea. I just tagged along really. Thought it might be a good experience. Our teachers were always telling us to make contacts.'

The screen showed am-cam footage from a travellers' site. A bonfire gathering, a child ladling lentil stew from a steaming pan, a sly young man in his early twenties grinning sardonically and making trigger fingers at the camera.

'When we got to the audition we had to act out this corny storyline. Well, I thought it was corny anyway. Chazzie had to play Kate's boyfriend, and I had to play his former girlfriend who had been killed in a car crash. But I had come back as a ghost and was haunting him. Quite spooky, really, when you think about it now.' Billy Morton put a hasty hand to her face to suppress an ironic smile.

'Only, the thing was, when it came to doing the acting, Chazzie was . . . useless, completely hopeless, and it shocked me, you know, because it had been his idea all along. He was always telling me how he and Kate were going off to drama college, and yet, when it came down to it he . . . he couldn't even do the basic facial expressions, mugging, reaction shots, stuff like that. He ended up having a right strop and walked out.'

Billy Morton ran the gamut of teenage mugging from A to B for the benefit of her TV host, who having not updated his mannerisms since middle youth had no real need of the lesson.

'I mean, he couldn't even do the walk. There was one shot where we were supposed to be walking by the side of this busy road, near where I'd been killed, and the cameraman kept saying, "Chaz, you're waddling," and "Chaz, have you crapped your pants?" And I started laughing, which made things worse. But he was right. When they showed me the contact sheets – they gave us contact sheets for our portfolios and you never saw a less convincing . . . he looked so awkward. You'd have thought it was impossible to get it wrong, wouldn't you, walking? But somehow he looked bandy-legged in one and like he'd got a wooden leg in another. So perhaps it all stems from that. You know. What came later I mean. Who knows?'

The TV ran stock footage of the victims. Long-forgotten faces from a bygone age. There's showbiz agent Maurice Went again, beaming bald and avuncular. There's poor old pools winner Sidney Dunne, a millionaire for all of four minutes before he supped from the poisoned chalice. There's the only library footage available of impresario Jermaine Shaft, half of the twentieth century husband-and-wife showbiz team Jermaine and Gizelle Shaft. The image comes from a charity luncheon, circa 1960. Jermaine Shaft has stray crumbs around the corner of his mouth. All the other guests at the long table seem to be wearing guilty looks, staring warily at the camera as if it's an intrusion, as if each one of them is a prominent gangster or dating someone else's wife. There's Kenny Cash, cool, calm and conceited in one of his soft-focus publicity shots, as perfectly parodied by Malcolm Drummond all those years ago. And there's Gizelle Shaft, in a white feather boa and little else, a memento of her pre-circus days as an exotic dancer. There's an inscription on the creased photo but it's been hazed to save the sensibilities of someone who must be over ninety now.

The TV voiceover pondered the unexplained gap of twenty years before the bloodlust began again. And there's the footage of the forensics team poking around for evidence among the squalor of Chaz's living quarters. They find a scrapbook of press clippings. Page after page logging the seventeen shootings that occurred since the resumption. Chaz and Kate liked to read their reviews.

They ran the footage of the girls again, being led out like a chain gang. The voiceover explains how in later years Chazzie sent his loyal harem out to do his dirty work for him. The smarmy TV host asks Billy Morton how much she knew. Didn't she once receive a letter, some sort of threat, some sort of demand for money? He had now turned inquisitor and grand jury.

'All I think now is: there but for the grace of God, you know,' said Billy Morton, deflecting the question. 'Those poor young girls, asylum seekers mostly, weren't they?' Pause. 'It makes me sick to think I knew him. I mean, how did he get away with it for so long? How could they have missed him? The guy had even changed his name by deed poll to Chaz Manson. I mean, for Christ's sake!'

'That all sounds very heavy.' Having allotted the full five minutes to Billy Morton's dark side, as required in his script, he was eager to get back to the familiar terrain of plugging and promotion.

'It was heavy.' She said it in the same baritone-deep parody of hippie-speak that Keith Gear remembered from that summer's day thirty years earlier when a young girl with shaven eyebrows and a missing earring helped him to carry his equipment across the fresh fields of Avalonia. Keith Gear thought briefly of that ancient pasture, now buried under a bypass.

The interview returned to the comfort zone and Billy Morton eased into publicity mode, puffing and gushing, playing the game, being a good girl for the camera. 'Well, obviously it's really exciting to be directing for the first time. There's so much responsibility and it's a challenge.'

'What's with the wig?' asked the host.

'Yeah, great, isn't it?' She laughed. 'That's great as in hideous, obviously.'

The TV host allowed himself an obsequious snigger, then glanced at his prompt. 'And of course you're currently appearing at The Third Hand theatre in *Put Down*, Eleanor Booth's harrowing tale of a battered wives' refuge. Set in the 1970s. Hence the hair.'

'Hence the dress too.' She fiddled with a strap.

'You're always doing things with your barnet aren't you?' said the host in his best old estuary accent, crassly reducing Billy Morton's rich theatrical repertoire to its attendant hairstyles. 'Everyone remembers that you had your head shaved for *Temple Of Cloud*, Antony Brevinski's epic tale of a group of monks who flee from Tibet in 1959 and end up taking refuge in Java.'

'That's right. The film appealed to me because the exiles go further east, rather than heading west, which is not normally the route they take. He's such an intelligent producer, Antony. He's a hard taskmaster but I learned so much from him, and of course he let me choose the music . . .'

They ran a clip. Billy Morton playing a western missionary gone native. She drifts ethereally through woodsmoke in a forest clearing, her head shaved to the bone. The soundtrack was Javanese gamelan.

'I first heard a gamelan orchestra in . . . 1989 I think it was, at the Avalonia festival. I'd never heard anything like it. It was hardly music. It sounded like a big bag of bells rolling down a hill.'

The host laughed genuinely at that description.

In his living room Keith Gear's face creased too. The

feeling was unfamiliar to him. Dry skin cracked at the side of his mouth.

'I also worked with Antony on *Horrors Arc*, three years ago.'

'Brevinski's moving story about concentration camp survivors,' interjected the host, nodding earnestly and plastically. 'And of course you had your head shaved for that as well,' he added, clodhopping through the sensitivity of the moment in size-nine jackboots. 'Do you think Antony might have a bit of a thing for bald actresses?'

'Actually, do you mind if I take this off? It's so hot.' She put her hands to her scalp and pulled off her wig with one tug.

There she was. The Blin Thing. Her face was somehow longer than it was in her sweetly tainted teens, but the moment she turned away from the camera and placed the wig on a table her profile revealed her younger self: the cheekbones, jawline, nose, lips, the lot.

They showed another clip from *The People Lab*. Billy Morton provided a halting circumspect summary, not wanting to give the plot away. The action was low-lit, all shadows and significant glances. The soundtrack music barely registered. She was trying not to reveal the narrative twist which linked the suburban animal liberationists and the Las Vegas Cosa Nostra and as she talked the music rose in volume. Its resonance came from way back, lapping at the shores of memory, invoking the ancient soul in the ancient seas, trees and rocks.

'I met this man. Well, I met a lot of men,' she quietly qualified. 'And got into scenes and situations I never should have.' She bit her lip.

'Maybe you were seeking a father figure.'

'Ecch, that's such a cliché.' She winced dismissively. 'I hate all that cod-psychoanalysis. Your parents died. You wanted a father figure.' She was back in the baritone-deep parody zone.

'Tell me about the soundtrack music. I gather there's quite a –'

'I tried to find him,' said Billy Morton, earnestly. A look of anguish crossed her face. 'I looked everywhere. I tried Net One. Net Two. I found a Keith Gear who was a sheep farmer in New South Wales, so I contacted him. I thought, yeah, that's the kind of thing he might have done. He didn't seem particularly career-minded, shall we say. I could just imagine him going off to Australia like that. So I wrote to this Keith Gear. *Are you the Keith Gear . . . ?* Etcetera. I convinced myself that it was going to be him. I sent this guy a rather personal letter, a bit indiscreet in the circumstances. Anyway, it wasn't him. He turned out to be a real Australian sheep farmer and not my Keith Gear at all. In the meantime though, I discovered . . . on the Web there's all these . . . thousands, well perhaps not thousands, hundreds of people buying and selling and burning his music. He did a few record disks and they all sell for a fortune now. They're like gold dust.'

'So you were never able to find him?'

'No,' she said sadly. 'I think he must be dead. He would have been seventy by now. At least.'

They showed another clip. There was some more *Tree Music*. Keith Gear sat alone in six up, six across and contemplated the thick sticky tears that clogged up his eyes. They felt more like conjunctivitis than longing and sorrow.

He missed the host's glib summary. The platitudes all blurred into one.

'Well this is the life I have chosen,' said Belinda Morton, actress, director, curator, keeper of faith, protector of the *Tree Music* for all those years.

Keith Gear went to a drawer and rummaged among mementos and debris and dust. All that remains. An outline of a life. An old gold watch left to him by his Uncle Lenny. A shard of plectrum shaped like lightning, gathered up in fan-haste after an incendiary performance by Hendrix. Numerous undeveloped photo-negatives of trees and rocks and railway lines and street lights and cityscapes. Inexplicable haiku drawn from the dream well. A letter from the warden's office asking him to attend a meeting. A yellowing obituary of Malcolm Drummond taped together from paper scraps. A single silver fish earring.

WHAT ABOUT THE HALF NEVER BEEN TOLD?

2019

Keith Gear spoke through a grilled window. A woman spun round in a swivel chair, stopped watching the porno-cam that she was illegally hooked up to in company time, smoothed her skirt and pressed a red buzzer. With difficulty, he shouldered open a heavy bullet-proof door and found himself waiting with two other men in a narrow airless corridor outside the warden's office.

One of the men was Constantine. He held his stringless guitar like a stranger and wiped thick glycerine tears from his red eyes with a small white handkerchief.

'Where's your sign, Constantine?' Keith Gear enquired.

'I nev-ra had no sign,' Constantine replied sharply, shaking his head in denial. 'Not for many years.'

'You had your signs when I came to the Crescents.'

'No, no!' said Constantine, adamantly. 'Not since many years ago.'

Also waiting was a tall, perspiring man in a long funereal overcoat who spoke only to the floorboards and said his name was Keith. 'Mr Gore, would you go in now,' said a disembodied intercom voice. Keith Gore got up hesitantly, avoided all eye contact, knocked on the warden's door and went in. He came out again almost immediately, backwards and bowing and gushing gratefully, 'Thank you, thank you. Yes, thank you. Thank you, yes.'

'What's this all in aid of?' asked Keith Gear.

'Nothing I know about,' said Constantine, glancing nervously towards the warden's door. 'Nothing I do, I am sure of it. Rosemary and the woman who is not her mother but she says she is, they are bad, they try to block up the waste pipe and get moved from here but it does not work. The only way is death. This is how Constantine will leave from here.' Constantine talked like his signs. 'They say I made sign for trouble but this Rosemary, I know about her and her falseness mother. They are bad people and everyone knows this. And I says this. I always says this. What about the half never been told? Ask Cain. Ask Able. What about the half never been told?'

'Mr Gear, would you go in now.'

Keith Gear left Constantine gripping his stringless guitar and denying his sign language, and went through to the warden's room. The warden, a Mr O'Brien, had the practised face of one who had scowled contemptuously from behind an administrator's desk for many years. He wore small steel-rimmed glasses and a look of seasoned irritation on his brow as he leafed disdainfully through the papers on his table. Finally, he fixed Keith Gear with a withering stare.

'Is this you?' he asked, holding up a photocopied image of a bedraggled man.

'It used to be.' He recognised the blurry reproduction of the *Music Maker* photo from all those blurry years ago. His heart skidded past a beat as he was confronted with the image of his younger self. His old hands gripped each other and locked tight, whitening the knuckles and reddening the finger tips. He tried to take deep slow breaths in an attempt to regain some semblance of composure.

'Mr Gear. You have caused a lot of trouble,' said the warden, exhaling gravely. 'I am a busy man. I have problems to deal with. Accommodations to allocate. Complaints to process.' He pressed a buzzer on his desk. A woman opened a door to another office and said, 'Shall I let Mr Hunt go now, Mr O'Brien?' The warden glanced impatiently at a notepad and said, 'Yes. But tell him I want to see him later, to explain those . . . signs of his.'

Keith Gear studied his cracked fingernails and thought about his next meal. The warden's secretary said, 'Go through.' Uncertain as to whether the instruction applied to him or Constantine, he rose hesitantly from his chair and started towards a partition door that led through to another office. There standing in the doorway were two old men, or to be more accurate, one man and an immaculately attired cross-dresser.

'It's taken us so long to find you,' said Guy Truelove.

Keith Gear cried into Guy Truelove's coat-clad shoulder. The two men held each other as if they had been lovers parted in wartime. Guy Truelove gently stroked Keith Gear's head as he sobbed out all the century's pain and sufferance. Keith Gear sniffed and regained his composure for long enough to say his first words to Guy, save prison visits and letters, in twenty years.

'Your coat stinks.'

'I told him,' said May Grey, tinted hair in a bun, hands encased in lace, slender shoulders shrugging in 'I told him' resignation.

'It's an Afghan,' said Guy. 'It's dyed.'

'Yes, but what of?' May Grey sighed wearily.

Keith Gear glanced at the warden, who was staring at May Grey with undisguised contempt – real 'get this fucking transvestite out of my office' seething hatred. May Grey, antennae ever sensitive to hostility and threats, suggested the three of them adjourn to a café.

'If I may say, it was very brave of you to come to the Crescents dressed like that,' said the warden's secretary, transfixed by the apparition in front of her.

'This, my dear is one of the most famous musicians in England,' said Guy Truelove.

'Tsh,' said May Grey, waving a dismissive lacy-gloved hand.

'This whole business has caused me untold trouble,' said

the warden. 'Paperwork. Investigations. Returned mail. Letters to a Mr Lyons. We had no record of a Mr Lyons. I have personally checked more than two thousand files.'

They left the warden to his procedures and walked out of the Crescents into brittle winter sunlight.

'We came looking for you, you know,' said May Grey, brushing dust from her blue silk jacket. 'Some time ago.'

And there was such a time. And they did come looking. Keith Gear, with his century sickness and his beaten-down, broken-down resistance, didn't grasp the significance of that moment when two travellers approached him in the Crescents. One who looked like Guy Truelove, a Guy Truelove sent from the Anglo-Saxon days, fashioned in sackcloth. The other who looked like May Grey, in silken threads and rickshaw drag, similar to the attire she was wearing now. The two of them, acting on a hunch, wandering the windswept Crescents in search of their friend. The viciousness and oppression of that insane place hounding them out soon enough but not before Guy had click-clicked Constantine's signs with his camera for his next exhibition.

There walked old Guy, his big hand wiping swirling grit from a half-closed eye, just as a bedraggled man shuffled by on his blind side, drifted past like a tortured tattered ghost and away into tenement shadows. Such tragi-farce. Such moments as these that renew bonds or break a life. Psychogeographic proximity to the notorious had left Keith Gear's mind criss-crossed with weary footprints and the wheel tracks of white vans. Dreams inverted and endlessly refracted through so many distorted mirrors, until the dreams invaded his daylight and the night was rendered empty of all but T'ang fragments and fading echoes.

The three of them went to a café called Larfs at the edge of the Crescents. May Grey took exception both to the stenography and spelling of the vomit-green sign above the door. Once inside she read the menu with pursed lips and incredulous eyes, finally ordering three 'koffee kups' and a spread of 'kup kakes'.

'Guy did all the detective work,' she said, shaking choco-bits onto her kemical froth.

'Aye, I heard your music,' said Guy, slurping through his froth moustache. 'On the radio.'

'He did,' confirmed May Grey, nodding assent. 'You gave me a tape of your album, the one that didn't come out. *Dusk Music*? Remember? You didn't master it properly. Or you taped over the master tape. I think it was when you were getting sick.'

'You mastered it onto an old video. VHS,' said Guy. 'That's all you had. And at the beginning there was this brief snatch of what was on there before. There was just this voice saying "Turn them into love junkies". It were Peter Sellers, man! Remember? It was that Peter Sellers film.'

The three of them sat naming Peter Sellers films till they conceded that none of them could remember which Peter Sellers film the line came from.

'You decided to incorporate it like a sample because you liked it, but it was an edit malfunction. That's all,' said Guy.

'The poetry of chance,' cooed May Grey.

'No, May, it worra faulty pause button. Shoorup and let me tell the story. Do you know the M-Com organisation?' said Guy. 'They own everything you ever hear, man. Every processed note on the planet. That's where I heard a snatch of your music. Kept hearing it on an M-Com station so I followed it up. Took fooking forever, man. What's it been, May? Two years? Idiots on the phone. You wouldn't believe how many e-mails I had to send. They all get rerouted and lost and bounced back and everyone's foocking lying to yer all the time. Anyway, finally we got a name. Some M-Com wonder kid, who as it turns out used to come and kneel at May Grey's stockinged feet when she wuz playing afterhours at – what were that club, May? The one they closed down. It was on the telly.'

'Mneepsnapes.'

'I spoke to him eventually,' said Guy. 'The lad, I mean. On the phone. A bit vague. Genuine enough though. He thinks they were part of a batch of tapes he picked up at a junk shack.'

'Everything was stolen,' said Keith Gear.

'Well, you're getting something back,' said Guy. 'You're owed.'

'It's true,' said May Grey. 'M-Com sent us a print-out this long. Sampled sequences. Ad music. Incidental music from TV programmes. There was even a film score.'

'*The Pink Panther*,' said the man behind the counter.

'Pardon me?' said May Grey.

'*The Pink Panther*. The Peter Sellers film you were trying to guess. Was it *The Pink Panther*?'

'Of course it wasn't *The Pink Panther*,' scoffed Guy True-love. 'Fooking Inspector Cloussaeu. "Turn tham eentoo lurve jurnkeys." I hardly think so.'

They all laughed. Gear, Guy, Grey. And the other customers, they larfed too. The café owner frowned and wiped his counter so clean he could see his dismay in it.

'Why?' asked Keith Gear. 'Why now? Now that . . . I've lost everything.'

'Redemption,' said Guy Truelove. 'Good deeds lined up against bad deeds. You never said anything when I borrad Helena's camera. Well, that camera helped me make my fortune.'

'It's true. He's a renowned photographer,' said May Grey. 'Exhibitions and everything.'

Now it was Guy's turn to go 'tsh' and wave a dismissive hand.

'And you were the only one who came to see me in prison,' he continued. 'May couldn't, to be fair. They-dah foking lynched her, wouldn't they, princess?'

'Are you two an item?' said Keith Gear.

'God, no.' May Grey recoiled. 'A bickering old pair of spinsters perhaps, but, Guy and his disgusting urges . . . urgh no.

Perish the thought. He just likes a bit of glamour around him, don't you, dear?'

'There were so many rumours,' said Guy to Keith Gear. 'Some people thought you were dead. Somebody thought you were a sheep farmer in Australia. That film producer we spoke to. Belinda somebody. Remember, May? She said she'd met you once, man. Didn't know whether to believe her or not. She seemed a bit, y'know, scatty.'

'Yeah, I did meet her once. It was many years ago. Everything was many years ago.'

'Yeah, well, like I said, you're owed, man.' Guy got up to pay.

They went back to his room, filled a couple of bin liners and boxes with his possessions, slung them into the boot of Guy's car and drove away from the Crescents forever.

As dystopia receded in the rear view, Gear and Guy and Grey talked about Drum. Drum's art. Drum's life. The way he even turned his death into an art work. They compared Drum's missing years with Gear's missing years. They compared silence and madness.

May discretely dabbed her eyes with a lacy glove. 'Do you remember the last words Drum said to you?' she asked quietly.

'Yeah,' said Keith Gear. '50p for a tin of mixed veg. 50p for a tin of kabli chana.'

'What was that?' Guy laughed. 'The name of his last LP?'

'He was telling me how you could eat really well on 50p a day,' said Keith Gear. '50 old pence, as was. He said, buy a tin of mixed veg for 50p and a tin of kabli chana, chickpeas in curry sauce. Also 50p. Heat them together in a pan. Result, two main meals for a quid.'

'I'd add some rice to that,' said May Grey. 'To make it a bit less watery, I mean.'

'I suppose. If you really wanted to splash out,' said Keith Gear.

'Yeah, you'd need a bit of rice with that.' Guy nodded. 'Oora naan bread at least.'

About the author

Rob Chapman has been a regular contributor to *Mojo*, *Uncut* and *The Times,* as well as a broadcaster with the BBC national network. He is the author of *Album Covers From The Vinyl Junkyard* and *Selling The Sixties: The Pirates And Pop Music Radio*, which was included in the *Guardian*'s top ten music books of the year in 1992. He was singer and lyricist with the Bristol-based post-punk band Glaxo Babies. John Peel was a keen supporter of the band and two compilations of their output, *Dreams Interrupted* and *The Porlock Factor,* have recently been released. Chapman is currently a Senior Lecturer in Music Journalism at the University of Huddersfield. He lives in Manchester and is working on a biography of the late Syd Barrett.